SAVAGE DAY

LEWIS KINMOND

SEVEN MONSTERS

Published worldwide
by
Seven Monsters Media Ltd.
www.sevenmonsters.co.uk

All Media Rights Enquiries:
Micheline Steinberg Associates
info@steinplays.com

Cover Design by Fiona Jayde Media
www.fionajaydemedia.com

ISBN: 978-1-9998750-0-8

For Mum and Dad

CONTENTS

PROLOGUE

The Angel and the Darkness

THEN

In the mirror there was darkness.

And the Darkness spoke:

The child still lives.

Huddled in the candlelit gloom of his most secret of chambers, the old tyrant choked out a gasp of shock and felt a sick, cold terror begin to seep into his gut. This could not be so. *Must* not be so...

Trembling in every muscle, he drew in a long, wavering breath and finally dared to raise his eyes. To confront the void in the ancient mirror he knelt before.

"No," he said. "You are mistaken."

Silence.

"My orders were explicit," he went on. "All children of two years and under— "

The boy child lives.

In the mirror, the Darkness rippled as it spoke, *pulsated—*

—and once again the old tyrant shrank into himself, lowering his gaze, gulping back the escalating terror. Black despair closing in on him from all quarters, he glanced down at his hands. The hands of a weak old man. Shaking. Withered. Diseased. The finest doctors in the land could do nothing for him. Time would have its merciless way. Unless...

"Tell me what I must do."

Let me in.

"No. Please, no. You do not... belong here..."

In the mirror, the Darkness rippled:

Let.

Me.

In.

Horror clawing at his innards, the old tyrant recoiled, tried to rise. But pain lanced through his ruined flesh, and he dropped to his knees once more. Tears began to spill down his cheeks.

"And... you will keep your promise?"

Yes.

With a last, defeated sigh, the old tyrant nodded, then drew himself up as much as the pain would allow... and reached for the mirror. His quivering hand crept towards the emptiness in the ancient frame. Closed in on the void. And when his fingers made contact, the Darkness surged. Erupted from the mirror like a living black mist. A seething cloud of featureless nothing, enveloping all.

For one brief moment, hope flickered in the pitiful soul the void engulfed.

Hope that somehow it might take away his pain there and then.

It did not.

And as the Darkness entered the world of man, the old tyrant screamed.

●●●

The traveller shivered. Not because the desert night was cold. That he was used to. Seven days he and his family had journeyed since leaving the town of their birth, moving always in the biting chill of these darkest hours—a time when they might pass... unnoticed.

No, it was not the cold that made the traveller shiver.

It was the shadow.

Up ahead lay the border crossing that was their journey's end, the moon-cast shadow of its roadside guardhouse spilling darkness across the dusty track. And in that shadow something seemed to swirl. To surge. A *greater* darkness. Denser somehow than the night alone could account for.

The traveller shivered again and pulled his robe close, stepping up onto a small rise by the roadside so that he might peer into the distance ahead.

And as he did, his frown deepened.

Because all the way down the road, for as far as he could see, every single shadow—of tree or hill or bush—seemed to churn with that same strange darkness. As if...

As if what?

"What is it, husband? Is something wrong?"

The traveller turned to his young wife, seated atop their laden donkey just a few paces behind. A gathering concern furrowed her brow, tarnishing her youthful beauty, while in her arms, the couple's infant child—their beautiful little boy— lay asleep in his swaddling. Tiny, perfect, at peace.

And in the gravest danger.

The traveller forced a smile. "It's nothing," he said. "We should— "

And then he saw it again. But nearer this time. In a *closer* shadow. His *wife's* shadow. The swirling. The deepening. The darkening...

Frowning once more, the traveller made to step down from the rise...

... and that was when it happened.

Suddenly, the same darkness that was in the shadows seemed somehow to swirl into the eyes of the traveller's wife. Moments later, she began to tremble, then to shake with increasing violence, the sleeping infant in her arms juddering with each worsening spasm.

With a gasp of horror, the traveller leapt back down onto the road. "My love, what's wrong! What's— "

But before he could reach her, a sound beyond all comprehension shattered the desert silence—a dissonant, musical thunderbolt that the traveller had heard only once before. And as before, light followed—a single, stupefying blast of it, filled with all the colours of the world. From the light's dazzling core the warrior angel leapt, tall and powerful and terrifying, slivers of the scattering radiance glinting from his battle-scarred armour, his cloak billowing behind him in tattered, bloodstained magnificence.

In one dazzling motion, the angel landed before the traveller's wife, snatched the baby from her arms, then took two further bounding steps away, finally coming to rest by the guardhouse door.

Almost instantly, the traveller saw the darkness leave his wife's eyes, her spasming body sagging into stillness...

... before stiffening again as fear and confusion surged into her face. "Husband...? What...?" Only then did she seem to become aware of the being who had taken their child, and with a cry of shock, she leapt down from the donkey. "No! My baby! Give me my— "

"Stop! Come no closer," the angel said, backing up farther still against the guardhouse wall and taking the baby with him.

Terror bright in her face, the traveller's wife stopped where she was.

"Please," the traveller said to the angel, "I do not understand. Why do you take our child? You *told* me to bring him here. That he would be *safe* once we were across the border."

"Things are not as they were," the angel said. "It is among you now. Within you."

The traveller's head swam in confusion. "What is?"

"The Darkness. If we are to keep your son safe, it is vital that we— "

But before the angel could say more, a border guard appeared suddenly at the door of the guardhouse, and even as he spotted the towering armoured figure standing there the guard gasped in shock, drew his sword, and sprang forward. Caught unawares, the warrior angel made a grab for his own blade, but before he could draw it, the border guard had brought the point of his weapon to bear on the angel's exposed neck.

"Don't," the guard said, and the warrior angel withdrew his hand from his sword.

"What's going on here?" the guard barked, his

eyes darting in confusion to the stirring baby in the angel's arms. "What was that sound? That light? Who— "

But then, for no reason the traveller was able to comprehend, the man stopped dead—simply froze where he was and stood there in silence, the point of his sword still pressed to the warrior angel's throat.

And only a moment later, the traveller saw the same terrible things as before:

The darkness from the shadows surging into the *guard's* eyes now...

The man's body starting to tremble, to convulse, to spasm...

And then...

Then the true horror of the Darkness finally revealed itself.

The guard's flesh began to ripple, to *pulsate*, his spasming torso broadening, bloating, distending with monstrous new muscle, his skin roughening, darkening, suffusing with a freakish shade of burnished red. Clutches of razor-taloned claws sprang from the man's hands. More still from his sandaled feet. Two monstrous horns drove themselves through his contorting, mutating skull. And mere moments after the darkness had entered his eyes, the border guard was gone, the thing that stood in his place no longer even remotely human.

All at once, the sword that was pressed to the

angel's throat fell away, fumbled by talons now too big to hold it, and at last the warrior angel was able to reach for his own blade, pulling it free just as the demon—for it could be no other thing—let loose a hellish roar of animal fury and brought one of its butcher hook claws slashing down at the angel's head.

In a single blinding blur of motion, the warrior angel's sword flashed upwards to block the demon's blow, and sparks exploded where blade met claw, raining down upon the baby still cradled in the angel's other arm. That was when the traveller's infant son finally began to scream, and the sound of that terrified cry seemed instantly to draw the creature's leering gaze, its black eyes darkening further, filling with a blind hatred as they fell upon the child. Howling in yet more fury, the monster raised its talons, and once more they came slashing down...

... this time straight at the shrieking baby writhing in the warrior angel's arm.

With a gasp of shock, the traveller lunged forward, reaching for his screaming son.

"No!" the angel cried, deflecting the monster's attack for a second time. "Stay back! You *must* stay back! The Darkness cares not whose flesh it uses."

And as the full, terrifying meaning of these words became clear to him, the traveller stumbled to a stop, watching in helpless horror while the demon creature once again threw itself forward and began to rain down blow after savage blow, all of them now aimed directly at the screaming baby boy clutched to the warrior angel's chest.

The angel's shining blade danced and whirled, darted and flashed, repelling each attack with bewildering speed, until at last, the heavenly avenger spotted an opening and rammed his sword forward, skewering the monster straight through its dark heart.

Howling and flailing, the demon staggered backwards, life spilling from it in a thick black flood. But even as the creature fell dead in the dirt, four more border guards, each as confused as the next, stumbled from the guardhouse door and lunged for the warrior angel. Grabbing him by both shoulders, the guards slammed the mighty figure down into the road, screaming infant still held tight to the angel's chest. Pinned to the ground, the warrior angel struggled and thrashed in the guards' grip until finally he managed to wrench himself free, leaping once more to his feet...

But too late.

Now four more of the snarling hell creatures stood before him.

In one heaving mass of demonic fury, the monsters launched themselves forward, hook claws reaching for the howling baby in the angel's left arm. Again, the warrior angel's sword slashed and stabbed, nightmare shrieks turning quickly to roars of agony as, one by one, the devil creatures fell. Fell until only one of their number remained.

But then, just as the angel turned to face the final demon, the back of the creature's flailing claw met the angel's jaw, and suddenly the warrior angel was hurtling backwards, slamming down onto the road—

—where finally he lost his grip of the baby. Screaming and kicking, the traveller's infant son slipped from the angel's arm, fell to the sandy ground, and rolled to a stop not four paces from the snarling, huffing monster.

Black eyes gleaming in triumph, the creature lurched up to the shrieking baby boy and raised a fistful of razor talons. But just as their lethal points came arcing down, the warrior angel hurled himself forward between monster and child, and with a hideous tearing sound the demon's plunging claw gouged a grisly path across the angel's shaven head, blood splashing the dirt road in a ragged fan of dark red.

Screaming in pain, the warrior angel snatched up the baby once more. Tried to rise. He had barely made it to his knees when the demon's claw came at him again, and hunched over the shrieking infant, the angel heaved his blade upwards. But it was a desperate, ill-timed block, and in the end it served only to seal the angel's fate. Heaven-forged steel met hell-spawned claw in a crashing explosion of sparks, and with a single ringing snap, the warrior angel's sword broke in two, its bloodstained blade half clattering to the dusty ground.

Towering over the now defenceless angel, snarling its monstrous, inexplicable hatred, the demon drew back a bloody claw to deal the final blow...

But even as it did, the warrior angel looked up... and locked eyes with the monster.

"No," the angel said, his voice barely a whisper now. "Do you hear me, creature? No. He is the light. And the light *will* shine." And swaying on his knees, the angel turned once more to the traveller and his wife. "I will return him to you," he said. "This I swear." Then, as if in prayer, the warrior angel bowed his head and closed his eyes, and all at once, an earth-shaking dissonance rang out as a pillar of multicoloured fire exploded from the sands beneath the angel, shooting up into the night sky. Caught in the blinding rainbow blaze, its deadly claw still raised to attack, the lone surviving demon froze where it stood, as if pinned there by the light... then the black of night came rushing back in, and the creature sagged to the ground, slumping horns first into the dirt of the desert road.

The silent desert road.

The *empty* desert road.

Because where, only moments before, the warrior angel had knelt in desperate prayer, a tiny, defenceless baby screaming and thrashing in his mighty arms, there was now... nothing.

The pillar of fire was gone.

So too was the warrior angel.

And with him, the little boy the angel had fought so fearlessly to protect.

For what felt like all eternity, the traveller stood there trembling, lost in an ocean of black despair that surely would have claimed him completely... if not for those nine words.

Those nine barely whispered words, echoing still in his reeling mind:

I will return him to you. This I swear.

Then, through the muffling dullness of his ringing ears, another voice reached the traveller. The voice of the woman he loved. But the anguish in it. The terrible, unbearable anguish:

"No! My baby! My baby..."

And as his wife collapsed weeping into his arms, the traveller turned his eyes to the heavens and prayed. Prayed that the warrior angel would live long enough to keep his promise. Or if die he must, that another, equally worthy, might take his place. Another warrior, sent from God to keep their little boy safe and bring him home again...

1

Samar

NOW

It wasn't the punch in the face that made Samar Chowdhury angry. His head guard took the brunt of that. It wasn't even the pain. And there was some pain, head guard or not.

No. It was the look on the boy's face. His smug, private-school grin. Dancing around the ring in his shiny two-hundred quid shorts and his top-of-the-range Everlast gloves and his—

BAM! Okay, now that really *did* hurt.

Samar stumbled, dropped to the mat, heard the crowd groan. Then an instant later, their hollers of encouragement: "Sam! Sam! Sam! Sam! Sam! Sam! Sam!"

Face flat to the canvas, Sam forced himself to stay down, waiting for his head to clear while Williamson knelt beside him and began the count:

"One... two... You with me, Sam?"

Sam nodded, willing the community centre's shabby gym hall back into focus—

"Three... four..."

Okay, yeah, there it was again—threadbare tinsel trimming its worn out equipment, drooping Christmas tree in one corner, the tiny but vocal home crowd cheering Sam on—

"Five... six..."

And not forgetting his own family of course, ringside front and centre as always—his mum and dad rigid with fear, too scared even to cheer, while his little sister, Asha, yelled her eight-year-old lungs raw and waved her trusty crayoned sign—
Go Walworth Warriors!

"Seven... eight..."

Sam wondered briefly if Asha even knew he was on the mat. His little sister had lost her sight when she was four. Sam could be dancing around the other boy's lifeless, bleeding corpse for all Asha knew...

"Nine..."

With a grunt of determination, Sam leapt to his feet again and raised his gloves. A thunderous roar of approval rolled through the hall. Then the boy in the two-hundred quid shorts was circling in

14

once more, tipping Sam a smug little wink, while ringside by the boy's corner, his private-school team-mates exchanged grins of delight. This was gonna be good...

"Oh, come on," the boy said to Sam, and his voice was as shiny as his shorts—polished, perfect, and just loud enough for Sam alone to hear. "Lord knows I expected it to stink in here. But hey, I thought we'd at least get a decent fight."

A jab, fast as a snake on a tight schedule. Sam dodged it. But barely.

"I mean, aren't you lot supposed to be tough?" Shiny Shorts said. "All that gang culture and rioting and stuff?"

Sam knew full well that the boy's words were pure strategy. Trash talk intended to wind Sam up, make him lose concentration. Knowing this however made zero difference, and a wave of hot red anger came surging into Sam's chest anyway. He felt his breathing begin to speed up, his teeth start to grind down, his—

No!

Just *no!*

Sam absolutely could *not* afford to let Old Red take the wheel now. Not here. Not in the ring. In the ring he *had* to stay cool. Wasn't that the whole bloody point of all this? An exercise in *Anger Management* or whatever the hell they were calling it now. A way to—

Shiny Shorts heaved a right at Sam but slower this time. Hah! An easy block—

Then BAM! The boy's left fist came from nowhere, slamming into Sam's chin.

Sam staggered back onto the ropes, cursing himself for failing to recognise that obvious right-hand feint. *Damn it*, he was *not* thinking. Old Red was doing his thang for sure. Sucking out the smart and pumping in the stupid.

And Shiny Shorts, he was *loving* it, dancing his way around the ring with that big shiny grin on his big shiny face.

"Pathetic," Shiny said. "Know what I see here?" The boy's eyes darted to the rest of the Walworth Warriors—all two of them—huddled ringside by Sam's corner and cheering their homeboy on. "Fat boys and freaks. *That's* what I see here."

And once again, Sam fought it back—that surge of crimson anger.

Ignore him. Don't let him get to you...

The boy circled some more. "Know what *else* I see?" and he fired off a second dismissive glance, this time at the cheering crowd in the hall. "Scroungers, losers, and no-hopers..."

Just keep it together, Sam. Head in the game. Don't let this guy—

But then Shiny Shorts's gaze fell on Asha, now up on her chair, going absolutely crazy, pumping her crayoned sign at the tinsel-draped ceiling—

"SAM! SAM! SAM! SAM! SAM!" And as the boy finally registered Asha's unfocused eyes, pointing not quite where they should be, he smirked. "Oh, and let's not forget the infirm, right? What is she, spastic?"

By and large, Old Red had never been that big on warnings, but the truly shocking speed of his arrival now surprised even Sam. The rage came roaring into his brain like a runaway freight train, bells clanging, whistles blasting, and before he even knew what he was about to do, Sam dropped his fists, drew back one booted foot, and drove it home—

—right into Shiny Shorts's oh-so-shiny groin.

The crowd gasped.

Then fell silent.

All except for Asha: "SAM! SAM! SAM! SAM! SAM!"

Shiny Shorts's eyes bulged, shiny themselves now too, glistening with shock and pain. And clutching his groin with both hands, the boy toppled forward like an overladen coat-rack, slamming into the mat with a painful CRUMP.

"SAM! SAM! SAM!" Asha chanted. "SAM Sam… sam…"

At last, she tailed off.

"Um… what happened? Did he win?"

●●●

Halfway down the litter-strewn alley, Roger "Rabbit" Crawford stood with his nose pressed against grimy glass, peering in the community centre window. Through it he could see everything but hear almost nothing, like watching a TV with the sound turned down. And as the scene behind the glass played out, Rabbit sighed, wishing he could change the channel. Sadly, grimy windows in South London community centres rarely came with remote controls.

Inside the centre, the gym hall had already been cleared, the last of the crowd sent on its tutting, gossiping way. The entire place was empty now except for Sam and his family.

And Williamson, of course.

Poor old Williamson.

Mr. Williamson—founder of the Walworth Warriors and the club's main coach—was one of those old guys whose complexion functioned like an early warning system. White: Conditions normal. Pink: Anomalous internal pressure detected. Red: Aaaarrgghh, he's gonna blow!

Tonight he was purple.

Hunched and scowling, the old ex-copper paced the floor of the gym, shaking his fists while he hurled saliva-laced rebukes at Sam. Rabbit found himself mentally dubbing in the inaudible tirade—easy enough, given the numbers of times they'd heard Sam subjected to it:

"...let the club down... a noble sport... laughing stock... how many times, Sam?"

And through it all, the slim, toned, fourteen-year-old that was Samar Chowdhury just sat there, slouched on a plastic chair, weathering the storm of spit, while behind him, his parents and his little sister stood in sombre, embarrassed silence.

Eventually, Rabbit could take no more. "We can't just *stand* here," he said. "We gotta *do* something, L-Man. We gotta go in there, stick up for him, yeah? Cos that posh kid, he were asking for it, right?"

No answer.

"L-Man? You listening?"

"Hunk-a-licious or Hunk-a-sonic?"

Rabbit paused, shook his head in frustration, then turned to frown at his friend.

Matthew Love—"L-Man" to the world at large—stood there lounging against the alley wall, scowling down at the constant companion that was his iPad Mini, two thumbs poised over its virtual keyboard. "New user name," he said. "Hunk-a-licious or Hunk-a-sonic?"

"L-Man, would you give it a rest! This is serious! Williamson's gonna kick him out!"

"Bruv, chill. They ain't gonna kick him out. Three strikes you're out, innit?"

"Yeah, and Sam's on, what? Strike nine? Ten?"

A pause... followed by a puzzled frown. Classic

signs that the L-Man brain had engaged at last. "Okay... so *maybe* they kick him out? What's the big deal?"

Rabbit gaped, unable to believe what he was hearing. "What's the *big deal?* Seriously? You gotta wake up, man! Sam's the only one in the club got any cool!"

Rolling his eyes in despair, Rabbit turned once more to peer through the community centre window... and in doing so managed to catch a passing (and frankly unwelcome) glimpse of his own reflection in its smeary glass—a timely, punch-in-the-face reminder of exactly how uncool Roger "Rabbit" Crawford really was. Oh, it wasn't *just* that Rabbit was small. Apparently, Tom Cruise was a dwarf and that bruv had done okay. No, it was all the other stuff, too. The acne-ravaged skin. The embarrassing Christmas hoodie knitted by his gran (Hey, she was the world's best gran! What was he gonna do? *Not* wear it?). And of course, the teeth, jutting through Rabbit's gums at all angles, like a row of Lego tower blocks built by a deranged toddler. Still, at least his afro was awesome. Not to say gigantic. No white kid would ever get that kind of volume.

In the end though, awesome afros only got you so far in this world. And even if it wasn't obvious to L-Man, it was to Rabbit—they *needed* Sam. *Needed* Sam's cool.

L-Man though? He seemed to have other ideas. Stupid ideas:

"Hey, *I'm* cool."

"L-Man, get real. You ain't cool."

Snorting in derision, L-Man presented his evidence on 7.9 inches of HD display. "Nine thousand foxy followers. Hanging on my every sexy little word," whereupon the bruv's thumbs returned to the iPad's virtual keyboard, resuming their life's work. "Gonna go with Hunk-a-sonic. Got a ring to it, yeah?"

Rabbit sighed, looking his mate up and down. Whatever the social media statistics might suggest, neither "Hunk-a-licious" nor "Hunk-a-sonic" would be the first word that sprang to mind when you took a moment to consider Matthew "L-Man" Love. That word would most likely be "fat". Or at the very least, "chunky". But then, you weren't really allowed to say stuff like that these days, were you? Apparently "big-arsed white git" was out, too. Not that any of it ever seemed to offend the ultra-laid-back L-Man, eternally protected as he was by his indestructible, vintage polyester shell-suit. Not to mention his even more vintage Ray-Ban sunglasses. In winter. At night. In a dark alley.

"Bruv, trust," Rabbit said to his poor deluded friend. "Right now, even I'm cooler than you. And I'm wearing a hand-knit hoodie that's got reindeers on it. *Reindeers!* Seriously, we gotta get in there and— "

Sadly, the rest of Rabbit's words never made it out of Legoland, because just then, a giggling, nattering posse of about a dozen teenage girls came tumbling into the alley, and what happened next was as inevitable as it was depressing. Rabbit felt his throat go dry, his chest tighten, and his breathing shrivel to a thin, rasping wheeze.

Panic attacks. Just another short straw in Rabbit's ever-expanding collection.

As the gang of girls headed inexorably towards them, Rabbit gasped and huffed, clawing at his hitching chest. Within seconds he was actually struggling to breathe at all.

Beside him, barely even looking up from his iPad, L-Man reached into one shell-suit pocket and pulled out an old scrunched-up crisp packet, thrusting it absently in Rabbit's direction. "Slow and shallow," L-Man drawled.

Rabbit grabbed the crisp packet with both hands and jammed it to his mouth, the little foil bag inflating-deflating like a crinkly salt'n'vinegar flavoured lung as he puffed into it. Almost instantly, the vice around Rabbit's own lungs began to slacken, thank God.

But the girls... oh God, the girls! The posse was now less than five metres away—almost on top of them—and as ever, L-Man was taking not one blind bit of notice. Guy was still just jabbing away at his stupid iPad with all the cool he didn't have.

Hiding the crisp packet behind his back, Rabbit drew himself up to his full height and tried heroically to pull "urban warrior" out of the bag as the posse flounced by. As usual, the only thing in the bag was "desperate geek". Damn, he had to get a new bag...

Then one of the girls caught Rabbit's eye, and Rabbit felt his heart lurch.

Whatever you do, don't smile don't smile don't—

Rabbit smiled at the girl—his gaping Lego grin.

In response, the girl raised one perfectly pencilled eyebrow then muttered something to her crew, upon which twelve pairs of lavishly mascaraed eyes flicked in Rabbit's direction. A microsecond later, the entire posse emitted a standard issue snigger before finally swanning out the other end of the lane.

Great. So that went well then.

As usual.

Slumping into the wall of the alley, Rabbit hauled out his crisp packet again and dragged in several more despairing but tangy lungfuls, at the same time enquiring silently of that God bloke how the hell this night could get any worse.

At which point the community centre's side door crashed open, and a lone figure in a Walworth Warriors hoodie barged its way out, storming off down the alley.

Apparently that God bloke had a freakin answer for everything.

Because there he went.

Samar Chowdhury—Rabbit and L-Man's only possible salvation from the hell of uncool— striding his way out of their textbook loser lives, quite possibly forever.

●●●

Storming off. A *loser* move if ever there was one. And Samar Chowdhury hated himself for it. Oh, he went back home again, of course. Eventually. He always did. Shuffled his surly way back along Walworth Avenue, crept in the front door of the flat, slunk into the bedroom he shared with his little sister Asha, and just hid out there for the duration, waiting for Old Red to pack the last of his bags and go.

Old Red had obliged eventually. Almost two hours ago in fact, though even now a vague unpleasant sourness seemed somehow determined to linger, festering in the warmer corners of Sam's mind, like dirty socks stuck behind a radiator...

"Sam, come on! Faster! What happens next?"

Sam sighed. It was Asha's voice, and if he was being perfectly honest here, the shrill note of frustration that it rang with was entirely justified. Perched on the edge of his little sister's bed, Sam was currently in the middle of reading Asha her bedtime story—something he did every evening at this time—but the plain fact of the matter was he was off his game tonight. Way off. And Asha knew it.

"Okay okay, keep your hair on," Sam sighed, dragging his attention back to the comic book in his hands—*Super Commando Dhruva*, of course. Asha's favourite.

Dredging up what meagre dregs of enthusiasm he could find, Sam pulled in a deep breath and gave it his best scary bad guy voice:

"*'And now, Dhruva, you die!'* says Grand Master Robo! And he fires his death ray, straight at Dhruva!"

Asha clutched at her quilt in excitement.

Okay, better, Sam thought and flipped on to the spectacular double page splash that followed. "FZZZAMM!" Sam said. "The beam blasts Dhruva right in the chest!"

Asha giggled. "FZZZAMM?"

"Yeah, FZZZAMM. And Dhruva, he goes flying across the room and hits a wall. And his costume, it's all torn and stuff."

"Uh-oh," Asha said, her eyes shining with excitement.

"Uh-oh is right," Sam shot back. "And then Dhruva, he struggles to his feet, yeah? And there's blood streaming down his face. And he's like... he can barely *stand*. Super Commando Dhruva is practically *dead...*"

Sam paused, finally allowing himself a smile. He was in the zone now. Totally. Asha agog at his every word. Lowering his voice almost to a whisper, Sam gripped his little sister's arm and continued: "But then Dhruva, he just sticks out his chin, and he's standing there, yeah, looking Grand Master Robo straight in the eye, doing that total hero pose of his..."

"Cool," Asha said. "Then what? Does he kick Robo in the nuts?"

Sam stopped dead, gaping in complete shock.

"Well?" Asha said, staring back at him defiantly. "Does he?"

Sam felt his jaw tighten. "You know Dhruva wouldn't do that."

"Uh-huh."

Silence.

"You're just being... stupid," Sam muttered.

Asha folded her arms and said no more.

Sam folded his own and scowled furiously. He didn't have to take this. No way. Gulping back a fresh wave of anger, Sam stood up, stomped over to his side of the room, and slumped onto his own bed.

And still Asha just sat there—rigid, silent, superior. His judge and jury in Spider-Man jim-jams.

Sam sighed. He loved his little sister, of course he did. But wilful? Sam could imagine Asha when God had been dishing out the stubborn, telling the Almighty she was *not* leaving until she got her fair share. Plus maybe a bit extra.

And idealistic? Sam's eyes roamed over the walls around Asha's bed. Walls papered floor to ceiling with posters of chisel-jawed superheroes— Dhruva, Superman, Wonder Woman, Captain America. A primary-coloured riot of derring-do and goodness triumphant. Ironically, most of the posters there had actually belonged to Sam himself not so long ago, donated to a delighted Asha after Sam had finally decided he'd moved on from all that stuff.

Moved on, yeah right...

Sam let his eyes drift to the walls above his own bed, all of them utterly bare now except for the odd blob of fossilised Blu-Tack. Acres of faded wallpaper he'd somehow never felt the urge to fill since giving Asha his posters...

Scowling once more, Sam made a grab for the heavy divider curtain that ran down the middle of the bedroom. Supposedly there to give him and Asha some privacy when they needed it, they'd rarely used the thing in six years of sharing a room, but Sam yanked it shut now.

Asha, of course, was having none of that. "No!" she yelled from behind the curtain, immediately hauling it back open again.

Scowl deepening, Sam was just reaching for the curtain a second time when the bedroom door opened... and Sam's heart sank a little more.

In the doorway stood Sam's mum, smiling in at him and Asha.

Under normal circumstances, a smile sat very naturally on Sam's mum's face, but somehow he got the impression that the one there right now was taking some serious effort to maintain.

"Samar," she said, "your father and I, we'd... we'd like to speak to you."

With a deflated sigh, Sam tossed the Dhruva comic onto Asha's bed and went to face the music.

●●●

The music, of course, turned out to be pretty much the same old song in the same old key—that timeless Mums & Dads classic about "self-respect" and "letting yourself down"—and for the next twenty minutes or so the three of them hunkered down in the kitchen and went to it, riffing wearily on their oh-so-familiar parts.

Now, with the entire tedious performance finally over and *nobody* looking for an encore, Sam's mum and dad just sat there hand in hand at the kitchen table, frowning across at Sam in the seat opposite, awaiting some kind of response to their proposed solution.

The silence dragged on, Sam slouching in his chair, head bowed, hands gripping a cold mug of tea he had barely put lips to. So far he'd at least managed to keep his voice down. To keep Old Red at bay. But *this?* His parents' supposed "solution"? This was gonna be tough. Both of them were in total agreement, of course. They always were. And what they were asking Sam to do, it sounded so completely reasonable. Maybe they were even right. *Probably* they were.

Except now it seemed that Old Red finally had something to contribute.

An edge crept into Sam's voice: "So... what? You're saying I should *beg? Beg* Williamson to let me back in?"

"Apologising is not begging," Sam's dad said.

"I didn't even want to join that stupid club in the first place."

"It's an outlet, Samar. You said so yourself. You need an outlet for this... this anger."

"You didn't hear what that boy said."

"That is no excuse. The boy was an idiot. Ignore it, forgive it— "

"Oh, please— "

"Rise *above* it. You're better than this, Samar. Your sister, you see how she looks up to you. She— "

"No! Stop!"

"Son, please, you have to— "

29

"I said NO!" Sam shouted, slamming his mug down onto the table and sending a tiny tidal wave of cold tea flooding over the pristine tablecloth. "People start looking up to you, that's when people stop looking where they're going," and before Sam could even think about holding them back the next words were out there. "That's when people get hurt."

Silence followed.

A long silence.

Eventually, both of Sam's parents lowered their eyes, and Sam felt a dark twinge of guilt. He really hadn't planned on raising this particular family spectre, and in his heart he was genuinely sorry he had, but did it have the desired effect? Oh yes, no question. The conversation was now most definitely closed. Asha's accident was *not* something Sam's mum and dad were willing to talk about.

Ever.

Shaking his head, Sam got up and stalked out of the kitchen.

In the hallway, he snatched his hoodie from a hook, began to reach for the front door knob—

—and felt a hand come to rest on his shoulder.

Sam looked around.

His mum stood there, trembling visibly but clearly trying really hard to stay calm.

Once again, guilt tugged at Sam's heart.

"Samar, please…" his mum said.

"Mum, no. Just… no. Don't you get it? I ain't Asha's hero. I ain't *anyone's* hero."

Turning away again, Sam made a grab for the front door and hauled it open—

—to find himself face to face with a startled Rabbit and L-Man, Rabbit's forefinger poised just over the doorbell.

"Yo, Sam!" Rabbit yelped. "Awesome footwork, bruv! Posh git got what was coming, right? You is like a total *hero,* man!"

Samar Chowdhury closed his eyes and sagged in despair.

2

The Baby and the Broken Sword

Hunched against the evening chill, hoodies pulled tight around their faces, Sam, Rabbit, and L-Man shuffled along through the icy streets of the Walworth Estate. As they walked, Rabbit outlined his plan:

"... so okay, maybe Williamson says, like, no way, yeah? He ain't *gonna* let you back in the club. So what do we do then? Well, here's the thing..."

While Rabbit yattered on, Sam found his eyes drifting once more to the Christmas lights twinkling in windows all around, their gaudy brilliance dragging a reluctant half-smile onto Sam's lips. As a kid growing up in South London, he'd always loved Christmas time. The lights in particular. He'd read once that Christmas lights actually had very little to do with Christian celebrations at all. That the idea of special lights at this time of year went all the way back into prehistory. It was almost as if there was some kind of deep, primitive urge in man. Some primal need to come together in midwinter, light up a candle or a flaming torch or a flashing LED snowman, and make a stand against the darkness...

"Oi, bruv, you listening?" Rabbit said, dragging Sam back into the moment.

"I'm listening."

"Okay, so then BAM! After that it's ultimatum time, innit?" and Rabbit proceeded to hit them with his big finish. "Either Williamson lets you back in the club, or me and L-Man, we are *gone*, yeah? I mean it, man. *Gone!*" Rabbit's eyes glowed with triumph as he punched this last bit home, and Sam could almost swear he saw the tiny kid's afro grow another centimetre. "Cos then he ain't got no club at all, get me?" Rabbit added. "So he's *gotta* let you back in, right?"

Sam wasn't so sure about that but nodded anyway as they all turned off the main street and into St. John's Lane—a shortcut to Williamson's house. On the long, narrow alleyway, darkness dropped in quickly around the three boys—a thick, clinging shroud relieved only by the perpetual glow of L-Man's iPad. As ever, the big lad continued to squint stubbornly through his

Ray-Bans at the tablet's hi-def screen, thumbing in some "sexy" new message while he ambled along silently in the rear.

"Swear to God," Rabbit went on, skipping and bobbing at Sam's shoulder. "If Williamson don't let you back in, we are walking."

Sam weighed this up. "You'd really do that?"

"Believe it. It's like a loyalty thing, innit? A *warrior* thing."

At last, L-Man found speech: "Plus Rabbit needs your cool if he's ever gonna get girls." Aaaaand back to his tablet. "Lovemachine, that all one word, right?"

Rabbit scowled. "Yeah, like you could ever actually talk to a proper *real* girl!"

L-Man's thumbs continued their stubby, darting dance. "Believe, bruv. When he needs 'em, the Loverman he got the moves."

"Uh-huh," Rabbit said. "We ever actually gonna see any of these famous 'moves' then?"

Sam knew that this one could rage until stars died, galaxies stopped turning, and the universe cooled to absolute zero. Best nip it in the bud...

"Hang on," Sam said, bringing the three of them to a halt beside a huge wheelie bin overflowing with bottles and cans. "So what you're saying is, you think I won't hang with you guys no more if we don't all do Walworth Warriors together?"

Silence.

Rabbit and L-Man gawped back at Sam like a pair of dead fish.

A haddock with an afro. A cod in sunglasses.

Sam shook his head and sighed. "Guys, we're mates now."

Whereupon Rabbit's eyes suddenly widened in delight, his voice shooting instantly into its uppermost of upper registers. "Really?" he squealed, and Sam found himself wincing involuntarily, surprised he could actually hear sounds that high without being a dog.

Spotting Sam's amusement, Rabbit attempted a hasty recovery, voice plummeting to a gravel-voiced grunt. "So we're still cool then, yeah?"

If anything, this sounded even funnier—like a Chihuahua trying to convince you it was a Rottweiler—and Sam had to fight back another smile.

In the end though, yes, they *were* still cool. Because when all was said and done here, these two guys—Roger "Rabbit" Crawford and Matthew "L-Man" Love—they were Sam's mates. His *best* mates. His *bruvs.* How the hell the pair of them couldn't know that by now, Sam failed to see, but since they both still seemed to be waiting for some kind of definitive pronouncement on the subject, Sam gave them one. The best one he had.

In the light of L-Man's glowing iPad, Sam raised one deadly serious eyebrow, stuck out a clenched fist to waist height, and growled, "Walworth Warriors, man."

The response, of course, was instantaneous. Rabbit and L-Man beamed at each other, glanced down at Sam's outstretched fist... and then launched into it.

Into the routine.

Because by now, that's what the club handshake had become. One crazily elaborate "routine", created entirely unspoken over months of training sessions and long walks home, with move after move added as the weeks rolled by. And as they worked their way through the insane choreography of it all now—fists dancing and bobbing, linking and crossing, dipping and darting—the Walworth Warriors chanted:

"All for one
One for all
Two for a tenner
And three for the show!"

Hands slamming together at the end for a final, three-fist "tower of power".

For several more seconds, they all stood there, grinning at each other like three cats who'd just ram-raided a creamery. Then Sam nodded, opened his mouth to speak—

—and that was when the explosion rocked the Walworth Estate, and the world changed forever.

The flash alone was brutal. It seemed to come

from somewhere up ahead, just past the end of the alley, and Sam felt it scorch the back of his eyes even as it whited out his world.

But it was the *sound* of the thing that truly shocked. A sound like nothing Sam had ever heard. Like nothing *anyone* had ever heard. A senses-shattering, near musical cacophony—part thunderbolt, part fanfare—filling Sam's world, bludgeoning his ears into submission—

—and then gone. Gone even before the swirling afterimage blotches dancing across Sam's vision had begun to fade.

For a long moment nobody spoke. All three of them just stood there, stunned into terrified, trembling silence.

"W-w-what the hell was that?" Sam finally stammered.

Rabbit managed a kind of shaky whimper: "Was that a… a bomb or…?"

"Bomb?" L-Man croaked. "That weren't no bomb, bruv. There was… there was… *trumpets* in it… What kind of bomb got *trumpets* in it…?"

Sam and Rabbit stared back at L-Man as if this were some kind of incomprehensible joke he was about to supply a punchline for.

I don't know, L-Man, what kind of bomb does *have trumpets in it?*

No punchline followed, of course. What *did* follow was another sound. But this time a far more familiar one.

It was the sound of a baby crying.

Sam whirled in the direction it came from...

... and saw a lone figure stumble into the alley up ahead.

In the dark of the narrow lane, his vision still recovering from the blinding flash, Sam found himself struggling to make out exactly what it was he was looking at. It was a man, that much was clear. But this guy was huge, *really* huge, maybe seven feet tall, while huddled in the man's massive arms, wrapped up in some kind of shawl or blanket, was the squirming, wriggling source of all the crying—one tiny little baby, maybe six months old at most, kicking and screaming like its entire world was coming to an end.

The stranger began to lurch towards Sam and the boys, and Sam called out to him down the alley, "Hey, you okay, mate? What the hell *was* that?"

But the man didn't answer. Just continued to stagger closer, gasping with each step, as if in pain. And as Sam's vision finally began to return to normal, he saw why. The stranger was injured, badly, blood oozing from a deep wound in his shaven head.

Sam took a startled step back. "Whoah, mate, we... we better phone you an ambulance, man. Maybe you shouldn't be walking. Maybe you oughtta lie down, yeah?"

Again though, no answer, the stranger just shambling closer still, grunting in pain with every laboured step, writhing baby screaming in his arms...

"Seriously, mate," Sam said, "ain't no way you should be on your feet, man. No way."

But still no response. Was this guy *deaf?* Did he speak *English?* Could he speak *at all?*

Eventually, just a step or two away from Sam and the boys, the towering stranger—seven feet *easily,* Sam saw now—lurched to a halt. And that was when Sam finally clocked that the guy's crazy height was far from being the craziest thing about him. Because what the *hell* was this dude *wearing?* Was that a... a *cloak...?* And... *armour...?*

Swaying dangerously on his feet, the silent stranger reached down and began to gather up the loose corners of the baby's shawl into one bloodstained hand...

"Mate, I mean it," Sam said. "You gotta lie down, man. Lie down before you— "

"Take him," the stranger said, thrusting the whole squirming, shrieking bundle of baby straight at Sam with a single powerful arm.

"Wh-wh-whoah!" Sam stammered, stumbling backwards in shock. "What do you think you're— "

"Keep him safe," the stranger said, and his

voice, though barely a choked whisper, somehow rang with a terrifying authority.

"Eh? What? No!" Sam gasped. "What are you— "

"I will return for him," the stranger said, forcing Sam back farther still, hard up against the overfilled wheelie bin, screaming baby dangling from the man's outstretched fist.

"Hey hey hey," Sam gasped, a white hot panic now starting to boil up through his chest. "You gotta chill, man. I dunno what's going on here but— "

Then the stranger's other hand shot forward and grabbed Sam by the collar, slamming him back into the side of the wheelie bin. "There is no time. Look at me."

Sam tried to wriggle free. But couldn't. Tried to prise the stranger's fingers apart. No chance.

"I said *look* at me," the man grunted. "Look into my eyes. *See* the truth."

And hanging there in the stranger's throttling grip, Sam could do nothing except stare back into those desperate, penetrating eyes. Eyes filled with fear and pain and—

And then he saw it.

In the stranger's eyes Sam *saw* it.

Saw the *truth*.

And the truth was darkness. The truth was despair. The truth was death.

Unless...

The stranger lowered his eyes, staggered backwards, and Sam looked down...

... to find that the baby was now in his arms. In his arms and no longer crying. Just lying there quietly, cuddling into Sam's chest. Had Sam taken it himself? He couldn't remember.

With another gasp of pain, the stranger turned, stumbled a little, then began to lurch off again. And as he did, something fell from beneath his cloak, hitting the litter-strewn ground with an echoing clang. Whatever the object was though, the stranger paid it no heed, just kept staggering onwards, back up the alley.

"Oi! Stop!" Sam yelled.

No answer.

"Hey you! Wait!"

Nothing. And the guy was already halfway to the end of the lane.

In a single frantic rush, Sam thrust the baby into Rabbit's arms and took off after the stranger. Hurtling up the dark alley, he saw the lurching figure ahead of him reach the end of the lane then stumble out of view around a corner. A split-second later, another blinding flash lit up the night sky, and a further blast of that incomprehensible noise battered at the air. The sound of it was still ringing in Sam's ears even as he rocketed from the mouth of the alley...

... and stopped dead.

For a long moment, Sam just stood there, his heart pounding, his eyes scanning all around him in confusion. Because what he saw made no sense. The broad residential street Sam now stood in was brightly lit for its entire length. But on it there was not a soul to be seen.

The stranger was gone.

No way, Sam thought. *Absolutely no way. The guy could barely walk...*

Just what the *hell* was going on here?

Shaking his head in bewilderment, Sam turned and began to jog back the way he'd come. Ahead of him he could once again hear the sound of the baby echoing down the shadowy lane. Kid was back in the crying game, it seemed, and louder than ever apparently. Though actually, "crying" didn't come anywhere near to describing the noise this baby was making. The relentless, heartfelt shriek of it seemed to hurt Sam's head in a way he found hard to make sense of...

Jogging closer to the spot where he'd left his two mates, Sam could make out Rabbit up ahead now, bouncing the wailing, wriggling baby up and down at arm's length. "Ssshh, it's cool," Rabbit was cooing to the kid. "Everything gonna be okay. Your Uncle Rabbit's here, innit? We gonna... Okay, this thing's leaking from both ends now," and with an appalled grimace, Rabbit thrust the crying baby unceremoniously onto a startled L-Man beside him. A bad move, as it turned out, the kid responding with yet more kicking and wailing...

... while in Sam's head, that strange pain seemed somehow to dig deeper...

Baby now thrashing in *his* arms, L-Man's reaction was both instantaneous and entirely predictable. "Whoah! Bruv! Dry-clean-only!" the guy yelled, gaping down in horror at the front of his immaculate vintage shell-suit and the drooling, leaking infant batting its snot-smeared little fists against it. "Get this thing off me, man! Now! I mean it!"

In response, said infant just shrieked louder still...

... while in Sam's head, that strange pain dug deeper again—deep enough this time to make Sam stumble as he jogged to a stop beside his mates once more. Head now positively pounding in agony, Sam reached out to steady himself against the wheelie bin, but before he could actually get a hand to it, L-Man shoved the screaming baby back into Sam's arms...

... and all of a sudden the kid stopped crying...

... while at the exact same moment, the blinding pain in Sam's head vanished.

Simply drained away in less than a second, as if someone had pulled a plug. Sam almost stumbled again just with the sheer unexpected relief of it.

"Hey," Rabbit said with a grin. "What about that then? Reckon he likes *you,* bruv."

"Wow! You ain't kidding," L-Man said. "*Look!*"

Still fighting to make sense of exactly what had just happened to him, Sam finally managed to blink away the worst of his confusion and glanced down at the baby in his arms...

... to find the kid looking right back at him, beaming forth one dazzling, gap-toothed, medal-winner of a baby smile while ten chubby infant fingers groped for Sam's nose.

For a long moment, Sam just stood there, at a loss as to how to respond. Oh, he knew perfectly well he should smile back. That's what you were supposed to do with babies, right? It was like some kind of law. In the end though, Sam *didn't* smile back. *Ignoring* the baby's smile, *ignoring* those ten tiny fingers reaching for him, Sam turned again to his mates. "Bloke's gone," he said.

"Huh?" L-Man grunted, already scrubbing away at the front of his shell-suit with a tissue, buffing its polyester shine back to peak nineties condition. "What do you mean gone?"

"Just gone," Sam said, hauling out his phone.

"Who ya calling?"

"Who ya think?" and jabbing three numbers into its keypad, Sam pressed the mobile to his ear. But even as the phone on the other end began to ring—

"Whoah… bruvs… *look*…"

It was Rabbit's voice, and for the second time tonight its tone was hushed and trembling, if anything even more so than before.

Great. What now? Sam thought, turning with L-Man to discover Rabbit on his knees by the overfilled wheelie bin, retrieving something from the shadows there.

"Whoah…" Rabbit gasped again. "Oh my *God*…"

And as the guy stood up, pulling what he'd found out into the open, Sam heard *himself* gasp, too, his lungs emptying like he'd just been sucker punched by Mike Tyson.

A thin voice trickled from Sam's phone:

"Nine nine nine. Which service do you require?"

Sam's reply did come, eventually, stammered and hoarse, but the words seemed barely to be his own—"P–p–p–police, please…"—and even as he explained the situation to the officer on the other end of the line, Sam still could not tear his eyes away from the object Rabbit held out before him.

The object the stranger had dropped as he ran off.

Clutched in Roger "Rabbit" Crawford's two trembling hands, glinting in the light of L-Man's glowing iPad, was the hilt half of a huge broken sword, its jagged stump of blade dripping with what could only be fresh blood.

•••

Sam, Rabbit, and L-Man hurried on through the Walworth Estate's night-deserted streets, frost crunching beneath their trainers, their breath condensing before them in swirling puffs. The broken sword now dangled from Rabbit's hip, thrust through one of his belt loops, while huddled in Sam's arms, the mysterious baby lay silent and shivering.

"I'm telling you," Rabbit said, "We shoulda stayed where we was. Scene of the crime, innit?"

Sam shook his head. "Kid's freezing, Rabbit. We gotta get him inside. What if he's got hypothermia or something? My mum's a nurse. She'll know what to do."

The baby had turned out to be male—a brief inspection in the alley had revealed that much at least, along with the odd (and oddly *disturbing*) fact that this tiny, dark-skinned little boy had, in the middle of a London *winter*, been wearing nothing more than what appeared to be a few scraps of cloth and a rough woollen shawl.

"What the hell *is* that stuff he's wearing anyway?" Rabbit said. "Them ain't no pampers, bruv. Them's like towels and stuff."

"Well... maybe he's, you know, really poor or

something," Sam said. "Like, some homeless family's kid. Or something…"

L-Man nodded. "Yeah, makes sense. That bloke? Homeless nutjob. Gotta be, right?"

Rabbit looked unconvinced. "Uh-huh. Know a lot of homeless nutjobs what are nine feet tall, wear armour, and carry a bloodstained sword then?"

L-Man mused. "Dunno. He asks if you wanna buy a *Big Issue*, you ain't gonna say no."

In truth, Sam wasn't all that convinced either, though to him, what the stranger or the baby were wearing seemed almost the *least* freaky part of all this. Looking into that guy's pain-filled eyes on the other hand… what Sam had experienced *then*— that feeling of paralysing despair, an eternity of darkness—now *that* had been a whole other level of freaky.

In the end though, none of this was really their problem, was it? Sam's house was just around the corner. They'd be there any minute. His mum could warm the kid up with a fan heater or something while they waited for the police, and the cops would take it from there.

Someone else's problem then.

"Hey, look," L-Man said as they hung a left onto Walworth Avenue and the flats that Sam lived in finally came into view. "They was quick."

L-Man wasn't wrong. Outside Sam's block, a

police car was already pulling up, and as the boys drew nearer, the car's front doors swung open, and two policewomen climbed out.

One of the officers—a hefty woman about Sam's mum's age—turned in the boys' direction, spotted Sam with the baby, and waved. Sam raised a hand in reply, and as the officers began to approach, the hefty one smiled, calling over, "You must be Samar then?"

"Yeah, that's me," Sam said.

Coming to a halt in front of the boys, the two policewomen glanced down at the shivering bundle in Sam's arms, and a concerned frown creased Hefty's brow. "So this would be the— "

But then, for no good reason that Sam was able to see, she stopped. Froze almost.

Just like that. Mid-sentence. Mid-*frown* even.

Beside her, the second policewoman looked puzzled for a moment and then turned to her partner as if about to say something. But before she could, she too seemed to freeze.

And there they stood. The pair of them. Rigid, blank-eyed, and completely silent.

"Um… hello?" Sam said. "You all right?"

Nothing.

Sam opened his mouth to speak again…

… and that was when he saw it.

At first, Sam could make little sense of what it *was* he was actually seeing. The policewomen's eyes, they seemed to be changing, *darkening* somehow, a strange kind of inky black stain swirling into them, leeching them of colour and life. What the *hell?*

Behind him, Sam heard Rabbit gasp and L-Man stammer out, "W-w-whoah, bruvs, are you guys seeing what I'm— "

Then all at once, the two policewomen began to shake—twitching, juddering spasms that escalated rapidly into a kind of wild, erratic jerking. Then more rapidly still into a full-on nightmare of convulsive thrashing.

What came next though? That truly went *beyond* all nightmare.

While Sam and his friends stood watching, frozen in utter terror, the women's thrashing bodies started to swell, flesh rippling and pulsating like simmering porridge as grotesque new musculature bulged and flexed beneath their dark uniforms. Sam heard tiny, machine-gun-like ripping sounds as stitches popped and fabric split, and then the officers' bloating torsos burst from their clothing: limbs lengthening, thickening, growing taut with powerful new sinew; skins roughening, scaling over, darkening to a hideous shade of devil red.

Somewhere, a trillion miles away, Rabbit whimpered, "Guys, w-w-what's happening?"

Freakish, knife-like talons sprang from the

49

policewomen's fingertips...

Black horns thrust their way through monstrous, broadening foreheads...

And now it was Sam who was shaking. Shaking with horror as his mind tried to deny the truth of what he was seeing. Tried to show him mercy.

But there was no mercy. Not tonight.

Because the policewomen were gone.

In their place now, leering down at the Walworth Warriors, evil boiling from their dark red hides like a noxious acid mist, were two hulking, horned demons.

3

Demons and Chips

Sam tried to run. But couldn't.

Tried to scream. But couldn't.

His entire body had seized up, every muscle in it straining against every other, every rational thought erased by sheer terror.

He could only watch as two pairs of demonic black eyes fell upon the baby in his arms. Could only listen as one of the creatures let out a low snarl. Could only stand there frozen to the spot as the monster raised a massive arm, spread its clawed fingers to strike—

—and that was when the baby screamed—a stab of raw uncomprehending horror that lanced straight into Sam's mind, finally unlocking his fear-numbed body.

"RUN!" Sam yelled at Rabbit and L-Man.

The three boys turned and ran.

Shrieking baby clutched to his neck, Sam hurtled back down the deserted street, his heart hammering wildly in his chest, his mind screaming for answers. What the hell was happening here? What *were* these things? What did they want? Were they following?

He shot a glance over his shoulder.

Oh God, *yes*, they were freakin following! Not even ten metres behind, the two creatures were now in full-on pursuit, galloping down the middle of the road with a kind of lurching, ape-like gait, each stride almost a leap on its own. Sam felt his stomach turn over at just the sight of it. Whatever the hell these things were, they were fast. *Really* fast.

Forcing the terror down into the soles of his pounding feet, Sam threw himself onward, the baby's screaming head battering against his shoulder as he ran, Rabbit and L-Man powering along at his heels.

Behind him, one of the creatures suddenly let loose a terrifying roar—a screeching, hate-filled bellow that seemed to tear at Sam's ears. *Way* louder than it should have been.

Way *closer*.

Sam shot a second glance over his shoulder—

—and felt another lurch of pure horror. Rabbit

was still there, thank God, keeping pace with Sam. But L-Man... L-Man was starting to fall behind.

And the two galloping monsters were closing in. Closing in *fast*...

Sam hurtled onward, his mind racing with electric terror: *No way are we gonna outrun these things. No freakin way. Gotta lose them somehow. Find someplace to hide...*

Hurling himself around a corner, Sam skidded wildly on the frosty ground, ricocheted off a parked car, raced on down the empty street.

Another quick glance back—

—and another jolt of shock. L-Man was even *farther* behind now, five metres at least. While behind *him*...

Wait...

Behind him *nothing*. Both creatures were now out of view, still somewhere back around the corner. Which gave Sam and the boys a few seconds to get themselves out of sight!

Sam's eyes whipped front again—

—and there it was. Next doorway down. *The Fishcoteque* chip shop, its cartoonish sign—a disco-dancing cod—glowing above the entrance.

Flinging himself headlong through the shop doorway, Sam vaulted the serving counter and dropped down behind it, wailing baby still clutched tight to his shoulder.

An instant later, Rabbit tumbled to the floor

beside him, totalling a waste bin on his way down, sending greasy food wrappers flying.

Huddled out of sight below the counter, Sam and Rabbit waited for L-Man...

And waited...

And *waited*...

Oh God. L-Man! Where the hell was—

Then the chip shop door slammed open again, and L-Man came careering through it.

"Bruv! Here!" Sam yelled, leaping to his feet with Rabbit.

As L-Man stumbled towards them, Sam and Rabbit leaned forward, grabbed the big guy by his shell-suit sleeves, and hauled him bodily over the chip shop counter, all three of them slumping into a heap on the floor behind. How the hell they managed to avoid crushing the terrified baby still clinging to Sam's neck, Sam would never know.

"Oh God!" Rabbit shrieked. "Oh God oh God oh God..." The bruv was hyperventilating again, his lungs whistling like a leaky tyre as he squeaked out words in staccato bursts: "What are they?— WHEEZE!—What are them things?—GASP!— Sam, what the hell *are* they?"

"Shut up or they'll hear you!" Sam hissed. "Stay down. Maybe we lost 'em. If we can just— "

But before Sam could finish, one of the doors behind the counter—the one leading out into the back shop—suddenly swung open, and a lone figure stepped through it.

"Samar? Samar, what do you think you're doing?"

Standing there in his fish-fryer's whites, Sam's dad gaped down in complete bewilderment at the three boys now cowering beneath the serving counter of his shop.

"Dad, sssshhhh," Sam urged. "Please, something's after us. Something's— "

"Enough," Sam's dad said. "Out you go. The lot of you. You *know* you can't be in the frying area. Seriously, Health and Safety would have a— " and that was when he spotted the baby on Sam's shoulder. "What on earth… Samar, what is going on here?" Shutting the door behind him, Sam's dad began to stride towards them. "Whose baby is that? What are you boys— "

But then he stopped.

Stopped dead.

Exactly like the two policewomen before him.

"Oh God…" Rabbit whimpered, scrambling backwards into a far corner. "Oh God no…"

Sobbing baby still clinging to his neck, Sam lurched again to his feet and stumbled towards his blank-eyed father. "Dad? Dad, are you okay! DAD! Speak to me!"

But Sam's dad didn't respond. Just stood there as that same strange darkness began to swirl into *his* eyes. As that same awful trembling began to shudder through *his* body.

Barely even thinking about what he was doing, Sam grabbed the nearest heavy object to hand and swung it hard like a club. With a dull thud, thick glass struck his father square in the side of his head, and like a puppet whose strings have been cut, the man sagged unconscious to the floor. For several more seconds, dead silence reigned in the empty chip shop. Eventually, L-Man's disbelieving tremolo drifted up from somewhere beneath the shop counter:

"Bruv... you just decked your dad with a jar of pickled eggs."

And then the entire chip shop window exploded inwards as half a ton of red-skinned abomination came crashing through it, slamming onto the shop floor in an avalanche of glass.

Sam barely had time to hear Rabbit's shriek of terror, to feel the baby on his shoulder grip him tighter still, before the creature's meathook claw came at him. Came at him faster than Sam would ever have believed possible, four razor talons slicing straight at his head.

No, not at *Sam's* head.

At the *baby's*.

Sam ducked. Pulled the baby clear. Watched the monster's claw whip by barely centimetres above them. Splayed talons ploughed through the shelf behind the counter, sending rows of glass salt shakers flying. One of them thunked hard into Sam's head, knocking him to the ground again. A second shaker smashed into a wall opposite, shattering on impact and spattering its powdery contents down the demon's lashing right arm…

… and even as the salt touched its skin, Sam saw the creature freeze.

Because where the salt landed, the demon's red leathery hide began to sizzle, to blister, wisps of yellow smoke rising from bubbling skin. A split-second later, the creature threw back its monstrous head and howled, clawing wildly at its burning arm.

For a moment, Sam just sat there on the floor, gaping in confusion… and then his head whirled to a low shelf beneath the countertop—a shelf stacked with catering-size plastic squeezy bottles of salt. Lunging forward, Sam grabbed one of the salt bottles, bit open its plastic spout, then leapt to his feet again, pumping a thick jet of white straight at the howling creature.

And with another ear-splitting scream, the monster jerked backwards, thrashing and writhing, yellow smoke now billowing from a pizza-sized patch of blistering skin on its chest.

Still cowering beneath the chip shop counter, L-Man sat there for just a moment longer, gawping in disbelief at the salt bottle in Sam's outstretched hands… and then the big guy leapt into action himself—jumping to his feet, snatching up another of the salt bottles, ripping off its entire cap, and then swinging the whole thing like a bullwhip. Sam watched a wide arc of salt lash from the container's open end to stripe the creature down one complete side...

... and for a third time the air shook with the monster's agonised howls.

"Rabbit!" Sam yelled over the unholy shrieking. "Rabbit! You with us?"

But Rabbit was still just sitting there, shaking and hyperventilating in a far corner of the serving area, while the howling monster flailed and thrashed on the other side of the counter.

"Rabbit!" Sam yelled again. "Back door! Now!"

Still no response.

"RABBIT!"

At last, the guy turned to look at Sam... but his eyes were dull, dead, hazy with shock.

"Rabbit! Go! Now! Back door!"

Eventually, Rabbit's glazed eyes drifted lazily towards the door to the back shop—the door that Sam's dad had entered through and now lay slumped beside. But still the bruv made no move. Sam really thought that the guy had totally locked up. That somebody would have to drag him screaming from his—

Then Rabbit was up on his feet and away, bolting for the door.

As the bruv ran, Sam and L-Man sprayed and lashed the raging creature on the other side of the counter, keeping its whipping claws back, away from Rabbit as he flew towards the exit. Vaulting over the body of Sam's unconscious dad, Rabbit threw himself at the closed door, wrenched its handle downwards, and shoved. But even as the door burst open, Sam saw his slumped father shift suddenly where he lay, then choke out a low groan and begin to spasm again, limbs thrashing wildly, head smacking against the tiled floor at Rabbit's feet.

With a squeal of terror, Rabbit hurled himself on through the open door, disappearing into the back shop beyond. At the same time, Sam snatched up two of the fallen glass salt shakers from the floor beside him and pitched one of them hard at the ceiling directly above the rampaging monster. Smashing into a central light fitting, the shaker practically exploded on impact, salt avalanching down onto the startled demon beneath, and as the burning creature howled and thrashed, Sam thrust L-Man towards the door. "Go!" he yelled.

L-Man didn't need telling twice. In an instant, the big guy was gone, dodging the writhing monster's flailing claws and throwing himself through the open doorway.

A heartbeat later, arms wrapped tight around the screaming baby on his chest, Sam leapt to his feet and followed—

—sprinting over the bottle strewn floor—

—lurching past his dad, still spasming on the tiles—

—scrambling onward into the open doorway—

—and that was when he slipped.

Brown sauce? Vinegar? Mayonnaise? Could have been anything, but Sam's front foot hit something wet on the tiled floor, and he went down hard. Only for a second, yes, but long enough, and even as he was dragging himself upright again, a flailing demonic claw came flashing straight at his face.

Sam screamed in shock—

Threw himself to one side—

But too late.

Four razor talons sliced through the soft flesh of Sam's cheek, and a shocking splash of dark red spattered the screaming baby in his arms. Molten agony surged into Sam's head, and his legs almost gave way there and then. But somehow, Sam buried the pain in rage and ran on, flinging himself through the open doorway, stumbling onward into the back shop.

Up ahead, he could see Rabbit now hauling frantically at a second door opposite—their only way out. Wheezing in terror, Rabbit wrenched at the latch. Pulled again at the handle. At last, the door flew open, its steel reinforced bulk slamming back against the wall——

——and there in the doorway stood the second demon.

Rabbit screamed. They all did.

And the demon in the doorway bellowed its triumph.

With unholy glee, the monster blocking their only escape reared up to its full nightmarish height, flashed a clawfull of deadly talons at the petrified Rabbit, and——

"Duck!" Sam yelled, lobbing his second salt shaker straight at the creature.

Rabbit ducked, and the shaker cannoned over the bruv's head to shatter against one of the demon's horn. Clouds of white caked the monster's face in an instant, and howling in agony, the creature clawed at its black eyes before falling backwards into the darkness beyond the door.

"Go!" Sam screamed, and Rabbit launched himself forward, out into the pitch dark of the alley behind the chip shop. Sam and L-Man barrelled through after him, dodging the lashing, whipping claws of the demon on the ground, then hurtling on up the alley, racing for the lights of the main street ahead. But before they were even halfway there, Sam heard yet another eruption of animal fury behind him and shot a glance over his shoulder——

—to see the fallen creature in the alley clambering once again to its clawed feet, just as two more monsters—one of them in fish-fryer's whites—lurched out of the shop's back door.

"Oh, man, demons, them's demons! Freakin demons! I'm not even lying, bruv!" It was L-Man's voice, the big guy babbling hysterically as he charged along at Sam's side.

"Just keep running!" Sam screamed back. "If we can just— " But then a second wave of agony surged through Sam's head, and just as he and the boys rocketed from the end of the lane, Sam stumbled, his entire body pitching forward into a wild freefall. Baby still screaming on his shoulder, Sam flung out a desperate hand at the ground rushing up to meet him, his head jerking to a stop only centimetres above the grimy pavement. Torrents of blood rained down from Sam's torn cheek, splashing the slabs below. Oh, God... so much blood! Had all of that come from *him?* From his *face...?*

But even as Sam's mind tried to process this fresh horror, Rabbit and L-Man were hauling him to his feet once more. At the same time yet another demonic roar pulled Sam's eyes back to the alley behind them. Back to the three creatures from Hell now thundering up it, their claws raking the walls on either side, throwing off showers of sparks, shards of redbrick shrapnel.

Sam tried to force his legs back into action, but again, blinding agony exploded in his head and he collapsed onto Rabbit and L-Man. Gasping with terror, the two bruvs began to stagger forward anyway, dragging Sam and the baby with them, step by laboured step.

But Sam could feel his senses dulling now. Sounds starting to fade, sights to blur...

He tried to speak. Tried to tell the boys to leave him. To grab the baby and run...

But no words came out...

... and once again, the oncoming demons howled, all three of the creatures still hurtling up the lane towards them.

Sam realised it was over now. All over.

Suddenly, he found himself wishing he hadn't been so mean to Asha earlier...

Wishing he'd been a better big brother to her...

Wishing he'd just—

Then the roar of an engine. A squeal of brakes. And a car screamed to a halt beside them.

Right *there* beside them. Wheels actually *on* the pavement. Door less than a metre away.

What the hell...?

Through the pain and the blurring vision, Sam tried to make sense of what he was seeing... but there was no sense to be made. The car that had pulled up looked like something out of a cartoon.

Gleaming and black and crazy long—a stretch limo but with the unmistakable engine grill of a Rolls-Royce.

"Get in!" a voice commanded through the car's open driver's window.

Behind them, still more howls of demonic rage rang out, the three galloping monsters now just twenty metres away. Less even.

"In the back!" the voice barked. "Now!"

L-Man began to heave Sam towards the limo.

"What? No!" Rabbit yelped. "We can't just…"

L-Man stared at Rabbit in disbelief. "What? Stranger danger? Big ass, poop-your-pants demon danger, bruv!" and yanking open the limo's back door, L-Man shoved Sam and the baby inside, diving in after them. Sam saw a gasping Rabbit shoot one final terrified glance over his shoulder then hurl himself headlong into the limo, too. And even before the bruv had pulled the door shut behind him, the car's engine roared and the vehicle took off again, brutal acceleration slamming all three boys back in their seats.

With the last of his ebbing strength, Sam somehow managed to drag himself round to look out the car's rear window, and as the limo powered away he saw the trio of demons finally burst from the mouth of the alley, leap out onto the main street—

—and then just stop dead, slashing at the empty

air around them while they howled their fury at the night sky. An instant later, all three creatures collapsed as one to the tarmac, jerking and spasming in the deserted road, and even through his rapidly fading vision, Sam could see that the monsters were transforming again. Horns receding. Torsos contracting.

They were changing back. All of them. Sam's dad, too. Becoming human once more...

Then the limo careered around a corner, and the rest was lost from view.

"All right, good," the man behind the wheel growled. "Now just stay back. Keep the baby as far away from me as you can. Too close and— "

L-Man gasped. "Oh God! You'll turn into one of them things! You will, won't ya?"

"Just... stay *back*."

Once again, the pain in Sam's head surged, and once again he felt his senses submit to it, dulling a little more. A *lot* more, actually. Sam could still make out his friends' faces, still feel the baby clinging to his shoulder, but it was all starting to recede now, as if the world were stepping slowly backwards into the shadows and taking the pain along with it...

L-Man leaned in and lifted Sam's sagging chin. "Bruv? You okay? Sam? Talk to me!"

"I'm... I'm okay..." Sam croaked. "I'm... I'm just..." But then his head flopped forward into L-

Man's hands, and he saw the big guy recoil with a gasp, the bruv's two upraised palms now covered in blood. *So much* blood.

"Oh God," L-Man babbled. "Sam, you're messed up, man! Seriously messed up!"

Still wheezing in terror, Rabbit banged on the smoked glass window of the driver's compartment, yelling at the shadowy figure behind it: "We gotta get him to a hospital, man! Hey you! You hear me! We gotta get him to a— "

"No. No hospitals."

Once more, Sam felt the pain surge... and once more the world took another of those slow backward steps into the shadows...

"We gotta, man!" Rabbit shrieked. "We gotta!"

"No hospitals."

Another surge, another step...

"He's messed up, man! He's freakin messed up!"

Sam felt the whimpering baby cling tighter around his neck...

Felt soft infant flesh press into the shredded remains of his cheek....

Heard a distant Rabbit wheeze out three more syllables: "Sam? Sam! SAM!"...

Then the world took a final step backwards... and the rest was lost in darkness...

4

Perdita

Sunshine and laughter.

Bright as each other and filling Sam's world.

Oh, there was other stuff, too. The happy bloat of a stomach full of sandwiches and cola. The earthy/oily smell of the tree Sam was climbing. The can-it-really-be-true awesomeness of all that lay ahead. Six weeks of summer holiday freedom!

But sunshine and laughter...

Somehow those two things just seemed more of a big deal today.

Locking his legs tight around the branch he'd just pulled himself up onto, Sam paused for a moment to take in the view below. The busy play park. His mum and dad flat out on a picnic blanket. Asha all but dancing a jig at the foot of the tree, gazing up at Sam in four-year-

old adulation. Hers was the laughter, of course. As ever, it bubbled from her in an endless stream, an effortless sparkle of sound that sometimes drove Sam crazy.

Not today though.

Grinning down at Asha on the grass below, Sam waved a brotherly hand, Super Commando Dhruva smiling in support from the front of Sam's well-worn T-shirt.

In response, Asha twirled and boogied, her laughter ringing out louder still—merry, mad and musical.

Truthfully, Sam felt just the teensiest bit sorry for his little sister right at this moment. He knew Asha would give anything to be doing what Sam was doing now.

But hey, the perks of being ten, right?

And with Asha's joyful laughter still jingling in his ears, Sam began again to climb...

"Sam?"

Asha's laughter began to fade...

"Hey! He's waking up! Sam?"

The sunshine was fading, too...

"Sam? Yo! You with us, mate?"

Whereupon two fuzzy shapes loomed into view, emerging slowly from the vanishing light of a summer sun four years in the past. They were human on the whole, these two shapes, though one of them—the shorter one—did appear to have a giant head...

(It's an afro, you wally...)

... while the other—a significantly *larger* human shape—appeared oddly... reflective...

(*Shell suit, you muppet. Get a grip, Sam...*)

Blinking several times, Sam let his vision come into focus...

"L-Man? Rabbit?"

The very same. Sam's two friends stood over him, frowning with concern.

"You okay?" L-Man said.

A question that made *zero* sense to Sam. Why *wouldn't* he be okay?

But then, as he blinked some more and turned his head to look around him, Sam finally began to realise that something was not right here.

Seriously not right here.

Sam seemed to be on a bed. Not his own bed though. Not even close. The object he was currently reclining on looked like something out of a movie—a huge, elaborately carved four-poster with a blue satin canopy and an entire mountain range of plump feather pillows stacked against its dark headboard. And as for the *room* the bed sat in... well, once again, any kind of "real world" that Sam knew was nowhere in evidence—fancy antique furniture, towering multi-paned windows, an honest-to-God *chandelier*...

Frowning in confusion, Sam turned again to his friends to question them... and as he did, became aware of a slight, itching pressure against his right cheek. Frown deepening, his fingers darted in to investigate the sensation… and found there what could only be some kind of medical dressing—a bunch of absorbent pads all taped to one entire side of his face.

Panic began to flutter deep in Sam's gut.

Had he been in an *accident?*

Sam couldn't remember.

How had he got here? Where *was* here anyway?

Sam realised now that he couldn't remember *anything.* "Guys…? What's going on? What is this place? How did we get here? I don't— "

That was when he finally clocked what lay beside him on the bed.

A baby.

A tiny baby. Fast asleep, thumb jammed in its mouth, head nuzzled into Sam's hair.

And just like that, the memories came crashing back in.

The crazy guy in the armour. The baby. The chip shop. The monsters…

"Oh God!" Sam gasped, dragging himself upright on the bed. "Them things! The demons! They— "

"It's okay, bruv," L-Man said. "Chill. I think we're safe here."

And then the worst memory of all.

"Dad! Oh God, my Dad! He turned into one of them things!" Sam's right hand flew to his pocket.

70

"I gotta phone home! Gotta— Huh? My phone! Where's my phone?"

L-Man shot a nervous glance at Rabbit before turning back to Sam. "Okay, look, don't freak out, yeah? She took our phones. Said she had to. Said the cops could trace us with 'em."

"What? Who? What you on about? What the *hell* is going *on* here?"

For a long moment, Sam's two friends just stood there, as if scared to answer, but eventually, L-Man heaved out a shaky sigh then turned to a low table by the bed. On it was a small stack of newspapers. L-Man grabbed the top one—a copy of *The Metro*—and passed it to Sam.

Scowling in complete bewilderment now, Sam unfolded the newspaper, raised his eyes to the front page... and felt the breath leave his lungs like he'd just been kicked in the gut.

The newspaper's enormous headline, taking up almost half the front page by itself, screamed, "BURNED! POLICEWOMEN INJURED IN BIZARRE ACID ATTACK", while below this, filling most of what remained of the page, were three individual pictures—grainy school photos of Sam, Rabbit, and L-Man. A further sub-headline beneath the three pictures read: "WANTED FOR QUESTIONING. HAVE YOU SEEN THESE BOYS?"

Sam looked back up at his friends, gaping at

71

them in utter disbelief. "Acid? What they talking about acid? That ain't what happened... Them things, they... Oh, God, they..."

"Bruv, I know," L-Man stammered. "Believe me, I know."

"Where *are* we? What *is* this place?" Sam began to haul himself out of the bed. "We gotta get back! Tell 'em the truth! We gotta— "

"Sam, wait," Rabbit yelped. "Just... wait. I mean... think about this for a minute, yeah? You really think the cops are gonna believe us? *Us?* Bruv, I was there and *I* don't believe us."

"She says we can stay here for now," L-Man said. "I think she's got some kind of plan. Maybe we should listen to her, yeah? Just, you know... hear her out?"

Sam glared back at his friends "She? Who? Guys, I *gotta* phone home! My Dad! He turned into one of them things! He— "

"Your father is unharmed, Samar. That much I am able to assure you."

The voice came from somewhere behind Rabbit and L-Man, and at the sound of it the two guys turned as one, parting like mismatched curtains to reveal a lone figure framed in the elegant arch of the bedroom's open door.

It was a girl. A teenage girl. Maybe the same age as Sam, maybe a little older, she stood there poised in the bedroom doorway, peering in at them all with a kind of detached curiosity, her straight blonde hair framing a composed, near expressionless face, her sky blue eyes as cool and as distant as the private-school reserve in her voice:

"By now your father will have recovered completely," the girl said, taking two gliding steps into the room. She moved gracefully, like a ballet dancer, and as she entered, a second figure stepped through the door behind her to stand protectively at the girl's shoulder. This particular figure was an elderly man, dressed all in black, like... well, like a butler, Sam supposed. Did rich people actually still have those? Another memory sparked in Sam's mind then. The limo driver. Was this the same guy? Something told Sam that it was.

"Unfortunately," the girl continued, "like the two policewomen, your father will also have no clear memory of exactly what happened to him. In all likelihood he will— "

"Enough!" Sam snapped. "Who are you? What is this place? What do you want?"

The girl paused, her face betraying just the merest hint of a raised eyebrow. "My name is Perdita," she said at last. "This is my home. And for now, I simply want your trust," at which point her cool blue eyes shifted and fell upon Sam's injured cheek.

"Remove your bandages," the girl said.

Sam shot a nervous glance at L-Man and Rabbit, but the pair of them now looked just as confused as Sam was. What the *hell* was going on here? Who did this girl think she—

And suddenly the girl called Perdita was in balletic motion again, heading straight for Sam. "Your bandages," she said. "Take them off."

Alarm flashed into L-Man's face. "Whoah, girl, no! Stop right there! He is *seriously* messed up, babe! You can't just— "

But before L-Man could make a move to intervene, the girl's hand darted forward and ripped the entire dressing from Sam's face. A cascade of absorbent pads tumbled to the hardwood floor, every single one of them caked with dried blood.

And if Sam thought he'd been confused before, the silence that fell on the room now left him utterly mystified. L-Man and Rabbit both just stood there, *gawping* at him.

"What?" Sam blurted at them all. "What is it?"

In response, the girl raised a hand to indicate a huge, gilt-framed mirror on one wall.

Shaking his head in utter frustration, Sam turned his angry gaze to the mirror—

—and froze.

Because what he saw in it made absolutely no sense.

Cocking his head to one side, Sam peered

harder at the mirror's gleaming surface. Walked towards it. Paused. Moved in closer still. All but pressed his nose up against it.

Nope. No sense whatsoever.

Last night, some kind of monster had practically ripped Sam's right cheek clean off. This morning, that same cheek ought to have been a grisly mess of torn flesh and clotting blood.

But it wasn't.

Sam's face had completely healed. There wasn't a mark on it. Absolutely none. Just perfect, unblemished, skin.

When he finally turned back to the girl, Sam's voice was barely a whisper. "That... that's impossible," he said, and for the briefest of moments, Sam thought he saw a hint of actual expression—just the faintest of smiles—flicker across the girl's tightly composed features.

"No, not impossible," she replied. "Just... miraculous," and pursing her lips thoughtfully, the girl called Perdita directed a brief, meaningful glance at the baby on the bed, before turning once more to Sam and his friends. "You really have no idea who this child is, do you?"

Sam looked across at his baffled mates, then drew himself up and locked eyes with the mysterious girl standing before him:

"Maybe you better tell us."

• • •

Half an hour later, she did, and Rabbit's response pretty much summed it up for all of them:

"Girl, you are having a laugh," the bruv blurted, jamming another sausage into his gob.

Sam and his friends sat together around a huge oak table in a vast, high-ceilinged dining-room, the baby perched close beside them in a high-chair. Clustered in the centre of the table was a miniature city of silver trays, all piled high with food—sausages, bacon, black pudding, eggs— while over at the table's distant far end, the girl called Perdita sat before an untouched bowl of muesli, her butler Travis standing protectively at her shoulder.

Sam stared across at the girl, his jaw still dangling, his brain still struggling to process what she had just told them.

Perdita let the moment settle then continued:

"It was only ever meant to be a temporary solution. The angel thought that, in the short term at least, the child would be safe here. Safe from the Darkness. The angel believed that he could go back to his own time, gather his forces, defeat the Darkness, then return here for the baby. But that was a mistake. A terrible mistake. Somehow, the Darkness managed to follow the baby here, and now any adult who comes within six feet of this child will find themselves enslaved. Possessed by the Darkness itself. Craving only one thing."

Sam laid down his fork and knife. Suddenly, he didn't feel like eating anymore. "To kill the baby," he mumbled, his eyes darting reluctantly to the little boy in the high-chair beside him. "Them things... that's what they wanted. That's *all* they wanted."

A beat of bleakest silence followed, during which the baby looked up curiously from his bowl of pureed fruit to spot Sam staring at him. As ever, that gap-toothed baby smile wasn't far behind— sunshine through smeary clouds of stewed apple and pear—and even after the terrible things he had just been forced to listen to, Sam almost found himself smiling back.

Almost.

"But this... this *angel* or whatever the hell he was," Sam said. "He can still come back, yeah? Do what he's gotta do and come back for the baby?"

"No. I'm afraid not. After passing the child to you last night, the angel did succeed in returning to his own time, but the effort of it took the very last of his strength. He died."

"So... what are you saying? That the baby's, what, *trapped* here now?"

"Yes. That's exactly what I'm saying."

Rabbit proceeded to stuff an entire fried egg into his face. "Girl, that bloke weren't no angel. No wings, innit."

Sam ignored the guy. "But this... this *Darkness*

thing. What *is* it? What does it *want?*"

"What the Darkness actually *is* remains unclear," Perdita said. "What it *wants,* on the other hand, could not be clearer. The Darkness seeks only two things—chaos and despair. It thrives on both. *Feeds* on them, you could say. And killing this baby would, as you might imagine, generate significant levels of chaos and despair."

L-Man whispered in Sam's ear, "Bruv, seriously, are you buying *any* of this?"

The million dollar question, Sam thought. *Was* he? And then, once again, he caught a glimpse of his own reflection in the sparkling silver of a coffee pot—his left cheek, smooth and unmarked where it should have been torn and bloody...

Shaking his head, Sam turned once more to Perdita. "How do you even *know* all this stuff?"

"My father was an archaeologist," the girl said and gestured to the room around them, all four of whose walls were lined from floor to ceiling with row upon row of glass-covered shelves, each and every one of them stacked high with a bewildering array of what Sam took to be ancient artefacts—sculptures, pottery, books, bones...

"In the early part of his career," Perdita went on, "my father's work was funded by the Roman Catholic church. Because of this he had privileged access to many rare documents in the Vatican library, and one of these—a fragment of a first century scroll called the Gospel of Benjamin—piqued my father's interest greatly. In the end, he devoted much of the rest of his professional life to retrieving further fragments of that scroll, piecing together as complete a version of it as he could. Travis, if you would be so kind…"

And in sombre silence, the butler at Perdita's shoulder nodded then took a single step up to the table. In the old man's hands were two fat, leather-bound folders, and with a respectful dip of the head, Travis set them both down on the dining table then stepped back again.

Perdita pushed one of the folders—the fattest one—towards Sam, and after a moment, Sam flipped it open. A thick, acrid smell wafted up from between its heavy leather covers—musty and ancient, filled with secrets somehow.

Dark secrets…

As Rabbit and L-Man leaned in closer to see, Sam began to leaf through the folder's pages. About half of them seemed to be flat pouches of clear plastic with ragged fragments of ancient parchment sandwiched between the two transparent layers. The remaining pages—interleaved between the parchment—were modern printer paper, every last sheet of it filled to the very edges with diagrams, tables, tiny handwritten annotations. Sam could read almost none of what was there, ancient or modern.

"Huge gaps still remain in the narrative," Perdita said. "Even now it's probably less than half recovered. But the story it tells is... fascinating."

Sam could feel the girl's eyes on him, as if trying to gauge his initial reaction to what she was showing him here. "Okay," he said finally, "so what's it say then?"

"In essence, the Gospel of Benjamin is an alternative account of the nativity story."

L-Man scoffed. "Let me guess. With big-ass monsters and time-travelling angels and— "

"Shut it, L-Man," Sam said.

L-Man shut it.

Sam flipped a few more pages, his eyes roving over the folder's incomprehensible contents. "And this... Gospel of Benjamin. *That's* what told you how to find us? *That's* how your butler dude there was able to swoop in and rescue us at *exactly* the right moment? Some ancient scroll told you what was gonna happen *last night?* In *London?* A time and a place?"

Perdita shook her head. "Not exactly. In truth, the gospel itself is somewhat sketchy on details, but there are... supporting documents, one of which did give a *very* exact time and place," and with her cool blue eyes still fixed on Sam, Perdita pushed forward the second folder, grabbed one corner of its gold-embossed cover... then flipped it open.

For several seconds, Sam could make no sense of what he was looking at.

Actually, no, that wasn't it.

Sam's mind simply refused to accept the *insanity* of what he was looking at.

Inside the second folder was today's *Metro* newspaper.

Except it wasn't. It was a copy.

Not a photocopy though. Oh no. What Sam and the boys were now gawking at in open-mouthed astonishment was about as far from a photocopy as it was possible to get.

The complete front page of this morning's *Metro* appeared to have been meticulously recreated—hand drawn and hand lettered—on what looked like ancient parchment. Recreated and *embellished* actually, the most notable case in point being the headline that filled the top half of the page (BURNED! POLICEWOMEN INJURED IN BIZARRE ACID ATTACK), the entirety of which had been artfully and elaborately ornamented with multicoloured swirls and curlicues, like some kind of medieval illuminated manuscript. Below the headline, the body text of the story itself also seemed to have been painstakingly copied, though not entirely accurately, Sam saw. Even at a cursory glance, the writing appeared to be rife with weird misspellings and oddly mirrored letters—

metrupolitan pelice, onti-sociol dehaviour—almost like whoever had transcribed it had been unfamiliar with the English language. With the English *alphabet* even. And as if all of this weren't bewildering enough, then there were the pictures—the three "school photos" of Sam, Rabbit, and L-Man. Each of these had also been replicated (quite brilliantly, Sam thought) in brightly coloured inks, right down to the finest detail. To the minutest wrinkle of L-man's skewed school tie. The actual likenesses themselves weren't perfect, Sam reckoned, but somehow he got the impression that they were never intended to be. It was almost as if their three faces had been... Sam struggled to find the word... *idealised,* that was it. *Romanticised,* his English teacher might have said. The impression was pretty much hammered home by the fact that each of those grinning, finely-etched mugshots also sported a bright shining halo of gold leaf.

It was Perdita who broke the silence this time. And a shedload of silence there had been.

"I imagine the original will have decomposed centuries ago," she said. "So at some point, evidently, this... copy was made."

"Centuries?" L-Man blurted. "But that's today's *Metro!*"

"Check it, bruvs," Rabbit murmured in wonder, letting his fingers trace the gleaming halo around his own saintly hand-drawn head. "Golden afro! Awesome…"

And even Sam had to smile at that. Cos yeah, okay, this *was* kinda funny. Weird and funny. (And with a go-large side of freakin terrifying, let's not forget that, right?)

But even as he smiled, Sam began to feel something else. An unpleasant tension in his gut. An idea that, comedy halos aside, he was *not* gonna like where all of this was heading.

Looking up again, Sam met Perdita's cool blue eyes and held them. "Okay," he said. "So what else then? What else does this loony tunes "gospel" of yours say?"

Perdita paused, as if trying to choose her next words with great care. And maybe she should've tried harder, because the words she eventually came out with were so completely ridiculous that Sam could barely believe he was hearing them:

"The Gospel of Benjamin tells us that the angel placed the baby in the care of three young… warriors."

"I'm sorry?"

"That these three warriors swore an oath to protect the baby with their very lives. That they made it their duty to defeat the Darkness and return the child to his— "

"Okay, *stop*. Just… stop," and Sam stood abruptly, the fronts of his thighs thudding into the edge of the table, toppling cups and rattling cutlery. In the high-chair beside him, the baby looked up sharply, his big brown eyes starting in surprise.

Sam took a deep breath. "That is *completely* insane!"

"Believe me, I know how this must sound, but— "

"We're not *warriors!*"

"Samar— "

"We're just *kids!* Kids from a lame boxing club no one else is desperate enough to join!"

"Please, Samar, if you'll just sit down we can— "

"L-Man there?" Sam jabbed a finger at his friend. "Only reason *he* joined Warriors is cos his mum said he were getting too fat!"

"Oi! I'm big boned," L-Man said. "And the laydeez, they love it."

"And Rabbit?" Sam barked out a laugh, immediately regretting the harsh, uncaring sound of it. "Only reason *he's* in the club is cos he got fed up getting the crap beat out of him by Jammo Benson!"

Rabbit gulped down another sausage, observing thoughtfully, "In Jammo's defence, I'd beat the crap out of me if I could."

Sam threw up his hands in despair. "Us three? *Warriors?* Swearing oaths? Protecting babies?

Fighting monsters? Girl, you are out of your freakin mind!" and thrusting both fists into his pockets, Sam turned on his heels then stomped over to a far window.

It was a bad move, and Sam knew it even as he set off. Before he had made it so much as halfway to the window, the baby in the high-chair started to cry, and in Sam's head, a familiar knot of pain began to form...

"Samar, please, you *have* to believe me," Perdita said, her voice hardening. "If you abandon this child now, he will die, and the Darkness will triumph."

Sam didn't respond. Just stood there scowling out the window, while behind him the baby's cries grew louder, and in Sam's head the knot of pain began to tighten...

Sighing in frustration, Perdita rose from her seat, extracted the screaming baby from the high-chair, and moved to the window to place the little boy on Sam's shoulder.

Instantly the kid stopped crying, and instantly the knot of pain in Sam's head vanished.

"Don't you see?" Perdita said. "He *needs* you. All *three* of you." A thoughtful frown stole onto the girl's brow then. "I think... I think he may have *chosen* you."

Still Sam said nothing, and after another moment, Perdita moved in closer, her lips only centimetres from his ear now. "Please, Samar…" she whispered, and Sam saw her eyes dart briefly to L-Man and Rabbit. "Your friends, I see how they look up to you. If you were to— "

That did it. Sam whirled on her. "NO! Get away from me! Just get the *hell* away!"

Perdita stumbled backwards, her eyes widening in shock.

"This is total B.S.!" Sam yelled, and already he could feel his breathing speeding up, his teeth grinding down. Could all but *see* a grinning Old Red crick his neck and crack his knuckles. "We didn't ask for this!" Sam shouted. "This *ain't* our problem!" and scowling in fury, he plucked the startled baby from his shoulder, thrust him back into Perdita's arms, and began to head for the exit.

"Samar, please, wait!"

Sam ignored her, marching full-tilt for the dining-room door where Travis the butler now stood in sentry-like silence, regally unperturbed even as Sam stormed towards him.

"You!" Sam barked at the man. "Take us home! Now!"

Without waiting for an answer, Sam yanked the door open and strode on through. And even as he stepped out into the hallway, he heard the baby's screams of distress resume behind him, the pain in Sam's head kicking in again almost instantly.

Except now it was more than just a knot.

Now it was a fist. Clutching and squeezing and twisting…

Hauling in a deep breath, Sam stashed the pain and set off down the hall. A quick glance behind confirmed that Travis was following. Rabbit and L-Man were too, the pair of them currently legging it past the butler to move in on either side of Sam.

"Bruv, wait," Rabbit squeaked, jogging along at Sam's shoulder. "Maybe we should— "

"Shut it. We're outta here."

"But— "

"I said shut it," Sam growled and stalked onwards, the baby's shrieks and wails echoing down the corridor behind him. Shrieks and wails that somehow refused to diminish in volume despite the ever increasing distance between Sam and their unhappy source. In fact, if anything, the kid's crying actually sounded even *louder* now. How the hell did *that* work?

Sam glanced left. Spotted a massive arched doorway down a short corridor.

Front entrance. Had to be.

Ducking down the corridor, Sam stomped up to the door and heaved it open. Bright morning sunshine smacked him full in the face, and as it did, the fist of pain behind Sam's eyes gave a sudden, extra brutal wrench. So brutal in fact that Sam actually staggered this time. Almost dropped to his knees right there on the front doorstep.

Swearing under his breath, Sam recovered, clenched his jaw, and just powered onwards, heading for the Rolls-Royce stretch limo parked only ten metres away on the gravel drive. Head pounding in agony, Sam stumbled up to the car, lurched to a halt by its back door. Rabbit and L-Man were right behind him, Travis bringing up the rear.

Sam saw the butler zap the limo with a key-fob. Heard the chirp of the vehicle's central locking. *Barely* heard it, if truth be told. Because in reality, Sam could *barely* hear anything now, his whole head ringing with screams and wails that, in any sane world, he should *not* have been able to hear at all. Screams and wails from a kid over a hundred metres away. A kid on the other side of at least *two* stone walls.

And there was something else now, too. Something *behind* the screams. *Beneath* the pain. Something deeper. Darker. A kind of terrible, soul-numbing sorrow...

Sam hauled open the back door of the limo. All but fell inside. Rabbit and L-Man clambered in after him, Travis sliding wordlessly into the driver's seat.

"Go!" Sam grunted, massaging his eyes with the heels of his hands as ever more agony spiked into his brain, as ever more of that unbearable sorrow clawed at his heart.

"Sam? Sam, you okay?" It was Rabbit's voice, the guy's frightened squeal cutting across the relentless shrieks still drilling into Sam's ears. "You don't look so good, man."

"I'm fine," Sam gasped. "Just go!" he yelled again at Travis.

And with a low rumble, the limo set off, accelerating smoothly down the sweeping arc of gravel drive, while huddled in the corner of its rearmost seat, Samar Chowdhury squeezed his eyes shut and gritted his teeth, praying that he'd never have to look at that crazy girl or that damn baby ever again...

• • •

Two minutes later, the dining-room door slammed back against the wall, and Sam stood there gasping in the doorway, his pain-filled eyes locked on the girl called Perdita and the writhing, screaming baby in her arms.

Stumbling his way across the room, Sam snatched the wriggling infant from the girl and collapsed into a chair, the little boy slumping forward onto Sam's shoulder and falling instantly silent.

In the end, the limo had driven only as far as the main road. Sam hadn't been able to let it go any farther. Had in fact ended up screaming himself.

Screaming for them to turn back.

In a strange way, it had felt a little like looking again into that dying angel's eyes... only a million times worse. As if the accumulated pain and despair of all humanity had been about to bury Sam alive. Oh, he knew how crazy that would sound if he ever tried to say it out loud. How extreme. But Sam could think of no other way to describe it.

And he knew something else, too. That the baby was *not* doing this to him on purpose. Of course he wasn't. How could he? He was just a *baby*. All he wanted was *baby* stuff. Fruity-goop in a Thomas the Tank Engine bowl. A warm blanket to snuggle into. His own mum and dad.

Especially his own mum and dad.

And if the kid couldn't have *them* at the moment, apparently Samar Chowdhury was the next best thing.

Slumped in the dining-room chair, baby yawning on his shoulder, Sam suddenly became aware of a strained silence all around.

He looked up.

Three anxious figures stood there looking down at him and the baby. Rabbit, L-Man, and Perdita. Travis the butler completed the picture, lurking just a little farther back, a safe distance from the kid.

The silence drew on, all four of them just staring at Sam in the chair, waiting, as if expecting him to say something.

Eventually, Sam got to his feet, drooping baby still cradled against his shoulder.

He turned to Perdita.

"I ain't the leader," he said.

"P-p-pardon," Perdita stammered.

"You got all the knowledge here. *You're* the leader. Understood?"

Perdita stared back at Sam in confusion. "I... yes, if that's what you—"

"Okay, good. So, what do we do now then?"

"I... don't know yet."

"How do we stop this Darkness thing?"

"I don't know."

"How do we get *him* back to his family?" Sam nodded to the baby on his shoulder.

"I don't know."

Shaking his head in despair, Sam looked Perdita up and down. "Permission to speak frankly, sir? You just better go get your posh blonde crap together then, yeah?"

And for the very first time since they'd met, Sam saw Perdita let her guard down, her jaw clenching in indignation and anger flashing into her eyes.

Sam almost smiled.

Maybe the girl was human after all.

5

Devine

Detective Inspector Marjory Devine slurped at her morning coffee and marched grimly over Walworth Road, striding past the busy forensics team scouring the broad section of street around the *Fishcoteque* chip shop. Scene of last night's delightful little "incident", the entire area was already cordoned off, surrounded by uniformed officers, a veritable hive of paper-suited, latex-gloved activity. Better yet, signs were even now looking good for a pretty decent evidence haul. Small mercies, Devine supposed. And once again she felt her stomach clench as the unpleasant details of the incident in question resurfaced in her mind. Up until ten o'clock yesterday evening, Devine honestly thought she'd seen it all.

Certainly as far as the group she liked to refer to as *bloody kids* was concerned. But what had happened here last night had shocked even her. *Acid?* And two days before *Christmas? Bloody kids* hardly seemed to cover it. Word was that both the officers who'd been attacked would recover fully, but nevertheless, as far as Devine was concerned, the whole thing marked a final nail in a child-sized coffin. Kids today? Sick little monsters, every single one of 'em, and DI Marjory Devine was going to find these vicious hooligans, find them fast, and put them away.

Spotting DC Jackson waiting for her across the road, Devine headed towards the young detective constable, nodded curtly to him, then marched straight on past, making for a block of flats just two doors down the street. "So what's the story then?" she asked Jackson as he fell into step beside her. "I wasn't expecting the hospital to let the father out for hours yet."

"Seems there wasn't a mark on him, ma'am."

"No acid burns?"

"No. Just on our two, as it turns out. But that's the other thing, ma'am. Whatever it was, it wasn't acid. Look." Jackson handed over a lab report, and Devine skimmed it as she marched.

"'Traces of sodium-chloride...'" A frown puckered Devine's brow. "*Salt?*"

"It's just a preliminary report, ma'am. They'll

have more for us later today."

Devine found her frown deepening anyway. "*Salt?*" she said again and shook her head in confusion.

Arriving at the entrance to the block of flats, Devine offered a further curt nod to the officer standing guard there then strode on into the building's main stairwell with Jackson.

"Apparently, the father still remembers nothing though, ma'am," Jackson said.

"Uh-huh."

It was Jackson's turn to frown. "You think he's protecting his son?"

Devine paused by the door of a ground floor flat and smiled cynically. If there was one group she knew even better than *bloody kids,* it was *bloody parents*. "What I *think*," she said to Jackson, "is that we've got a boy here who collects asbos like football cards and a father who knows how this could end. Families of kids like this? They close ranks. Every time." Devine rang the doorbell, nodding sourly to the door's nameplate as she did so. "Believe me, lad, we'll get no help from this lot. Nothing but a stone-cold wall of— "

The door flew open, and a distraught, middle-aged Asian woman rushed forward. "Have you found him?" the woman gasped, all but throwing herself onto Devine's chest. Her frightened face was wet with tears. "Please, have you found our son? Oh God, you haven't, have you? Tell us what we can do! Please! We'll do anything. *Anything!* You *have* to find him!"

Devine opened her mouth to speak... but nothing came out. In truth, this was about as far from the reception she'd been expecting here as it was possible to get.

A second or two later, a middle-aged Asian man stepped up to place an arm around the woman's heaving shoulders. Devine recognised him immediately as Ali Chowdhury—the acid attack's third victim and father of one of the three main suspects.

"It's okay, love. It's all gonna be okay," Mr. Chowdhury said to his wife before turning to acknowledge Devine and Jackson in the doorway. "Come in, please, officers."

Mr. Chowdhury led the way into the flat's narrow hall, pausing by an open kitchen door at the end of it. "Could you just... give as a moment, please?" he said to Devine.

Devine nodded, and Mr. Chowdhury gently ushered his shaking wife into the kitchen, pulling the door closed behind them.

Silence fell.

Devine could see Jackson frowning, his eyes filling with questions. But before the young detective could pose any of them, a small, weary voice piped up from behind:

"Excuse me…"

Devine turned.

In a doorway halfway down the hall, a little girl stood. She looked to be about eight years old, her tiny drooping form swamped in Spider-Man pyjamas at least three sizes too big for her. Something about the girl's eyes seemed to draw Devine's attention. They looked dazed somehow, unfocussed… and then Devine remembered that Asha Chowdhury was blind.

"Um… hey there," Devine said. "You must be Asha, right?"

The little girl nodded, grimy tear tracks streaking her solemn face.

"Nice to meet you," Devine continued. "My name is— "

"Can you give this to him?" Asha Chowdhury said, her voice a tired, toneless croak.

Devine looked down.

Clutched in the little girl's hands was a Christmas present. Probably the worst-wrapped Christmas present Devine had ever seen—layers of crumpled paper and copious lengths of twisted Sellotape, all plastered around some awkwardly-shaped item about the size of jam jar.

"To Sam, I mean," Asha said. "Can you give this to Sam? When you find him?"

Devine felt her throat go dry and the beginnings of a scowl etch its way into her brow…

"I got it special," Asha explained. "I wrapped it myself."

"Well, um…" Devine cleared her throat and then forced herself to look back up at Asha Chowdhury. "When we find him, you can give it to him yourself, can't you?"

"How?" Asha said. "You're going to put him in the jail. You think he's bad. You don't even *know* him and you think he's *bad*."

Detective Inspector Marjory Devine felt her scowl deepen and two familiar words begin to form unbidden in her mind…

Bloody kids…

6

Secrets and Skulls

"I'm telling ya, Sam, *that* ain't normal."

Rabbit stared down at the contents of the discarded nappy with a kind of twitching horror, as if what lay there might suddenly spring to oozing life and reveal a homicidal resentment of afros and bad teeth.

"Relax, Rabbit. It's normal," Sam said, plucking another wet-wipe from the plastic tub by his side.

The two boys sat together cross-legged on the floor of the cosy, first-floor nursery that Perdita's butler had led them to after breakfast. All around, faded pictures of teddy bears and cuddly dinosaurs beamed down from walls the colour of strawberry yoghurt, while between the boys, on the immaculate deep-pile carpet, the baby lay naked on a plastic changing mat, kicking and gurgling as Sam cleaned him.

And smiling, too, of course. Let's not forget that.

Smiling that big, gap-toothed baby smile of his. Smiling it right at Sam.

Who once again did everything he could to avoid meeting it.

Catching hold of the baby's two air-dancing feet, Sam pulled gently, lifted the little boy's lower half, and applied wet-wipe to soiled backside.

Rabbit, meanwhile, continued to squint nervously at the reeking load in the used nappy. "*Normal?* Seriously? Are you blind? It's green!"

"Yup. Completely normal."

"Yeah, if you're, like, an alien! Whoah! Do you think— "

"No."

"Cos I seen this thing on YouTube— "

"Rabbit, he ain't an alien. He's just a baby. You know? A poop-machine with a siren."

Rolling his eyes, Sam balled up the used wet wipe and dropped it into the dirty nappy...

... while on the changing mat before him, the little baby boy continued to kick. Continued to gurgle. Continued to *smile*.

At Sam.

Only at Sam.

Shaking his head, Sam grabbed another wet-wipe and went in for a final polish. "Let's get this thing done, okay? That way we can all— "

But just then the baby's waggling fingers suddenly found Sam's thumb, clenching tight around it.

Baby feet boogied and bopped.

Baby eyes beamed up at Sam.

Baby fingers tugged at Sam's thumb. *Shall we have this air dance?*

Yanking his hand free, Sam completed a hasty last swab and threw the used wet wipe into the discarded nappy.

When he looked up again, Rabbit was frowning. "Yo, bruv, he's just being friendly."

"Bucket," Sam snapped, thrusting the used nappy at his reproachful mate.

Distinctly unimpressed, Rabbit pulled out the broken sword still hanging from his belt loop and hooked the dirty nappy with it. "Just saying, man," the guy muttered, and with the entire soggy bundle dangling from the stump of broken blade, Rabbit strode over to a corner of the nursery and dumped the whole lot into a nappy bucket on the floor there. Lounging in a comfy armchair nearby, L-Man offered a brief grunt of disgust in response but otherwise seemed barely to have registered the ill-tempered proceedings. Predictably,

Walworth's whitest gangsta was once again thumbing at his iPad, looking for all the world as if actual horns-and-everything demons hadn't tried to rip them to shreds last night.

Rabbit scowled down at the glowing tablet. "You sure the cops can't trace us from that?"

"GPS is off," L-Man said. "It's cool, bruv."

"Ain't no K in ecstasy, bruv."

"Cheers, bruv."

Seating himself on a low window ledge, Rabbit glanced thoughtfully around the room for another moment or two... before his forehead creased again in a frown. This time of puzzlement. "Hey. You notice something weird here?"

An arch of eyebrow darted above the rim of L-Man's Ray-Bans. "Um... time-travelling babies? Miracle healing? Bloodstained angel swords. You wanna narrow it down, bruv?"

"Look around," Rabbit said. "No tinsel, get me? No reindeers, no snowmen, no inflatable Homer Simpson Santa."

"So?"

"Ain't just this room neither. Whole house. You even seen a Christmas tree? I ain't. Christmas-free zone, innit?"

Sam put down the talc he was using to dust the baby's backside and looked around. Rabbit was right. Now that Sam thought about it, he hadn't seen a single Christmas decoration since they got here. Not one.

L-Man just shrugged. "Too classy for that, ain't she."

"Too posh for Christmas? Man, that is sad," Rabbit said, turning again to L-Man in the armchair... at which point Rabbit's eyes seemed to pause. And linger thoughtfully. *Deviously* even, Sam thought. A moment later, he saw a sly grin creep onto Rabbit's face.

"So..." Rabbit said, "reckon we're finally gonna get a chance to see some of them famous Loverman "moves", yeah?" and he nudged L-Man's shoulder. "We are, ain't we?"

L-Man looked up, his pudgy brow knitting in confusion. "Huh?"

"Posh," Rabbit said.

It took a moment for L-Man to get it, and even when he did, his frown just seemed to deepen. "Um... Sam got first dibs there, man. You seen the way he looked at her."

Sam choked back an actual guffaw. "Eh? Where the hell you get that from? You like her, you do your thing."

Rabbit grinned, waggling his eyebrows at L-Man, but the big lad just continued to scowl back, offering a muttered, "Sorry, bruv. No can do. Ain't got no wing man, yeah?"

Whereupon a grinning Rabbit simply plonked himself down next to L-Man on the armchair and grinned wider still: *You do now*.

Outmanoeuvred on all fronts, L-Man finally heaved out a defeated sigh.

"Excellent!" Rabbit squeaked.

Just then, the nursery door swung open, and Travis the butler stepped into the room. "Miss Perdita would like to see you all now, please," the old man announced, aloof as ever.

"Yeah, well, tell Her Majesty she'll have to *wait*," Sam said. "It's time for his feed."

And there it was again. That petulant, pointless, angry tone. Even the baby had noticed it, the kid's big brown eyes blinking up at Sam, not exactly upset but certainly confused.

If Travis was offended though, he didn't show it. "Fifteen minutes?"

Sam nodded, and the butler turned on his heels and left.

After another moment, a frowning Rabbit hopped off the armchair and strode up to Sam, tutting like a little old lady. Disapproval pursing his lips, the guy leaned in to beam down at the tiny naked boy wriggling on the changing mat. "Yes. Yes he *is*," Rabbit cooed at the baby. "Uncle Sam is just a big old grumpy pants, innit? But you? *You* is just the cutest thing ever."

And then the cutest thing ever peed in Rabbit's face, an arcing jet of dandelion yellow squirting from the baby's business end to hit the bruv straight between the eyes. Drenched from afro to Adam's apple, Rabbit leapt back in total shock, screaming and spluttering and shaking his head wildly, sending twinkling droplets of baby-pee sailing gracefully through the sunlit nursery.

And for the first time today—for the first time in weeks really—Samar Chowdhury cracked an actual, genuine smile.

•••

Fifteen minutes later, Sam, Rabbit, and L-Man were following Travis down wood-panelled corridors, past battered suits of armour and crumbling statues, heading who-knew-where for their scheduled appointment with the Queen of the Castle. The baby, now fed and fast asleep, lay slumped over Sam's shoulder, snoring faintly as the boys trailed along after the butler.

Eventually, Travis brought the group to a halt before a grand arch-topped doorway, pulled open the heavy oak door there, and moved silently aside to usher the boys through.

Stepping over the threshold, Sam found himself in a large, gloomy library—endless rows of darkwood shelves stuffed with countless ancient books and box files. A vast, green-topped desk dominated the centre of the room, and as the boys entered, Perdita rose from a chair behind it, offering them all a formal smile before glancing at the baby on Sam's shoulder.

"If he's sleeping now, you can put him here," Perdita said, indicating a small cot that had been set up beside the desk. Crisp white sheets, thick woollen blanket, even a cuddly toy. You had to hand it to her, Sam thought. Girl was thinking ahead.

Sam laid the sleeping baby in the cot, tucking the blanket around him, and in the accompanying silence, he saw Rabbit nudge L-Man. *The moves, bruv. The moves...*

With a heavy sigh, L-Man sidled up to Perdita, his mighty-afroed wingman apparently superglued to his shoulder. "Hey... so... um... you like music? Who's your favourite— "

"What on earth is that *smell?*" Perdita said suddenly, her face twisting in a grimace as the outer regions of Rabbit's still damp afro wafted just centimetres beneath her twitching nose.

Sam couldn't resist. "Holy water," he muttered, giving the baby's blanket a final tuck.

The girl threw Sam a bewildered glance.

"Never mind," Sam said, and silence fell on the room once more, the "moves" apparently concluded for the time being as L-Man threw murderous looks at Rabbit.

Shaking off her confusion, Perdita turned and began to make her way to a corner of the library. "This way, please," she said, stopping in front of one of the massive bookcases there.

Sam and the boys exchanged puzzled looks before moving in behind the girl in mystified silence. This way *where?* It was a *bookcase*.

"Travis, if you'd be so kind…" Perdita said, upon which the butler appeared suddenly at the girl's shoulder, where he proceeded to undo his tie, reach down his shirt, and remove a thin silver chain from around his neck.

On the end of the chain was a key.

A key in the shape of a tiny sword.

Turning to the bookcase, Travis reached for one of the tatty, leather-bound volumes stored there and tugged. But the book didn't come out. Instead, its spine flipped back to reveal a smooth steel plate, in the centre of which was something as ordinary as it was unexpected.

A keyhole.

In sombre silence, the butler inserted the sword-shaped key into the hole, gave it a quick half turn, and with a muffled whirring sound, the entire bookcase began to slide back.

Rabbit's jaw sagged. "Whoah! Seriously? You got a lair? Bruvs, she's got a lair!"

"Ain't a lair, you muppet," L-Man sneered. "Girl ain't the Red Skull."

"So what is it then, smart arse?"

The bookcase slid to a stop, whatever lay behind it still hidden in darkness.

L-Man cocked his head. "I think it's a... a *safe*."

"You're quite correct," Perdita said, just as banks of spotlights flashed on to reveal a steel-lined room, about the size of a large walk-in closet, shelved all the way up both sides.

"This," Perdita said, "is where my father stored all his more... *sensitive* acquisitions," and dismissing Travis with an all but imperceptible nod, the girl stepped forward into the safe, beckoning Sam, Rabbit, and L-Man to follow.

Glancing nervously at his friends, Sam took a deep breath and then lead the boys in. With his eyes growing wider by the second, Sam scanned the racks of shelves on either side of the safe's central aisle—shelves stacked high with yet more artefacts: books, maps, paintings, scrolls; a gruesome stone gargoyle that was the image of those creatures from last night; a black decaying skull leering out from a windowed casket made of what had to be solid gold.

"Essentially," Perdita said, "everything you see here is related in some way either to the Gospel of Benjamin itself or to the religious brotherhood that came to be associated with it."

Sam frowned. "Religious brotherhood? Like monks? What's monks got to do with this?"

"Oh, these were far more than just monks. This was a very particular monastic order. Very small. Very obscure. And *very* secret. My father believed that it was founded by the warrior angel himself just before he died. Its name alone is certainly suggestive of that."

"Its name?"

"They called themselves the Order of the Broken Sword."

A hush fell then, and all eyes darted to the stump of sword still dangling from Rabbit's belt loop, its broken blade glinting in the stark halogen spotlights.

"Okay..." Sam said, "so this... *brotherhood*... Where do they fit into all this? What did they *do*?"

"That," Perdita said, "is where things start to get a little more obscure. The order, along with many others, was forcibly dissolved by Henry the Eighth around 1540. Most of its archives were either lost or destroyed. The little that did manage to escape Henry's purge—every known surviving item in fact—is now actually here in this very safe, located and purchased by my father over a period of thirty years. Even so, the overall picture remains... patchy."

L-Man hauled a huge, leather-bound tome from a low shelf and began to flip through it, its yellowing pages filled with reams of indecipherable text and obscure diagrams...

Perdita continued: "There *are* a couple of things we do know for certain. One is that the order's spiritual base was located here in London. Another is that, over and above any day-to-day ecclesiastical role they might have played, the Order of the Broken Sword appear to have been sole custodians of one extremely important and closely guarded religious secret."

Sam let this sink in. "A way to defeat the Darkness and get the baby back home."

"That is what my father believed, yes."

"But you don't know what this secret actually is?"

"Not entirely, no. However, a number of the documents here allude to the existence of a certain... ritual."

Sam frowned. "What kind of ritual?"

"Unfortunately, surviving texts tell us very little about it. Only two things really. One is that it seems to be a way of focusing spiritual energy."

Sam shook his head. "I don't even know what that means."

"Yes, well, frankly, I doubt even the brotherhood knew exactly what it meant either," Perdita said. "Their few surviving depictions of it are all somewhat fanciful," and turning towards the far end of the safe, the girl pointed out a dark, flaking oil painting stacked on a top shelf. In the painting, several robed, monk-like figures stood in a circle on a low hilltop, their hands raised in religious adoration, while from the centre of the circle, a broad pillar of multicoloured light extended upwards into a starry night sky filled with legions of white-winged angels playing trumpets and harps.

Yep, "fanciful" was certainly one way of putting it.

"And this *ritual* thing…" Sam said, "*that's* what's gonna defeat the Darkness and get the baby back home to his mum and dad?"

"My father believed so. I do, too."

"You said there was *two* things you knew about the ritual. What's the other one?"

Perdita took a deep breath and locked eyes with Sam. "That it has to take place tonight."

A loud clatter echoed through the safe as L-Man dropped the ancient book he'd been studying, several of its pages bursting from their bindings and fanning out across the floor.

"Whoah! Tonight?" L-Man said. "Why tonight?"

All three of them stared at Perdita in disbelief.

"It's Christmas Eve," she said.

Because, of course, that cleared everything up, didn't it? Sam scowled at the girl.

Perdita sighed. "For a significant number of the world's religions, spiritual energies have always surged in midwinter. When days are darkest. When faith seems like all we have. Christmas, Hanukkah, the pagan festival of Yule, the Roman festival of Saturnalia. Dozens more, hundreds even, all the way back into prehistory. At midnight tonight, when Big Ben strikes and London greets Christmas day, *that* is when this annual midwinter surge of spiritual energy will peak here. *That* is what the ritual is designed to focus."

"But you have no idea what this ritual actually *is*? What we're supposed to *do*?"

"Well... no. But I'm hopeful that— "

"Okay, stop," Sam said. "Just stop. Girl, can you even *hear* yourself! You've had years to try and figure all this out! *Years!* You couldn't do it. And now you're giving *us*, what, fourteen *hours?* This is completely— " Sam bit back the rest. The word "insane" was getting *really* old here.

"*Vide vero,*" Perdita said, breaking the bleak silence.

Sam looked back at her. "What?"

"*Vide vero.* It's Latin. It means 'See the truth.' Many of the artefacts here—*most* of them in fact— display those same two words in some form or other." The girl nodded towards a small tapestry hung on the safe's far wall, and sure enough, woven into its elaborate, medieval design, front and centre, were the words in question. *Vide vero.* "It seems to have been some kind of motto for the brotherhood," Perdita continued. "Maybe even— "

"Wait," Sam interrupted, staring at the girl now. "It means *what?*"

"'See the truth.' Of course, quite possibly I'm

taking it all too literally, but for a long time now I've wondered if those words might in some way be referring to the three of you. That *you* were the ones who would *see the truth*. That, somehow or other, if I just brought you all down here to examine what we have, you might be able to... Samar? Samar, what is it?"

Sam could feel his throat starting to go dry, could *hear* his heartrate cranking up a gear, and turning on his heels, he darted back down the safe's central aisle, lurching to a stop beside a low shelf next to the door. For a long moment, Sam just stood there, staring at the object stashed on that shelf.

The skull. The skull in the golden casket.

Running a forefinger over the small plaque on the casket's base, Sam wiped away several layers of dust to reveal an intricate inscription engraved beneath. Just two words:

Vide vero.

See the truth.

No way. Just no way. It couldn't be that simple. Could it?

Squatting down to get a better look, Sam peered through the casket's glass front...

... and finally saw all that he needed to see. In one swift motion, Sam snatched the golden casket from the shelf and began to haul at its ornate top as if it might be a lid—

"Samar?" Perdita cried out. "What are you doing?"

—but the casket's top wouldn't come off, so with his heart racing faster still, Sam thrust an elbow straight through the front of the thing. The thin glass there shattered easily, and stuffing his hand into the box's dark interior, Sam grabbed the ancient skull inside, yanking it free just as L-Man appeared at his shoulder:

"Sam? Sam, you okay? What— "

And then L-Man froze as *he* saw it, too.

Saw what Sam had seen as he'd stared into the casket.

In the left side of the skull's cranium.

Running all the way from front to back.

A long, deep... *groove*.

Wide-eyed and open-mouthed, Sam reached out to trace the groove with the trembling fingers of his other hand, and as he did, a memory flashed through his mind:

Last night in the alley. The crazy guy in the armour. Blood trickling down his face. Blood from a long gash in the left side of his shaven head.

A gash that ran all the way from front to back.

"Samar? Samar, what is it?" Perdita again, her voice dim and distant now, like she was broadcasting from another planet...

"*See the truth*," Sam murmured, as much to himself as in reply to Perdita. "It's what that guy said to me last night. That... *angel*. Those exact words. But..."

"But what?"

"Before he said it... *right* before he said it... he said something else..."

Another flash of memory. Again from last night. The angel's choked whisper:

"Look into my eyes..."

And Sam could almost swear he actually *heard* the guy's voice then, right there beside them in the safe, whispering directly into Sam's ears. *Look into my eyes...*

Lifting the skull to eye level, Sam peered into the dark of its two gaping sockets...

...and frowned.

The rear wall of the left eye socket... it seemed to have crumbled away, empty brain cavity visible behind it, black and filthy, caked with grime...

Obscured by grime...

Sam brought the skull closer...

Raised it a little more...

Angled it so that light shone through the split in the skull's crumbling cranium...

And there!

Yes!

There it was!

On the rear of the brain cavity wall, all but hidden beneath the filth of centuries.

Writing!

7

London Stone

"Up a bit..." Sam said. "Bit more. Little to the left. *Other* left, Rabbit..."

It was fifteen minutes later, and they were all back in the library. The skull now sat on Perdita's desk—blackened teeth gnawing at the green leather of the desktop—while Rabbit stood hunched over it, listening to Sam's instructions and adjusting the position of a small webcam they'd wedged into the relic's left eye socket. At the same time, L-Man fiddled with an adjustable desk lamp, directing its beam through the long crack in the skull's cranium.

Behind the desk, next to the baby still fast asleep in his cot, Sam and Perdita sat together, the pair of them peering intently at the screen of a high-end laptop. "Okay," Sam said finally. "Everybody hold it *right* there."

Rabbit froze, L-Man withdrew his hands from the lamp, and Sam darted in to jam several blobs of Blu-Tack around the barrel of the webcam, holding it in place in the eye of the skull.

"Perfect," Perdita said and began to mouse her way through some of the laptop's display settings, tweaking the webcam's image on the screen. As she did, the boys moved in behind her to get a better look... and once again, all three of them shook their heads in amazement.

Sam could still scarcely believe what they'd found inside the warrior angel's skull. After they'd brought it through from the safe, Perdita had spent several long minutes with a soft brush, dusting the skull's interior through the eye socket, the process eventually revealing that, at some point in the distant past, the whole of the skull's brain cavity had essentially been polished flat, creating what amounted to a blank canvas of bone for the incredible work of art that had subsequently been engraved there.

In the engraving, legions of angels, etched in minute and painstaking detail, soared and swooped through a starry night sky so finely drawn that, even on the laptop's UltraHD screen, the indentations for the stars appeared like pin pricks. In terms of them learning anything useful from their discovery though, it had been the area of the engraving directly behind the eye socket that had looked the most promising—the area now displayed in dazzling high-definition on the laptop's screen. In this section, angels soared outwards from a central point occupied by a strange, abstract symbol—circular, almost flower-like, a cross between a dandelion head and a burning sparkler. Directly below this symbol was the writing that Sam had glimpsed when he'd first looked into the skull—three lines of a delicate, flowing script so neatly inscribed it could have been done on a computer. What that writing actually *said* however, Sam had no idea. At least half the letters there he didn't even recognise.

"Do you even know what language it is?" he asked Perdita.

"Yes," she said. "It's Greek. Koine Greek. Or at least a form of it. The first language of the Christian New Testament."

"Can you read what it says?"

"Give me a moment," and picking up a pencil, Perdita began to scribble in a small notepad, her eyes darting every now and then to the three lines of text on the screen. "Okay, here's the gist," she said finally and began to read from her notepad:

"In the centre of the centre of the centre,
Two become one that a light may shine,
A beacon through infinity."

Silence.

"Great," Rabbit said. "Anyone here speak bollocks? Like, more than usual?"

The silence stretched on...

"What about that symbol thing then?" L-Man said to Perdita. "You ever seen that before?"

Perdita's gaze returned to the laptop. To the mysterious symbol just above the text...

"No," she said at last, "I'm afraid not." But then she frowned... "Interesting though..." and once more, she reached for her pencil. "This may be entirely irrelevant, but the whole symbol does appear to be made up of just the one single figure repeated. Here, see..."

Grabbing her notebook, Perdita quickly sketched a thin meandering line down the length of a fresh page, and Sam saw immediately that the girl was right. The strange flower-like symbol inside the skull was indeed made up of repeated copies of this single looping line, all of them anchored together at one end and fanned out in a full circle.

Perdita shrugged. "It still means nothing to me though. Anyone else?"

Sam, L-Man, and Perdita scowled down at the notepad...

Once again, it was Rabbit who broke the silence. "Seriously?" he said. "You're not *seeing* it? What are you lot, braindead?"

In perfect comedy unison, two pairs of eyes and one pair of Ray-Bans turned to Rabbit.

"Eh?" Sam said.

Rabbit smirked, relishing his moment. "No *'Enders* fans in the house then?"

"Rabbit, *what?*"

And with a grin of pure triumph, Rabbit reached for Perdita's notebook then launched into a perfect imitation of the cliffhanger drum sting that came at the end of every episode of TV soap opera *Eastenders*—DOOF – DOOF – DUM-DUM-DUM-DUM. At the same time, the bruv rotated the notebook through ninety degrees so that the single looping line, drawn vertically by Perdita, now lay horizontally.

Sam was the first to get it. "Oh my…"

Then L-Man. "Holy crap! It's the Thames!"

And it was. The looping figure, seen horizontally, traced a line identical to the winding course of the River Thames, east to west, through central London. There was absolutely no doubt about it—the river's contours were unmistakable, seen in aerial view by millions almost nightly during the opening titles of *Eastenders*.

"Okay," Sam said. "I still don't see how that helps though."

But then Perdita let out a sudden gasp and grabbed the notebook, flipping back a page to her translation of the text. And as she stood there re-

reading what she'd written, Sam saw the girl's eyes widen, something bright stealing into her stunned face. Realisation? No. More than that. *Brighter* than that.

Revelation.

"You know what it means now, don't ya?" Sam said.

Perdita's eyes were getting wider by the second—glowing like someone had just stuck a trillion watt electric light bulb in her head. "Not everything," she said, "but the first part..." Her gaze darted once more to the symbol on the laptop screen. "Maybe..." and glancing down at the baby asleep in the cot beside them, Perdita chewed her lip for a second more then stood abruptly. "Come on," she said. "While he's sleeping. It's only twenty minutes' walk from here."

"Wait! What?" Sam felt a hot spike of fear stab at his chest, his own eyes widening now. Widening and then flicking anxiously to the snoozing baby. "We can't just... just *leave* him. What if he wakes up?"

"It'll be fine," Perdita said. "We'll be there and back in under an hour. And he's just had his feed yes? Surely he'll be asleep for a while yet."

Eyes still fixed on the baby, Sam felt another surge of panic but then shoved it back down. The girl was right. If Sam knew babies—and Sam was pretty sure he knew babies—the kid would be out for a couple more hours easy. "Okay. So where exactly are we going?"

"There," Perdita said, jabbing a finger at the exact centre of the symbol on the laptop screen, and when Sam shot her back a none-the-wiser frown, he could almost have sworn he saw the corners of the girl's mouth curl upwards into something approaching an actual smile. Snatching up her notepad again, Perdita flipped back to the looping line she'd just drawn and scrawled a tiny "x" at the "western" end of it, where the line's anchor point would have been if it had been part of the whole symbol.

"See?" she said.

Sam nodded. "Okay, yeah. But why? What's there?"

Again that shadow of a smile. "Cannon Street."

Sam threw a mystified glance at L-Man and Rabbit but saw immediately that his mates were just as baffled as he was, and when he turned back to question Perdita further, the girl was already heading for the exit.

"Why there?" Sam called after her. "What's in Cannon Street?"

Perdita paused in the doorway, turned to Sam and the boys, and this time there was absolutely no mistaking it—Perdita, the Queen of Cool, the Empress of Aloof, full-on *grinned* at them.

"London Stone," she said.

•••

Ten minutes later, Sam, Perdita, Rabbit, and L-Man were hustling their way on foot through the hectic heart of a central London packed with last-minute Christmas Eve shoppers and heaving with all that was festive. Reams of fake snow clung to window after window, the bittersweet reek of hot chestnut stalls hung heavy in the frosty air, and through open shop doorways competing speaker systems sparred in a cacophonous yuletide audio showdown—Wham! vs Wizzard, Pogue vs Womble. Slade would no doubt be lacing up their gloves soon.

London Stone, Sam wondered as he walked. So how come he'd never even heard of this thing? A mysterious, one-of-a-kind, ancient artefact, just sitting there, out in the open, right in the middle of central London? The whole idea seemed ridiculous.

"It's just down this way," Perdita said, turning a final corner and leading Sam and his friends onto the bustling battleground that was Cannon Street in the lunch hour.

"Hoodies up, eyes down," Sam reminded the boys darkly. On the way here, they'd spotted their pictures on almost every single newspaper stand. Frankly, being out in the open at all felt like madness to Sam now. This London Stone thing had better be worth it...

Moments later, at the foot of what appeared to be some featureless sixties office block, Perdita came to an abrupt halt, and Sam and the boys stumbled to a stop behind her.

"Well, here it is," Perdita said. "London Stone." And so saying, she stepped aside to reveal the exalted object itself in all its epic and wondrous awesomeness.

Or not.

Sam wasn't really sure what he'd been expecting to see here. A towering standing stone perhaps? Inscribed all over with indecipherable magical symbols? Or maybe some kind of prehistoric sacrificial altar slab, its deep cut channels stained with ancient blood?

What he *actually* found himself looking at... well, Rabbit's deflated mutter pretty much summed it up:

"It's a big rock in a cage."

Yup. Nailed it. London Stone turned out to be nothing more spectacular than a featureless lump of rough-hewn rock, about the size of a microwave oven, set behind a wrought iron grille in the wall of a branch of W.H. Smiths.

"I don't get it," Sam said, squatting down to stare through the bars of the grille at the object in the alcove behind. "What the hell even is it?"

Perdita opened her mouth to reply, but L-Man was already on the case, reading aloud from the glowing screen of his iPad:

"'London Stone. A historic landmark found at 111 Cannon Street in the City of London, England. Thought to be the last remaining part of a much larger object that stood in the street for several centuries before building work eventually necessitated its removal. While precise details of the stone's origin and purpose remain shrouded in mystery, myths and legends surrounding the artefact abound. Some have claimed it was once part of an ancient stone circle that originally stood on Ludgate Hill, while others maintain that the fate of London itself rests upon London Stone. That if the stone is ever stolen or destroyed, the city of London itself will fall. Still other legends assert that London Stone is in fact the actual stone itself from which King Arthur pulled the sword Excalibur.'"

Sam rolled his eyes at Perdita, "Seriously?"

"Just… listen, okay?" Perdita said and turned back to L-Man. "Go on."

L-Man continued: "'As to the stone's true archaeological origins, several competing theories continue to vie for academic attention, the most widely accepted suggesting that the object is in fact nothing more mysterious than an old Roman milestone, erected back when London was regarded as the *centre* of Roman Britain, with London *Stone* marking the very *centre* of London

124

itself.'"

And there it was.

A jolt of excitement rang through Sam's body. The text in the skull! *In the centre of the centre of the centre...* Sam could feel Perdita at his shoulder, waiting for his response. Her grin of triumph. Her eyes lasering into him...

"Okay," Sam said finally, "the centre of the centre. I get it. But the inscription in the skull said the *centre* of the centre of the centre. I don't see how that— "

The truth hit him like a fist to the forehead, and Sam's mouth fell open.

He turned to look again at the ancient bulk of London Stone...

Turned back to meet Perdita's wide, glowing eyes...

"It's inside!" Sam said. "Whatever we're looking for, it's *inside* London Stone! It's— "

And then a world of misery and torment exploded in Sam's head.

First came the screaming—a shrieking wail of infant horror, louder than bombs, sharper than a scalpel—and all at once Sam was stumbling into Rabbit.

"Whoah! Sam!" Rabbit yelped. "You okay? *Sam!*"

Next came the pain—a tidal wave of crimson agony—and Sam stumbled again.

"Oh God, Sam, what is it? Sam, what's *wrong?*"

Finally, there came the despair—that infinite, unbearable sorrow.

"Sam! Sam, *talk* to me! Oh God, what do we do? L-Man, what do we *do?*"

Somewhere in Sam's darkening world, a phone rang.

He saw Perdita haul hers out. Press it to her ear:

"Travis? Travis, what is it? What's happening?"

But those were the last words Sam heard. Like a single titanic entity, Screams-Pain-Despair reared in him one final time, and Sam collapsed to the frosty ground of Cannon Street, waves of numbing grey washing the agonies into a welcome oblivion...

8

Gearing Up

For Sam, the fifteen minutes that followed were a fragmentary, disjointed blur—a dark, distorted jigsaw puzzle with most of the pieces missing:

Rabbit and L-Man's arms around him, hauling him to his feet...

A girl's voice (What was her name again?) calling for a taxi...

Then screaming. Agony. A maelstrom of despair...

Bundled into a cab...

L-Man's urgent whisper: "Keep your hoodie up. Driver recognises us, we're dead..."

Infinities of black. Eternities of pain...

Then running. Trainers pounding gravel drive...

Up ahead, the girl's house...

But the screaming. Oh, God, the screaming. Just one baby boy, lost in the dark...

Crashing through the front door. Stumbling down corridors...

Into a room. Some kind of library...

There's a guy there. He's dressed like a butler. (Why isn't he doing *anything?)*

And next to a desk, a little wooden cot bed...

In it there's a baby...

The baby!

Yes!

The baby is Sam's way back!

Back into the light! Back into—

Sam launched himself at the cot, swept the shrieking infant up into his arms, and collapsed to the floor of the library, hugging the tiny quivering bundle tight to his chest. Sweat coursed down Sam's burning face. His heaving lungs pulled in retching gasps of musty air. His pounding heart felt like it was about to punch its way out through his ribcage.

But Sam didn't care.

Because the baby had stopped crying.

The screams were gone. The pain was gone. The despair was gone.

Seconds later, Sam heard the thud of running feet and looked up to see Perdita, Rabbit, and L-Man burst into the room, stumbling past an ashen-faced Travis in the doorway.

"I... I couldn't..." the butler stammered. "He just woke up, there was nothing I could..."

"It's all right, Travis," Perdita said, laying a hand on the butler's arm. "Samar is here now. It's all fine. You did everything you could. Really. Samar's here..."

And slumped on the library floor, still numb with horror, Sam began to rock the baby on his shoulder, the little boy's trembling arms clinging ever tighter around Sam's neck...

●●●

Growling in frustration, DI Marjory Devine shut her eyes and sagged deeper behind her document strewn desk. Stupidly or not, she really had thought that a few minutes alone in her own office—just her and the evidence so far—might spark some kind of glorious crime-fighting epiphany.

But *stupidly* it had turned out to be. Seriously, just what the *hell* was going on here?

With an exasperated sigh, Devine hauled herself upright once more, then forced her attention back to her computer, tapping its spacebar to restart the CCTV loop.

Again.

And for the squillionth time today, the grainy, black and white footage began to play:

Night. A deserted South London street. Three

teenage boys dart into view. One of them has visible injuries to his face and a crying baby in his arms. A car pulls up. Not just any car mind you. Oh no. An actual Rolls-Royce stretch limousine, if you very please. Boys pile into car. Car races away. And back to the start of the loop.

Honestly, the harder Devine looked here, the more mystifying this case seemed to get. Acid attacks that weren't really acid? Stretch limos? Two officers with full-blown amnesia? And as for the *baby*... No scenario that Devine's overworked brain came up with went any way towards explaining the damn *baby*. The boys had *called* the police *themselves*. Actually *brought* the baby *to* the two officers. A baby they claimed they had *found*.

Which raised yet *more* question. Why no report of a missing infant tonight? Why wasn't there some distraught mother in the station right now, pounding on desks, crying her eyes out, demanding that the police find her child? Who the hell *was* this baby?

Just then, the office door clattered open, and DC Jackson stepped in, freezing in the doorway as he spotted Devine's scowl of irritation.

"Um... sorry, ma'am," the young detective said, raising a sheepish knuckle to administer the knock he'd forgotten to give.

Devine rolled her eyes and waved him in. "Tell me."

Scooting to Devine's side, Jackson jerked his head towards the CCTV footage still looping on the computer. "Positive I.D.s from all next of kin, ma'am. It's definitely them."

Them. Three fourteen-year-old boys from the Walworth Estate. One with a handful of cautions for antisocial behaviour, the other two completely clean. Not exactly the sick and irredeemable examples of *bloody kids* today that Devine had been anticipating in this case.

"And the car?" Devine said.

"No luck, ma'am. Plates are false."

This positively demanded another eye-roll. "Jackson, it's a Rolls-Royce stretch limousine. How many of those can there be? Even in London?"

Jackson opened his mouth. Shut it again. Nodded. "I'll get right on it, ma'am" he said and scooted back out.

As the door closed behind the young constable, Devine stifled a further sigh of exasperation and dragged her attention back to her computer—to the CCTV footage still looping there. But after several more seconds of fruitless study, she just sagged again and let the sigh have its way, pausing the loop with a petulant slap to the spacebar. Shaking her head in despair, Devine snatched up her mouse, traced a rough square around the Asian boy onscreen, then jabbed once more at the keyboard to zoom in hard on the blurry bundle in the boy's arms.

On the baby.

That damn, no-sense-in-any-scenario-what-so-ever baby...

Just who the hell are you, little one? Who...?

●●●

Roger "Rabbit" Crawford would never claim to be a chemistry wiz. World conquering afro? He was your bruv. Unparalleled knowledge of what not to say to girls? Ring for Rabbit. Exactly how much salt you could add to water before the stuff started not dissolving? Rabbit had no freakin idea. Not one. Huddled over the table in Perdita's kitchen, box of Saxa in one hand, jug of water before him, Rabbit considered the problem for several more seconds before finally he just shrugged, emptied the last of the salt into the water, then resumed stirring.

And hey! Damned if every last grain of the stuff didn't just disappear! Excellent!

Meanwhile, from behind Rabbit, the unholy shriek continued—the unholy shriek in question coming from the heavy-duty cordless angle-grinder that L-Man was currently trying to get to grips with, testing out its various settings and controls. Grinning like the Joker out of Batman, the big lad stood there in the kitchen doorway, waving the howling power tool around like he was taking down zombies in a video game, while Travis and Perdita watched from a far corner, safely out of limb-lopping distance.

"I was assured that these will be more than adequate for the job at hand, miss," Travis bellowed over the din, before reaching down into one of several shopping bags at his feet to pull out two more of the angle grinders.

"Excellent," Perdita yelled back at the butler. "Thank you, Travis."

"I beg your pardon, miss?"

"I said— "

L-man finally switched off his angle-grinder, a look of deep satisfaction on his face, and with a conspicuous sigh of relief, Perdita continued: "I said *thank you,* Travis. I'm sure these will be up to the task. Now I think if we just— " at which point the girl paused as something in another of Travis's shopping bags caught her eye. Extracting said something, Perdita turned to the butler with a puzzled frown. "And, um… this would be?"

"For the young gentleman, miss," Travis said, passing the object to Rabbit.

And as he scooped the thing eagerly into his arms, it was Rabbit's turn to grin like the Clown Prince of Crime. Okay, yeah, so the gaudy packaging did make it look a little, well… childish, but it was what was inside that counted, right? And what was inside was the Aquablast 3000—a top-of-the-line super-soaker water rifle. High-pressure pump-action, 10m range, and a huge back-pack water-tank for all the "ammo" you could ever need.

"Alfred, my man, you're the mutt's," Rabbit said.

"That's Travis, sir."

Ripping the toy gun from its packaging, Rabbit unscrewed the cap of the water-tank and began to empty the jug of salt water into it, ignoring L-Man's sceptical sneer as he did so.

"Seriously, bruv," L-Man said, shaking his head. "You're wasting your time. We ain't gonna need that thing." L-Man's gaze darted nervously to Perdita. "We ain't, right?"

"No, I shouldn't have thought so," Perdita said. "Samar and the baby will be staying here for the time being. This part of the plan we can accomplish without them, and it would be foolish to risk any further demon manifestations if we can possibly avoid them, yes?"

"Girl, you are too freakin right," L-Man replied, before turning back to Rabbit. "See? No baby, no monsters," and he nodded again at the super-soaker. "Waste of time, bruv."

"Yeah, well, you know the old saying," Rabbit said. "Better safe than get your balls ripped off by the spawn of Satan."

L-Man, though, was not to be swayed by such irrefutable wisdom. With eye-rolling disdain, the guy simply shook his head again then ambled off to help Travis and Perdita empty the rest of the shopping bags. And even as Walworth's Shiniest began to shuffle in shoulder to shoulder next to the posh girl, Rabbit found himself once more suppressing a sly grin...

Catching L-Man's attention, Rabbit waggled his eyebrows suggestively—*The moves, man! The moves!*—then watched in glee as his shell-suited mate stiffened, gulped, and shot back the darkest of scowls. Rabbit was sure the big guy was gonna bottle it this time. Dead sure.

But then, after several more seconds of his trademark scowling, the bruv just sighed, turned to Perdita, opened the L-Man gob to let the magic become words, and—

"Maybe I should go check on Samar," Perdita said and left the room.

Rabbit snorted with laughter, spilling the last of his salt water all over the kitchen table. "Crashed and burned, bruv! Crashed. And. Burned."

And right about then, Rabbit could quite easily have believed that a pair of vintage Ray-Bans were all that stood between him and an actual, fully-functioning death stare.

●●●

Midday sun filtered its way down through the leaves above, sending splotches of golden light crawling over Sam as he climbed the tree. From far below, Asha's merry laughter drifted up, but a tinkle now rather than a jangle, fading with distance...

Higher and higher Sam climbed.

Then higher still.

And the higher he climbed, the more the real world around him began to recede...

To dissolve...

To transform...

Below Sam now, not a London park on a bright summer's day but deadly, monster-infested rainforest!

And Sam himself? He wasn't Sam anymore. Oh no.

He was Super Commando Dhruva on a daring, near-impossible rescue mission!

With a mighty thrust of his powerful legs, Dhruva leapt up onto the topmost branch of the towering kapok tree. One final heave, and at last he was able to push his head through the rainforest canopy. Eyes glinting like polished steel, Dhruva glanced about him...

... and there! There it was!

The ancient Aztec temple that was Grand Master Robo's secret jungle lair!

Suddenly a scream rang out from one of the temple's windows, and Dhruva gasped, recognising the sound of that scream immediately. It was her! The President's daughter! The girl that Dhruva had sworn to protect with his very life! Now a prisoner of the diabolical Grand

Master Robo!

Then more screams rang out, louder this time—much louder—and Dhruva's heart began to race. He had to save her! Had to get to her before—

But wait...

The screams. There was something about them...

Something... odd...

And in Dhruva's mind, a strange faraway alarm bell began to clang...

Because the screams... somehow they didn't much sound like screams now... Not really...

They sounded more like—

Ten-year-old Samar Chowdhury hauled himself back to reality, his head whirling towards the ground of the park below—

—and fourteen-year-old Sam lurched awake to find himself in a world the colour of strawberry yoghurt, teddy bears and cuddly dinosaurs smiling down from all around.

Sam blinked several times. Shook his head. Looked about.

He was in the nursery in Perdita's house (of course he was), slouched on the comfy armchair, his heart still hammering wildly as old memories slinked their way back into the shadowy corners of his mind. Against Sam's chest, the baby lay fast asleep.

Hauling his slumped body back upright, Sam

pulled in a deep breath then took a moment to gather himself... before frowning in confusion when he saw that the nursery's lights were now on and its curtains drawn, a sliver of dark sky—*night sky*—visible where two of the drapes didn't quite meet. *Night?* How long had he and baby been—

"Are you all right?"

Sam turned.

Perdita stood in the nursery doorway, her brow furrowed with concern.

"What?" Sam said.

"Are you all right?" Perdita said again. "You look like you— "

"I'm fine. Just a bad dream."

Perdita cocked her head at the sleeping baby in Sam's arms and took a tentative step into the room. "I see you finally got him to go over. Did he— "

Sam raised a finger to his lips—*Ssshhhh*—and Perdita paused where she was.

Baby sagging over his shoulder, Sam got to his feet, tiptoed to the small cot bed in the corner, and gently laid the little boy in it.

Perdita kept her voice low: "You're very good with him, you know."

"Yeah, well... had plenty practice," Sam murmured and turned to see Perdita raise a questioning eyebrow.

For a moment Sam said no more. But then, "I

got a little sister," he mumbled. "She's only eight. When she was small, my mum and dad, they was pretty busy so…"

"You looked after her."

Sam felt his stomach tighten, immediately regretting saying anything at all now, and turning away again, he grabbed a blanket from a nearby shelf, draping it over the sleeping baby. He could feel Perdita's eyes following his every move…

"You're very lucky," she said. "To have a sister, I mean."

"I'm lucky. She ain't."

"Why do you do that? Put yourself down all the time?"

And there it was. Final button pushed. Sam whirled on the girl. "And why are *you* giving me this poor lonely rich kid crap all of a sudden?" The words were out of Sam's mouth before he was even aware he'd thought them, and he saw Perdita's eyes fly open in shock.

"Wh-wh-what…?" she stammered. "I… I… I wasn't…"

Somewhere deep inside, Sam was dimly aware of another part of himself—some *better* part maybe—trying to intervene, wanting to stop what was about to happen. But it was already too late— *much* too late—and Old Red came bouncing up from his corner, dancing and jabbing and looking for an opening.

"Oh, come on," Sam said. "What was it? Only child? Parents never home?"

Perdita stumbled backwards. "Wh-wh-why are you attacking me?" The girl looked more than shocked now. She looked *wounded*. Ten seconds ago, Sam wouldn't have believed she was even *capable* of looking like that.

But did the ref step in even then? Not a chance.

"Packed off to boarding school when you was little?" Sam found himself saying. "Never got no cuddles from Mummy and Daddy?"

"STOP IT!" Perdita yelled back—

—and all at once the baby in the cot bed opened his eyes and began to cry. The sound of it cut through Sam's anger like the clang of a ringside bell, and just like that Old Red was gone, leaving Sam to stand there with both hands clamped over his mouth, terrified now of what else might come out of it.

Perdita just stared back at him in complete bewilderment...

... while in the cot bed in the corner, the baby mewled and whined, kicking at the air.

Turning away from Perdita yet again, Sam took a step towards the cot, picked up the wriggling little boy, and began to rock him over one shoulder, using the moment to calm *himself* as much as the baby. He'd been out of order. He knew that. *Seriously* out of order. He had to

140

apologise.

Drawing in a deep breath, Sam turned back to Perdita—

—and almost cried out in surprise when he found the girl standing directly behind him, her face centimetres from his. Blue fire raged in Perdita's eyes, her voice a fury-laden whisper. "Does it make things easier for you?" she hissed. "Reducing me to a cliché? *Does* it?"

It was Sam's turn to stumble backwards now. "Okay, look, I didn't mean to— "

"Yes. Fine. Cut me off if you have to. Put up your idiotic barriers. But don't you *ever* treat me—treat *anyone*—like their feelings don't *matter!*"

Perdita held her ground for a moment longer, her chest heaving, her blazing eyes locked on Sam's. Then she turned on her heels and marched to the baby-changing station in the corner, snatching a tissue from a box to dab at her eyes.

And Sam? Sam just stood there watching her, shame coursing through him, his brain groping for something—*anything*—to say...

At last, a few stammered words found their way out of his mouth:

"H-h-how long you been...? I mean... your folks... When did they...?"

Perdita ditched the tissue, plucked another from the box, and turned once more to Sam. For a long moment it looked as if she might not answer. But then:

"My mother when I was a ten, my father when I was twelve."

"I'm sorry."

"Sorry they're dead? Or sorry for reminding me why I don't care?"

"I... just meant," Sam's voice shrivelled, first to a whisper, "I just..." and then into silence.

On his shoulder, the baby squirmed and whimpered...

"Look..." Sam said eventually, "what I said just now... it was... I don't even know why I... I'm sorry..."

In Perdita's eyes that blue fury seemed to give one final flash... then all at once it faded. A moment later the girl sighed, offering Sam an almost imperceptible nod.

Seems he was forgiven. Sam doubted he deserved it.

"And I'm sorry I woke him," Perdita said, balling up the second tissue and tossing it into the waste bin.

On Sam's shoulder, the baby gave one last restless wriggle then finally began to settle again, stretching and yawning, tiny hands groping at the air. At the same time, Sam felt the tension twisting at his guts start to loosen, too, and let out his own shaky sigh. But then, just as he was about to lay the little boy back in his cot, five chubby infant fingers suddenly found Sam's thumb again, closing around it with a startling firmness, exactly as they had done this morning when Sam had been changing the kid. With a resentful scowl, Sam once more yanked his thumb free, and was just beginning to tuck his hand out of the baby's sight... when he paused.

And looked across at Perdita.

The girl was standing before a wall mirror now, clutching tissue number three and dabbing discreetly at her red-rimmed eyes, her tear-smudged makeup...

Glancing down once again at the baby, Sam pondered in silence for a long moment...

... then gently slipped his thumb back into the little boy's tiny, clutching fingers.

And beaming up at Sam, the baby gurgled in delight, nuzzling deeper into Sam's chest.

After another moment, Sam turned again to Perdita, intending to ask her how the plan was shaping up. But in the end, he never got the chance, because just then the nursery door crashed open, and Rabbit and L-Man practically fell through it, the pair of them gasping and panting, their eyes wide with fear. Sam barely had time to register the ridiculous toy rifle that Rabbit appeared to be clutching to his shoulder before the guy's voice sailed into the upper registers he reserved for the purest of pure terror:

"Problem, bruv! Big freakin problem!"

Sam gaped back at his friends. "What is it? What's wrong?"

L-Man hauled open the nursery's curtains, and Sam saw all that he needed to see.

Two police cars were coming up the drive.

9

Into the Night

It was Perdita who finally broke the frozen horror of the moment. In one balletic whirl of motion, she darted to a nearby cupboard, yanked it open, pulled out a baby car-seat, and all but threw it at Sam. "Put him in this. Now!"

A microsecond later, the nursery door crashed open again and Travis strode in, all razor-edge trouser creases and stiff upper everything. His arms were laden with coats, hats, gloves. "The van is by the back gate, miss," the butler announced. "Everything you'll need is inside."

And suddenly the nursery was a blur of darting bodies and flapping limbs—coats hauled on, rucksacks filled with baby supplies, little boy strapped into the plastic car-seat.

Downstairs, a doorbell rang, shrill as a scream, and all eyes darted to the sound of it.

"Go," Travis said. "I'll delay them as long as I can. But *please* promise me you'll be careful, miss." A waver crept into the butler's voice then. "If anything were to— "

"Wait!" Perdita said, her eyes flashing wide. "Travis, we can't go without you!"

"Miss Perdita, please, you *have* to! If the police— "

"Travis, we *can't!* Not without *you!* Who's going to drive?"

Once again, everyone froze, and Sam felt his stomach clench. The girl was right. The brutal truth was that almost everything they'd discussed since the trip to Cannon Street—their entire plan in fact—had just been shredded, pulped, and recycled into toilet paper.

Sam and the baby were meant to be staying here.

Not now. Not unless they wanted a house full of demon cops in the next few minutes.

Travis was supposed to be the one heading up the Great London Stone Caper.

Not anymore. If they were to have any chance of escaping here at all, Travis was gonna have to stay behind, try and delay the police.

And oh yes. That other tiny detail. Now they had no driver!

Downstairs, the doorbell rang a second time. A third. A fourth.

And still no one moved, all five of them paralysed with sheer terror.

Then, bizarrely, like some schoolkid who needed to go to the toilet, L-Man raised a tentative hand. "Um… I can drive," he said.

Sam stared back at the guy. The idea that L-Man could drive seemed beyond ridiculous. Had to be some kind of joke, right? Indeed, Sam actually opened his mouth to say exactly that, but in the end he never got the chance.

"Okay, good," Perdita said, "follow me," and then raced out the nursery door. Without another word, L-Man charged headlong after her, Rabbit following, and for a moment, Sam just stood there, utterly dumbfounded. Then he snatched up the plastic car-seat with the baby in it and bolted after the others, out into the upstairs hall.

Car-seat hooked in the crook of his arm, Sam hurled himself down the stairs, scrambling along behind Perdita and the boys. Seconds later, all four of them shot out onto the ground floor, sprinting past the main front door just as heavy fists began to pound on it from outside.

"Police! Open up!" a muffled voice behind the door shouted.

Sam flew on down the hall after the others, car-seat battering against his hip as he ran.

"Police!" the voice at the door bellowed again. "Open up now!"

Firing a glance over his shoulder, Sam saw Travis take a step down the short corridor that led to the front door, the butler drawing himself together, preparing to let the cops in...

... while up ahead, Perdita launched herself through a door at the far end of the hall. The boys piled in after her, scrambling down yet more steps, through yet more doors, before finally tumbling over one last threshold and out into the face-slapping chill of the night.

Before them, a white van stood waiting by the open gate of a neat back yard, and charging up to it, Perdita hauled open the passenger door then leapt inside. Rabbit threw himself straight in after her, and Sam followed instantly, shoving the baby's car-seat through the open door into Rabbit's reaching hands before pulling himself in next to the bruv and Perdita.

On the opposite side of the van, L-Man yanked open the driver's door and vaulted into position behind the wheel, the vehicle rocking as eighty kilos of fake gangsta hit seat leather. Sam saw the guy's left hand close around the gearstick, while his right darted for the keys dangling in the ignition. A wrench of the stick, a twist of keys, and all at once a painful grinding noise rattled through the cab. Half a second later, the van kangaroo-ed forward a few metres... and then died.

Jagged panic staked Sam in the ribcage. "L-Man, you said you could— "

"Chill! I'll get it. It's just a bit... different."

"Different? Different from what?"

"A bus."

Okay, seriously, gotta be a joke this time, right? *Right?* "You can drive a *bus?*"

The L-Man lips pursed in concentration. The L-Man brow wrinkled like Play-Doh...

Stick. Keys. Wrench and twist. Aaaaaand...

... a healthy purr from the engine below!

Well, okay then! Maybe it really was all gonna be—

And then the van took off.

Literally.

The vehicle shot forward, hit some kind of bump, and Sam felt it leave planet earth entirely, before slamming back down again, hurtling headlong now for the open gate.

In the van's bouncing, lurching cab, Sam, Rabbit, and Perdita ricocheted off windscreen and walls, struggling in vain with their yet-to-be-fastened seat-belts. A split-second later, the van slalomed through the gate then swerved wildly into traffic, its trio of terrified passengers scrabbling desperately for something, *anything*, to keep themselves upright. But upright was not to be, and shrieking with terror, all three of them skidded over slick leather seats to slam face first into the passenger side door.

Meanwhile, through it all, the bruv responsible for this jolting, rattling madness just sat there huddled over the steering wheel, wrenching at the gearstick and grinning as if his shiny-suited self had been waiting for this moment his entire life.

Which, as it turned out, seemed more or less to be the case.

"All I ever wanted to do since I was a kid!" L-Man shouted to the tangle of arms and legs now plastered against the passenger door. "Drive buses, I mean! Did this Bus Driving Experience thing for me birthday last year, yeah? Got to drive a real Routemaster round a big track for like half an hour. Sweet!"

Another screeching swerve. Another thud from the passenger side of the van.

"H-h-hang on," Rabbit said, his horrified face emerging from the pile of bodies now pulling itself out of the passenger footwell, "so, what you're saying is... you've had, like, half an hour's wheel time? In a *bus?* Not even on a proper road!"

L-Man peeked over his Ray-Bans at Rabbit. "Bruv, I'm fourteen. You want Jenson Button, you got four hours to speak to Santa. Now shut up and let me—AAAARRRRGH!" and L-Man wrenched the van into another brutal swerve, sending the others crashing into the passenger door yet again, while outside the driver's window, a lorry the size of a tower block thundered past with millimetres to spare, its horn blasting a furious $%@!£*&!!! at them as it roared away into the night.

Dragging himself out of the passenger footwell for a second time, Rabbit ran a trembling hand through his afro and spoke on behalf of the sane:

"What's deader than dead? Cos bruvs, we are *so* that."

● ● ●

Pursing her lips thoughtfully, DI Devine settled back in her chair and studied the silent figure seated across the table from her. With an almost forensic precision the harsh white lighting of the police interview room laid the old man bare, as indeed it was intended to do: late sixties, groomed to a shine, impeccably attired in dress evening wear, like a traditional, high society butler. Which, it turned out, was more or less what this man happened to be. And quite the shining example of old-school reserve he was, too. For over an hour now the man called Travis had sat there, straight-of-back and achingly formal, saying not a single damn word, his professionally composed features betraying nothing.

No. That wasn't quite true.

Betraying *almost* nothing.

Devine glanced down at the small photograph

in her hand—a snapshot of the man seated before her beside a little girl with long blonde hair. In the photo, the girl held up some kind of sports trophy, smiles gracing both her face and Travis's. Hers was the uncomplicated beam of a happy, excited five-year-old, while his revealed a rather more sophisticated emotion—a kind of quiet, paternal pride.

Devine placed the photo back on the table before them, next to the wallet she'd taken it from—the one the attending officers had removed from Travis when they'd brought him in.

"So," Devine said finally. "I'm getting the feeling that this girl is more than just an employer to you. Would that be correct?"

The man across the table neither confirmed nor denied. At least not in words. His eyes on the other hand... More of that *almost* nothing...

Fear, Devine was now beginning to conclude. Fear for the girl's safety.

"If you really care about her," Devine said, "you'll tell us where they've gone."

No response.

"You do know what these boys did, right? What kind of company this girl of yours is keeping now? You seriously think she's safe with a bunch of lowlife thugs like that?"

Silence.

"Oh, for the love of God, man!" and Devine

stood, kicking her chair back across the room. "There's a *baby* involved here! An innocent *baby!* I swear, if those children hurt that little— "

"They're *not* going to hurt him."

Six words. The first the old man had spoken since they'd brought him in. And as they emerged now from his thin, tight lips, he looked up and locked eyes with Devine. "These are *good* children, Inspector. Surely such a concept cannot be *entirely* alien to you."

Devine scowled. Sat back down. Decided to ride out the silence that followed...

Eventually, she saw Travis's gaze drift once more to the photograph of the little girl, and for another long moment the old man's eyes lingered there, before, finally, he sighed then dipped his head in a slow nod, as if some kind of internal judgement call had just been made. "I suppose all I can really do now," Travis said, "for *them* as well as you, Inspector... is try to prepare you for what you may encounter if you *do* succeed in finding them."

Devine's scowl deepened. "Just what in the name of God are you talking about, man?"

Travis studied Devine for several seconds longer. Then, slackening his immaculate tie, the man dressed like an old-school butler reached down the front of his shirt, removed something from around his neck, and held it out for Devine.

153

It was a silver neck chain, and attached to it was a key.

A key in the shape of a tiny sword.

10

L-Man and the Law

With a deafening screech, the angle-grinder's whirling blade ripped into the wrought iron of the cage surrounding London Stone, blasting a shower of sparks straight at Sam's safety visor. Instantly, Sam was wincing. They all were. Even through the ear defenders the noise was excruciating, and that was with just one of these things running. A few seconds later, as Perdita and Rabbit set to work with the other two grinders, the resulting din was like the world's biggest fingernails down the world's biggest blackboard, and the inside of the cramped workmen's tent lit up like a miniature firework display.

Sam clenched his teeth and bore down harder on the howling power tool. The quicker they got this done the better. Their luck couldn't last forever. Truth be told, the journey here had probably used up most of it already, what with L-Man struggling to master driving on an actual road with actual other vehicles and an actual highway code. How they'd managed to get to Cannon Street without attracting the attention of the police—or indeed Death—was no small mystery. But hey, here they were, right? And a lot quicker than Sam had expected, too, so kudos to the big guy and his crazy bus-driver dreams.

In the end, setting everything up had also been much faster than Sam had anticipated. The workmen's tent (Travis really had thought of everything) had taken only minutes to erect and was now placed hard against the wall of W.H. Smiths, completely concealing the small alcove that London Stone rested in. They'd spent just a couple of minutes more surrounding the tent with perimeter tape, traffic cones, and Men-at-Work signs, and Sam reckoned the whole setup looked reasonably convincing, so long as no one got too nosy. Fortunately, Cannon Street was pretty quiet now, its few less-than-interesting shops closed, the gathering Christmas Eve crowds gravitating towards the bars and night clubs of the West End.

Bracing one shoulder against the wall of the shop, Sam leaned in harder on his revving angle grinder, easing it into the rusting metal of the cage. Sparks erupted, dust billowed, and only a few seconds later he felt the power tool's blade jerk forward as it completed its first cut.

One bar down. Seven to go.

Less than five seconds after that, Perdita's grinder jerked forward too, her own first cut complete, and Rabbit's followed almost immediately.

Okay, good. Once more, it was all going a lot faster than Sam had dared hope.

Firing up their angle grinders again, the three of them set to work on the rest of it, and not even a minute later, Perdita had severed the final bar, the entire front panel of the wrought iron cage toppling forward and clanging onto the pavement at their feet.

Crouching down to peer into the opening, Sam took a further brief moment to examine the thick window of safety glass that still lay between them and London Stone, then grabbed a hammer, shattered the glass with a single blow, and reached into the two-foot-square alcove to grasp the top of ancient artefact. Sam gave the rock a brief, experimental tug, but the thing didn't budge. Not that he'd really expected it to, of course.

"Here," Perdita said, handing him one end of a heavy-duty webbing strap. And together, Sam and Perdita began to loop the strap around the massive bulk of London Stone.

As they did, Rabbit turned towards the door of the tent. "I'll go check on L-Man..."

●●●

Matthew "L-Man" Love sat slouched behind the wheel of the parked white van, resplendent in hard hat and hi-vis jacket, slurping tea and reading a copy of the *Daily Star*.

The classic workman-on-a-break look? Nailed it, bruvs.

Originally, the plan had been for Sam to stay in the van with the baby and act as lookout, but when the kid had fallen asleep again—little guy was now snoozing in his car-seat on the passenger side of the cab—L-Man had become the better option, since everyone had agreed that he looked the oldest and, to the casual observer at least, might just about pass for an actual workman. In the dark. At a distance. If he kept his head down.

Or indeed buried in a copy of the *Daily Star*.

Pulling in another "workmanlike" mouthful of tea, L-Man raised the newspaper again for some further study, and had just begun to wonder if any of its pages actually *didn't* contain pictures of half-naked women when a sudden flicker of movement outside the van caught his eye. Shock lanced through L-Man's body, and his heart lurched brutally in his chest...

... before quickly slumping back to its former

uneasy idle. It was only Rabbit. On the other side of the road, six inches of afro and two startled eyes were poking from the flap of the tent, along with the yellow plastic barrel of Rabbit's super-soaker water gun (maybe not such a stupid idea after all, L-Man was finally beginning to concede). Eyes narrowing, Rabbit glanced about warily for a few seconds before shifting his gaze to L-Man in the van.

In response, L-Man lowered his newspaper, stuck his head out the van window, and peered up and down the road for several seconds more. But as before, there wasn't a single living soul visible the entire length of Cannon Street. Not one. Passing cars were sparse. Passing buses even sparser.

Satisfied, L-Man gave Rabbit the all-clear signal and watched the bro' with the 'fro return a steely-eyed thumbs-up then disappear back into the tent.

Well, okay then. So far so good.

Settling back into his seat once more, L-Man took what he confidently judged to be another "manly" slurp of tea, before finally he raised his newspaper again and—

"You are so nicked!"

Shrieking in fright, L-Man launched half the contents of his mug at the van's front windscreen as he whirled towards the source of the unexpected voice...

... and in that moment, Matthew "L-Man" Love became eighty shell-suited kilos of liquid terror. Because there, on the pavement outside the open driver's side window, not even four metres away, stood the biggest policeman L-Man had ever seen.

• • •

London Stone was having none of it. Damn rock was just *not* moving. Sam, Rabbit, and Perdita heaved and hauled at the webbing strap they'd looped around the thing, but still the huge lump of limestone stood its ground. Sam was beginning to wonder if it might actually be cemented in place. Maybe someone should go fetch L-Man. Get *him* in here, too. Give them a bit more muscle. Cos let's face it, the big guy was probably just sitting there in the van, drinking tea and doing bugger all that was useful...

• • •

L-Man thought he might have wet his pants. Hot pee or spilt tea? Jury was still out.

"*So* nicked," the gigantic policeman growled again, raising one shotgun-sized pointing finger and aiming it through the van window...

L-Man opened his mouth to reply... and suddenly found that he'd forgotten how to speak. Also how to breathe. With warm liquid seeping slowly through his boxers (please be tea please be

160

tea please be tea), all L-Man could do was watch in helpless horror as the cop's granite face fractured in a deadly scowl, darkened to a seething shade of stony-grim…

… and then broke abruptly into an affable smile:

"You only got here ten minutes ago, mate. Tea-break already?"

Huh?

It took L-Man's stuttering brain a full five seconds more to process the cop's meaning, but when it finally did, a titanic flood of relief swept through him, and he gasped in a lungful of cool air, willing his liquefied innards back to some kind of semi-solidity. Okay, so there was still a chance he could talk his way out of this. A slim chance maybe, but still a—

Then the baby beside him farted like an angry trombone, and terror sucker-punched L-Man in the gut again. The baby! Oh God! The freakin baby! Cops *had* to be on the alert for mysterious babies tonight, right? Had to be looking out for—

Enough! Calm down, bruv. Just calm down and think…

Dragging in another deep breath, L-Man glanced up at the policeman. Okay, didn't look like the guy had heard the baby fart, and at the moment the kid was still out of the officer's eyeline. Good. All good. As long as the cop didn't get any closer—

The cop strolled closer. "Right bloody part-timer you are, mate."

Stifling a completely unworkmanlike yelp of terror, L-Man hauled himself erect in his seat and practically *threw* his newspaper over the baby beside him...

... and almost miraculously, the paper's flapping pages landed in such a way that they completely concealed both kid and car-seat. L-Man could barely believe it.

Okay. Nicely done, bruv. Now just stay cool. *Gonna be fine as long as the baby doesn't*—

The baby squirmed under the newspaper, rustling its pages.

Aaarrrrrrgh! Game over, man! Game totally freakin—

But just as the cop drew level with the driver's side window, the baby settled again.

Heart now pounding like a pneumatic drill, L-Man somehow found enough breath to attempt the gravelly "workman" voice he'd been practising: "Yeah, been on since two, mate. Gaggin for a brew, you know?"

"Tell me about it," the policeman said. "Christmas Eve an' all, eh? I been— " But then the officer paused, squinting at L-Man in sudden puzzlement. "Hang on... How old are you? Ain't you a bit young to be on the roads?"

Fear sucked every last sensible word from L-Man's brain.

Long silence.

Crazy long.

But then divine inspiration! "W-w-work experience," L-Man stammered.

"Yeah?" The gigantic policeman seemed to consider this new information carefully. *Too* carefully, L-Man thought. But eventually, the officer just grinned again, nodding to the mug of tea in L-Man's hand and the *Daily Star* on the seat beside him. "Well, you got the tea-drinking and tit-watching down pretty good."

L-Man had a stab at a grown-up guffaw, flicking his eyes to acknowledge first the tea then the newspaper... and all at once he heard his own fake laughter croak to stop.

Because screaming out from the front page of the *Daily Star* beside him, in what was surely the world's biggest goddam font, were the words, TEEN ACID GANG STILL MISSING. And *below* this extremely helpful information? In *full view* of the gigantic policeman? What else? The three school photographs. Of Sam, of Rabbit... and of L-Man himself.

• • •

Every muscle in Sam's body howled in agony as he strained still harder on the webbing strap they'd

163

wrapped around London Stone. Opposite him, Rabbit and Perdita's faces twisted with exertion as they jerked and heaved on the strap's other end. But still the huge chunk of limestone refused to move. Still the damn thing wouldn't even—

Then the rock shifted, just a little, and Sam heard the faint rasp of stone on stone.

"I think it's coming," Sam hissed to the others, praying that he hadn't just imagined it. "Together, after three, yeah? One... two... THREE!"

And all at once London Stone was shooting forward, toppling over the alcove's front edge, Sam hauling his feet clear of the crash zone just nanoseconds before a quarter ton of solid limestone slammed into the street, shattering the paving slab beneath.

With a groan of relief, Sam dragged his aching body back into an upright position, hands on hips, gasping for breath. Beside him, Perdita and Rabbit did the same, and for a long moment, all three of them just stood there, gulping in air and staring down at the mysterious object that was London Stone.

Not that there was much to stare at even now. The huge lump of rock just sat there on the cracked pavement, as featureless and unremarkable as ever.

Actually, no, that wasn't true. At least not completely.

Because along the top surface of the stone, Sam could now make out a series of deep, straight grooves. Slashes almost. Lots of them...

Sam ran his fingers over the marks. "What's all these from?"

"Sword blows," Perdita said. "For centuries London Stone was regarded as the heart of the city. To strike it was seen as a powerful symbolic act. Shakespeare actually wrote about it in Henry the Sixth, Part Two. There's a character called Jack Cade who leads a rebellion against the king, and when he finally gets to London, he strikes London Stone to claim the city for his own. Over the centuries, hundreds, maybe even thousands of people have performed that same ritual act on this one block of stone." Perdita let her voice drop to a whisper, staring down in awe at the huge lump of rock. "Incredible when you think about it really. All that history in one piece of limestone. It really is a unique and priceless— "

A huge sledgehammer came smashing down onto the top of London Stone, sending Perdita and Rabbit leaping back together with twin gasps of shock.

"What?" Sam said to the stunned pair, heaving the sledgehammer back up and over his head again. "Whatever this thing is we're after, it's *inside*, innit? How else we gonna get to it?" And with a determined grunt, Sam brought the massive sledgehammer crashing down once more onto the scarred and pitted surface of London Stone, the ear-jarring clang of metal on rock ringing out through the night...

●●●

... but still the gigantic policeman just stood there nattering, grinning his affable grin, his eyes all but pointed directly at the newspaper draped over the sleeping baby. The newspaper with that blaring, damning headline. The newspaper with that unmistakable mugshot of the very boy that Officer Chatty McChatsworth here was jabbering to. How the hell the guy hadn't clocked the photo by now, L-Man had no freakin idea. Absolutely none. And through it all, from the tent across the road, CLANG after CLANG continued to pound at the air, echoing down the deserted street like some kind of medieval alarm bell...

Think, L-Man, think! You gotta get rid of this guy. And quickly, before he gets any closer.

The policeman stepped closer, now actually *leaning* on the edge of the van's open window, poking his grinning cop head *into* the cab!

"Yeah, didn't have no work experience when I were at school," the officer said. "We all just had to— "

Then the cop froze, and L-Man felt his bowels loosen as he saw it again. Saw that terrible, supernatural darkness swirling into the officer's eyes. Saw the policeman's gigantic body begin to tremble, to shake, to *spasm*.

Barely even thinking about what he was doing, L-Man thrust his mug out through the van's open window. "Tea?" he blurted, the mug colliding with the cop's massive chest and shoving the officer backwards, one step... two steps...

... and just like that, the spasming stopped, the man's jerking arms sagging to his sides. A second later, the swirling darkness left his eyes, too, and for another moment the huge police officer just stood there like a paused video...

... till finally he returned his attention to L-Man in the van... and the quarter mug of cold tea he was apparently being offered. "Um... er... no... ta," the policeman mumbled at last, shaking his head in confusion before eventually drawing himself up to his full epic height once more. "Well... um... I'd best be off then," he said. "Don't work too hard now, eh?"

"Not me," L-Man somehow managed to croak.

And with a final, slightly uncertain grin, the policeman tipped L-Man a playful salute, right-turned in mock-military style, then began to move off.

Heart still slamming in his chest, L-Man snatched up his newspaper again and pretended to read it, peeking over its trembling top edge at the departing officer as he strolled away.

But the nightmare, thank God, was over. The huge policeman ambled on down Cannon Street without a backward glance. Ten metres away now. Then twenty. Now thirty...

L-Man slumped in relief and let out the mother of all sighs.

Then the policeman stopped.

And glanced down to his right.

Beside him was a locked-up newsagent's stand, the huge text on its headline board visible even from where L-Man sat:

TEEN ACID GANG STILL MISSING

And below the headline? What else? The photos. The damn photos.

In the silent, sodium-lit gloom of a deserted Cannon Street, Police Constable Godzilla stood for a long long moment, staring down at the headline board...

Then he turned...

...and looked back at the van.

11

The Centre of the Centre of the Centre

Once again, sledgehammer met rock with an ear-jarring clang, a puff of dust rose, and... nothing. Absolutely nothing. Sam's entire body was now one sweat-soaked mass of exhausted flesh. With every hammer blow his muscles howled and his lungs burned. And still the huge lump of limestone just sat there. Sat there in a single, unbroken, screw-you-kid piece.

Grunting his fury, Sam let the hammer slam down one final time then threw the tool to the ground, leaning on his knees to catch his breath. "What the hell kind of rock *is* this?"

Rabbit ran a nervous hand through his afro. "Can't we just stick it in the back of the van? Smash it open later?"

"Yeah, right," Sam said. "You got the Incredible Hulk on speed dial then? Cos this thing ain't moving, bruv."

Just then, the tent flap flew open, and L-Man staggered in, car-seat dangling beneath his elbow. In it the baby lay fast asleep still, thumb in mouth, snoring faintly.

"We gotta get outta here," L-Man gasped. "Now!"

A shocked silence fell in the tent. Sam dashed up to the door flap to peer outside—

—and felt his guts clench in fear.

Halfway up the street, a policeman roughly the size of King Kong was standing by a locked up newsagent's stand, shooting dark glances at the van while talking into his radio.

Cursing under his breath, Sam began to pace, his mind racing. Eventually, he just shook his head, his eyes darting once more to London Stone, then up again to Perdita. "Okay, end of the day, we don't get whatever's inside there right now, it's all over, yeah?"

Perdita gulped. "Well, t-t-technically speaking we have until midnight, but— "

"Yeah. Like I thought. Now or never," and Sam snatched up the sledgehammer.

"Oh God," L-Man whimpered. "Sam, no! We gotta get outta here, man! We gotta— "

"Shut it!" Sam growled. "We can *do* this!" And once again he began to pound at London Stone. Blow after brutal blow, jolts of agony ringing through his bones with every strike.

Rabbit's eyes flew wide with terror. "Sam, come on! L-Man's right! If that cop— "

"I said *shut* it!" Sam barked, pounding still harder, sparks flying, rock dust billowing, the air shaking with every impact. "We can *do* this, bruvs! We can— "

"Wait!"

The cry was Perdita's—as close to an actual yell as Sam had ever heard from the girl—and freezing mid-swing, Sam turned to find her standing there with her mouth wide open.

"Oh my God..." Perdita gasped. "How stupid *are* we?"

"Eh?" Sam said. "What is it?"

But Perdita didn't answer. Just whirled on her heels—

—and lunged straight for Rabbit. Came at him so fast the poor startled guy slipped on a patch of melting frost and fell sprawling on his backside.

"So unbelievably *stupid*," Perdita hissed, her eyes fixing Rabbit where he'd fallen.

"Huh? Wh-wh-what you on about?" Rabbit stammered. "I ain't done— "

But before Rabbit could finish, Perdita's right hand darted out, shot towards the terrified bruv slumped there on the ground—

—and grabbed the handle of the broken sword stuck through Rabbit's belt loop.

In one smooth motion, Perdita yanked the half-sword free, dropped to her knees by London Stone, and raised the broken weapon high over her head.

"What the hell you doing?" Sam said. "That thing ain't gonna— "

"Hundreds of years!" Perdita said, and the girl's eyes were aglow again, shining with a kind of awestruck wonder. "Hundreds of years people have been striking this thing with swords! Everyone thought it was just symbolic. It *wasn't* symbolic."

Perdita grasped the broken sword with both hands—

"They just didn't have what we have."

—and plunged it towards London Stone.

With a dull clang, the jagged stump of blade struck the rock dead centre, and all at once the tent was filled with light—a dazzling, multicoloured swirl of it that receded again almost instantly to reveal a series of glowing cracks now spiderwebbing the huge lump of limestone. A second later, the entire rock disintegrated into a smoking mound of rubble. But not *just* rubble, Sam saw. Half buried amongst the crumbling remains of London Stone was something else.

172

Some kind of package, maybe fifty centimetres long by ten wide, wrapped in what might have been leather.

While Sam and the boys stood there frozen in astonishment, Perdita shoved the broken sword back into Rabbit's hands and snatched up the leather-wrapped package.

"Right, let's go!" she said.

L-Man was the first to haul himself back to reality. "Okay, as long as that cop ain't moved we can still make a run for the van, yeah?" and dashing to the tent door, L-Man drew back the flap, peered out... but then stopped dead, the blood draining from his face. "Oh God..."

Sam darted forward to see for himself—

—and yet again felt his heart lurch. The policeman *had* moved. And not just a step or two. The guy was now right next to the van, scowling into its empty cab, stepping back, glancing all around, his eyes scanning the length and breadth of Cannon Street for any sign of—

Then the officer's eyes paused, fixing themselves firmly on the workmen's tent across the road, and with his scowl deepening, the gigantic policeman began to cross the street.

Fighting back waves of panic, Sam pulled his mind into focus. Okay, they had one chance here that Sam could see. One chance of getting out of this before the whole situation descended into claw-sprouting, flesh-ripping, demon-copper mayhem.

Sam grabbed Rabbit's shoulder, turned him towards the wall, and shoved him. "Go!"

For a moment, Rabbit didn't get it, just stood there, totally blank. Then, at last, the penny dropped, and Rabbit launched himself forward... straight at the empty alcove they'd just dragged London Stone from. The empty alcove that was in reality a *hole*. Almost a low window in fact. A two-foot square opening that went all the way through the building's exterior wall to the newsagents shop on the inside!

In a second, Rabbit was gone, wriggling snake-like through the opening, super-soaker hugged tight to his chest. And even as the guy's feet were disappearing, Sam snatched the car-seat from L-Man, thrusting it into the hole after Rabbit. Baby still fast asleep in its padded interior, the seat vanished in an instant, yanked the rest of the way through by the bruv on the other side, and a heartbeat later the others followed—first Perdita, then L-Man, then finally Sam himself, his slim body barely touching the alcove's smooth sides as he hurled himself through.

Slamming hard into the floor of the newsagents on the other side, Sam tucked and rolled, then scrambled to his feet again, glancing forward to see L-Man now kicking and shoving at a door beside the shop's main counter—their only exit, as far as Sam could make out.

"Stop right there!" a booming voice bellowed, and Sam whirled to find the gigantic policeman now hunkered down outside the hole in the wall, glaring in at them.

"I mean it," the cop growled. "*Stay* where you are," and with a determined grimace, the officer thrust one huge arm into the narrow opening, squeezing his head in after it.

Terror exploding in his chest, Sam turned and launched himself across the room. "Move!" he yelled at the others, charging headlong for the door that L-Man was still kicking at.

The big lad leapt clear just in time, and Sam rammed the door dead centre, hitting it shoulder first with everything he had. Timber groaned and hardware clattered against the splintering doorframe, but the door itself held fast.

"Seriously, kids," the gigantic policeman snarled, "you don't wanna do this," and the guy thrust a second arm into the hole in the wall, at which point any hopes Sam might have had that the cop would be too big to fit into the opening vanished in a puff of unwelcome reality. Catering-size or not, this dude was coming through.

Stepping away again from the door, Sam shot L-Man a meaningful look and saw the big guy fire back a single grim nod—*message received*. Then, turning as one, both boys lowered their shoulders... and hurled themselves at the door together.

That did the trick. With a room-shaking crunch, one hundred and forty kilos of precisely targeted Walworth Warrior battered home, ripping the entire door from its hinges. Sam and L-Man tumbled on into the shadows beyond, Rabbit and Perdita scrambling after them.

Up ahead a sign glowed red in the dark—FIRE EXIT—and Sam barrelled straight for it, slamming into the heavy fire door beneath, punching the heel of his hand into the panic bar across its centre. With a screech of hinges, the door flew open, crashing back into a wall, and somewhere an alarm began to shriek.

Great. Just what they needed...

Leaping out into the dark of a litter-strewn alley, Sam shot a glance left, a glance right. One end of the alley was walled off. The other led back onto the main street.

So much for choices.

Heart pounding like a jackhammer, Sam took off for the lights of Cannon Street, burning up twenty metres of frosty tarmac before lurching to a stop at the end of the lane. Seconds later, the others came careering in behind him, and as they did, a soft infant moan drew Sam's attention back to the car-seat slung below Rabbit's elbow. In it the kid was now squirming unhappily, finally starting to wake up again.

Sam grabbed the seat back, hooked it under his own arm, and frowned at Rabbit. "You okay?"

Rabbit nodded, even offered a kind of shaky thumbs up, but Sam had his doubts. *Serious* doubts. He could already see that haze of shock creeping back into Rabbit's eyes. And the *sounds* the bruv was making. The guy's breathing was *way* too fast. *Way* too noisy.

Sam laid a hand on Rabbit's shoulder. "We got this, man. Just keep it together, okay?" Again Rabbit raised a single trembling thumb, and Sam nodded back in support, before crouching low, then edging forward to peer around the corner into Cannon Street—

—and there once again was the newsagent's shop, the workmen's tent still hard against its exterior wall. Through the tent's gaping flap Sam could see that the huge policeman seemed to have got no farther. In fact, from the look of it, the guy actually appeared to be wedged solid in the hole, unable to move. *Finally*, Sam thought, a break in their luck.

And that was when the sirens started.

Police sirens. An entire squad of them, it sounded like to Sam. Brutal spikes of sound, stabbing at the air over the wail of the shop alarm. And getting closer every second.

Sam scoured the street before them, searching for an escape. Anything that might—

His eyes narrowed. There! Yes! And pulling the car-seat tight to his chest, Sam bolted from the mouth of the alley, racing across the empty street for the only available cover he could see—a deserted bus shelter below a dead street lamp. A dozen pounding paces later, Sam skidded to a stop behind the shelter's graffitied side, ducking down to stay hidden below the transparent top section. A split-second later, the others came rocketing in behind him, a wheezing, whooping Rabbit bringing up the rear and collapsing at Sam's feet just as five police cars came screaming onto Cannon Street, two from one end, three from the other.

Fighting back the panic again, Sam raised his head to see, and through the bus stop's grubby windows he watched the five patrol cars screech to a halt right in front of the newsagents, teams of uniformed officers leaping out, heads whirling, eyes scanning the area.

"Oh God," Rabbit wheezed. "We move, they spot us. They spot us, we're Monster Munch!" Rabbit's breathing was getting noisier by the second, his lungs now rattling and rasping like a broken vacuum cleaner. How a sound like that could come from an actual person Sam had no idea. Worse yet, if it got any louder, one of the cops was surely gonna hear it, and then—

L-Man hauled a crisp bag from his pocket, shoved it at Rabbit, and like a drowning man the bruv pounced on the thing with both hands, jamming the foil packet to his mouth. Almost immediately, his rasping whoops and wheezes began to subside.

Sam heaved a sigh. Okay, good. Cops hadn't heard.

Then the baby started to cry.

Sam almost screamed at the kid in the car-seat. *Seriously, bruv? Now?*

They *had* to get away from here. And fast. But how? The bus shelter they were all crouched behind was their only cover. Move and they'd be spotted instantly, and then it would be—

Suddenly a huge red shape loomed into view above the shelter, and Sam's heart leapt with terror, his body steeling itself for fight or flight.

But the huge red shape wasn't a demon.

It was a bus.

A bus now parked directly between them and the police across the road.

Hearing the vehicle's front door clunk open, Sam risked a glance around the edge of the bus shelter and saw a lone passenger hop off what now appeared to be a completely empty double-decker.

"With me!" Sam hissed to the others and then

leapt to his feet, car-seat tucked under his arm.

Perdita gasped. "What! Are you crazy? We can't— "

But Sam was already gone, racing for the bus, the vehicle's front door pausing halfway closed before clunking open again as the driver spotted Sam hurrying up.

"Sorry, mate," the bus driver said. "Didn't see you there."

Drawing in a deep breath, Sam forced himself to return the driver's smile. "No worries," he said. "We *was* all gonna walk, but looks like his majesty here needs his dinner. Kids eh?" and rolling his eyes at the crying baby beneath his arm, Sam hopped quickly aboard the empty bus, whisking the car-seat past the driver as fast as he could, praying it would be fast *enough*. It was. Just. For a brief moment, the faintest of tremors did seem to rattle through the guy behind the wheel, twisting his cheery grin into a dark sneer, but by the time Sam was slumping into a seat at the back of the bus the driver was fine again.

"Yeah, I read ya, mate," the guy called over to Sam. "Got one like that at home myself. Still need a fare from you mind."

Damn! The bus fare! Had *any* of them even *thought* to bring their Oyster cards? Sam certainly hadn't, and by the looks on Rabbit and Perdita's faces—

"I got that," L-Man said, stepping up to the driver and waving the electronic payment screen of his iPad at the bus's card reader. "Four, please."

L-Man. Genius in polyester. No question.

While L-Man paid the fares, Perdita and Rabbit jumped aboard the bus together and hurried down the aisle, collapsing into the seat opposite Sam and the baby.

"This is insane," Perdita whispered. "What if someone else gets on?"

"We only need to stay on long enough to get clear of the cops," Sam said, slumping lower in his seat in case any of the police across the road happened to glance over at the bus. "Two stops and we're off, yeah? Just two stops."

Perdita gulped but nodded, sinking lower into her own seat, and still gasping into his crisp bag, Rabbit did the same. Moments later, with a gentle lurch and a hiss of pneumatics, the double-decker rumbled back into life and pulled away from the bus stop.

Almost immediately, the shriek of the shop alarm across the road began to lose its strident edge, fading with distance as the bus set off down Cannon Street...

A few seconds later, the sound was barely audible at all above the crying of the baby...

And a few seconds after that, it was gone completely, lost in the darkness behind them.

Sam unclenched his fists. Rolled the tension from his neck. Breathed out.

Okay, good call, Samar. Good freakin call.

With his revving heart finally starting to throttle back, Sam ran a sleeve over his sweat-sodden brow and turned at last to tend to the wailing infant beside him. Not that junior was currently limiting himself to mere wailing though. Oh no. Red-faced with misery, the little boy now seemed intent on cranking everything up to eleven—thrashing wildly in his car-seat as he howled his distress, punching at the air around him in a grimacing, gurgling fury.

With a weary sigh, Sam began to reach for the clips on the car-seat's multiple straps—kid almost certainly just needed burping—but then, before Sam could actually undo any of the clips, the baby gave a sudden, extra-contorted grimace, squeezed his eyes hard shut—

—then hitched up one almighty gutful of puke.

And just like that—as if by some strange, barf-powered magic—the little boy stopped crying. With a merry *Gaaah!* the sun broke out once more on his chubby, dark-skinned face, and there he lay, vomit caking his Teletubbies bib, beaming up at Sam as if they hadn't all just narrowly escaped death-by-demon-copper and the world wasn't really gonna end in under three hours.

Yet again, a resentful scowl began to tug at

Sam's brow, and yet again he found himself turning away from that drooling, gap-toothed baby grin. Turning away from those...

... but then Sam paused.

And sighed.

Cos maybe—*maybe*—it was time he just... Just *manned-up*.

Manned-up and met that drooling, gap-toothed baby grin head on, right?

Right.

Nodding to himself, Sam drew in a slow breath... then turned back to look at the baby.

To look into those eyes.

Those two shining brown eyes.

Impossibly huge.

Impossibly... *trusting*...

And after a long moment, Sam just sighed again.

Cos look... in the end, it was just a baby, right?

Just a baby... and what could you do?

Shaking his head, Sam carefully removed the little boy's vomit-splattered bib, then pulled a wet wipe from a pocket and began to mop sick from the baby's chin. "It's okay, kid," Sam mumbled. "We got this. Me and the Warriors, we got this. Everything gonna be fine, yeah? Everything gonna be okay now... Little Bruv..."

"He chose right, you know."

It was Perdita's voice, and Sam turned to find

the girl peering over his shoulder.

"Whether you want to believe it or not," Perdita said, "he chose right."

A moment later, L-Man finally stumbled up, pausing momentarily to frown down at the crisp bag still jammed to Rabbit's mouth. "You okay, man?" he asked.

Rabbit presented another raised thumb, marginally less shaky than the last one.

Satisfied, L-Man plonked himself onto the seat next to his mate and then turned to Perdita. "Okay then," he said, pointing his Ray-Bans at the leather-wrapped package tucked under Perdita's arm. "So… what exactly do we got?"

For a second or two longer, Perdita just sat there looking back at the boys' eager faces. Then she took a deep breath, placed the package on the seat beside her, and began slowly to peel off the leather. The stuff came away easily, in long ragged strips, almost crumbling beneath the girl's fingers as she tugged at it—a single protective wrapping, dry and brittle with age after who-knew-how-many centuries encased in solid limestone.

Eventually, the last of the leather wrapping fell away to reveal a wooden box—long, thin, and so ornate it almost hurt your eyes to look at it. Ultra-fine gold inlay sparkled across every square millimetre of the box's gleaming, darkwood surface—a mind-numbing swirl of text and symbols, weaving its way around several beautifully rendered images of warrior angels.

One single gold clasp appeared to be all that held the box's hinged lid shut, and reaching down with trembling fingers, Perdita paused for just a moment, then flipped up the clasp...

... and opened the box.

With the faintest creak of its golden hinges, the lid fell back, and as Sam caught his first glimpse of what lay inside, his lungs released in one long gasp of astonishment.

And then...

Then Sam smiled. They all did. Had to, really.

Because, in the end, what else was it gonna be, right?

What else could they possibly have been expecting here?

Inside the wooden box, on a bed of purple satin, was the blade half of a broken sword.

12

Piecing it Together

For a long moment, no one said a word. As block after block of London-by-night scrolled by in the windows of the moving bus, all four of them just sat there, gaping in stunned silence at the object in the wooden box. Sam couldn't pull his eyes away from the thing.

Unlike the piece already in their possession, no demon blood stained this half of the broken sword. It was polished and immaculate, gleaming there on its bed of purple satin like a shard of starlight. It looked... cared for.

And it had been, of course.

Cared for by an ancient secret society that almost no one on earth had even heard of. Held in their possession for who knew how long, before somehow… *somehow* being encased in solid limestone then hidden away for centuries, right in the middle of London. This incredible, impossible object. Just lying there waiting. Waiting for this precise moment…

It was Perdita who finally broke the silence.

"Yes, of course!" she blurted. "Of *course!* It all makes complete sense now!"

Sam and the boys looked at each other then turned to Perdita, L-Man speaking for all:

"Sense? Seriously? On Planet Posh maybe."

Perdita ignored the bruv. "I can't believe we didn't *see* it!" she said. "Listen…" and hauling out her notebook, the girl flipped to the translation of the text they'd found inside the skull then began to read: "'Two become one, that a light may shine, a beacon through infinity.'!"

Sam shot her back a none-the-wiser frown.

L-Man shook his head.

Rabbit gave a shrug and carried on wheezing into his crisp bag.

"Oh, come on! Really?" Perdita said. "The 'two' *must* refer to the two halves of the broken sword, yes? We have to *bring them together*. Reunite the two pieces. 'Two become one'. *That's* the ritual we have to perform. *That's* how we create this 'beacon'."

Sam's frown deepened. "Sorry… beacon?"

"Don't you see? He's *lost*. The baby is *lost*."

"You and me both, Little Bruv," L-Man said, fist bumping the smiling baby beside him.

Voice now trembling with excitement, Perdita continued: "Think about it. The angel brought the baby here to hide him from the Darkness, yes? After that, he went straight back to his own time. But before he could tell anyone where he'd hidden the baby, the angel died. And now no one but us— well, us and the Darkness, unfortunately—knows exactly where or even *when* this baby is. Our little friend here is *lost*. Lost in an 'infinity' of spacetime."

Sam began to understand. "But if we perform the ritual— "

"—by reuniting the two sword pieces— "

"—we'll create this beacon thing..."

"A 'beacon through infinity'!"

Sam found himself grinning. "It's a distress call. An S.O.S.!"

"Exactly! They'll see it and they'll come! Come to defeat the Darkness!"

"And take Little Bruv here back to his mum and dad!"

By now, L-Man was grinning, too. "Well okay then! So let's do it!" he said, snatching the hilt half of the sword from Rabbit's belt loop and reaching for the blade half in the box—

"No, *stop*," Perdita said. "The ritual *has* to be performed at midnight, remember? Midnight *exactly*. When London's spiritual energies surge. That's our power source. Without it, the ritual won't work. And we can't do it just anywhere either. It must be performed in— "

"—the centre of the centre," Sam muttered, and all at once his smile began to falter, vanishing altogether as he turned to look out the rear window of the moving bus, at the empty lanes of Cannon Street unspooling behind them...

"Back there?" L-Man said. "Where we just *come from?*" and the big lad's smile evaporated, too. "No way, bruvs. Place gonna be swarming with cops by now. How we supposed to— "

"Wait..." Perdita said, her eyes narrowing.

Sam turned to her. "What?"

"Back *there*..." and she too shot a glance through the bus's rear window. "That *wasn't* London Stone's original location. It's been moved at least twice in its history. Once in the eighteenth century. Again in the nineteen sixties."

"Okay," L-Man said, "so what *was* its original location?"

Perdita chewed her lower lip. "Well, back in the 16th century, several sources place it— "

"No, that ain't it," Sam mumbled.

Perdita cocked her head. "What do you mean?"

Sam paused. Rubbed his temples. He was on the verge of something here. He could feel it... "The writing in the skull," he said. "Can you put a date to it?"

"Well, um, up to a point, yes. Its dialect would place it maybe first or second century A.D., certainly no later."

"Okay, so... *The centre of the centre of the centre.* That's *gotta* be talking about where London Stone was *then*, right? Back in the first century A.D."

Perdita sat up straighter. "Yes. Yes, of course, you're right." But then she sagged. "The problem is, no one really knows for sure where London Stone actually— "

The answer lit up Sam's mind like the last firework in the display. "Oh my God..."

"Samar? What is it?"

Sam's heart began to race. "What that website said! The one about London Stone! How some people thought it might originally have come from— "

"Oh my goodness, *yes!* An ancient stone circle on top of Ludgate Hill! That's *it!* It's *got* to be! Samar, you're a genius!"

"Whoah whoah whoah, hang on!" L-Man said. "That were thousands of years ago! Ain't no stone circle on top of Ludgate Hill no more."

"Maybe not," Sam said, "but you know what *is* there now, yeah?"

Sam gave it a moment...

... then finally watched the lights come on in both L-Man and Rabbit's eyes. And a second later, in perfect unison, all four of them turned to look once more out the windows of the moving bus.

But not at what lay behind them.

Not this time.

This time, all eyes were drawn to what lay *ahead*.

Because there it was, less than a block away, thrusting skyward atop the gentle rise of Ludgate Hill, the pale grey surface of its illuminated dome stark against the velvet black of a starry Christmas Eve sky. Of *course* they knew what was on top of Ludgate Hill now. After Big Ben and Tower Bridge it was probably London's most famous landmark.

"St Paul's?" L-Man gasped. "But... but that's— "

"Yeah, I know," Sam said. "The next stop," and with a full-on grin of triumph returning to his lips, Sam began to rise, reaching for the bell push by his seat.

But then...

Perdita's eyes narrowed as she saw Sam freeze. "Samar? Samar, what is it?"

"The bus. Can't you feel it? It's slowing down."

"Well, um, yes, because we need to— "

"No. It's slowing down, and I *ain't* pressed the bell yet."

Perdita frowned, still not getting it.

L-Man did though. "Oh God! People! There's

people at the next stop!"

And all at once, as if a thousand volts had just been shot through the bus seats, the four of them leapt to their feet. Sam grabbed the baby and made a dive for the bus's central exit. Perdita and L-Man snatched up bags and sword pieces. Rabbit wrestled himself into his super-soaker's backpack, crisp bag still clamped once-handed to his mouth as he tightened the straps.

Poised by the exit of the slowing bus, Sam took a deep breath and shoved the fear back down where it belonged. This should *not* be a problem. The new passengers would be getting on at the *front* of the bus, while Sam would get off using the door in the *centre*. He and the baby would be out onto the street before the boarding passengers got anywhere near them. *Not* a problem. They all just had to stay cool...

But as the bus pulled up to the shelter, and Sam saw what lay waiting for them there, terror raked again at his guts. At least a dozen people were crammed together at the stop—a rowdy, raucous crowd of Christmas Eve revellers, waving beer bottles, swaying drunkenly, cheering and jeering as the bus braked to a halt beside them. Sam watched the driver heave a sigh at the sight of the rabble then brace himself visibly before reaching for a button on his dash.

Once more, Sam fought back the rising panic.

Just stay cool. This was *not* a problem…

Then the bus's front door clunked open, and like a tinsel-draped human tidal wave, the crowd of revellers rolled aboard, stumbling and jostling, shouting and singing, waving Oyster cards and debit cards…

Sam shot a glance at the central exit door and waited.

And waited.

What the *hell?* It wasn't opening. Why wasn't the door *opening?* Why wasn't—

And then it hit him.

In the end, Sam hadn't actually *pushed* the bell! And with a crowd like this one about to board his bus, the driver simply hadn't clocked Sam and the others moving to the exit!

"Oi! Driver!" Sam yelled. "Door!" and he slammed his thumb onto the bell push.

But the driver didn't respond, up to his eyes now just dealing with the unruly mob.

The new passengers began to tumble up the aisle, shrieking with drunken laughter, hollering carols out of tune… and heading straight for Sam and the baby.

Heart battering wildly against his ribcage, Sam bellowed again, "Driver! Door!" his thumb pounding at the bell push, Perdita and the boys yelling now, too.

At last the driver turned. "Oops, sorry folks,"

he shouted across, jabbing at another button on his dash.

And with barely a second to spare—just before the first of the oncoming crowd reached Sam and the baby—the bus's central exit door finally clattered open.

All but drowning in relief, Sam tucked the car-seat under his arm and darted forward—

—straight into the massive, convulsing bulk of a half-transformed demon.

The creature stood there spasming on the pavement next to the bus, completely blocking the exit. In its shaking left claw it clutched a bottle of lager, beer foam spewing out over sprouting meathook talons. From one still erupting horn there hung a pound-shop musical Santa hat, the bobble on its end flashing jolly Christmas red while it bleeped out a ghastly *Rudolf the Red-Nosed Reindeer*. And even as the shocking metamorphosis juddered to its climax, the hulking horror turned on the group in the bus doorway, let the bottle of lager crash to the pavement—

—then lunged for the baby.

13

Hellbus

Frozen with horror, Sam watched the demon's nightmare claw arc downwards at Little Bruv in the car-seat, a slashing blur of bone white and devil red, trailing beer foam in its wake...

... and once again, it was the baby's piercing shriek that shocked Sam's stuttering brain back to life. Hauling the car-seat clear, Sam hurled himself backwards into the bus, slamming hard into L-Man and Perdita behind, and with a collective yell of terror, all three of them went down, collapsing to the floor of the vehicle in a twisted tangle of limbs.

At the front of the bus, the drunken party crowd began to scream, stumbling back the way they'd come, tumbling out the vehicle's front door, while at the same time, the demon in the

Santa hat roared its fury and made a second lunge for the baby, one monstrous arm thrusting its way through the system of poles and guardrails around the central exit.

Sprawled belly up in the aisle, car-seat hugged tight to his chest, Sam once again scrambled clear of the plunging demonic claw and felt the entire bus shudder as the creature's hulking torso slammed to a dead stop behind the thick tubular steel of the guardrails. One meathook talon now just a knuckle's length shy of its shrieking, wailing target, the demon howled in frustration and forced itself forward, jamming its massive red bulk deeper into the rails. In turn, its lunging claw stretched farther, reaching for the car-seat clutched to Sam's chest, groping for the tiny, bawling figure strapped inside.

"NO!" Sam screamed, trying to back away for a third time but coming up hard against the bus seat behind him. Then again, "NO!" as the reaching claw stretched farther still, talons clattering against the pale blue plastic of the car-seat's head rest. "GET AWAY FROM HIM! GET AWAY FROM— "

And then the scrabbling claw closed hard around the seat's roll-bar handle.

Wedged behind the guardrails, the demon creature snarled in glee and began to heave backwards, dragging car-seat and baby towards it.

Towards the exit.

With fury and terror flooding his brain, Sam locked both hands tight around the section of handle he still had a grip of. An instant later, Perdita and L-Man came hurtling in behind him to clamp their own hands below Sam's, and screaming their rage together, the three of them dug in their heels and held on, taking the strain against half a ton of demonic resistance.

The demon huffed and howled. Hunched its shoulders. Heaved harder.

Sam, L-Man, and Perdita clung tighter still, their faces twisting with pain and horror. Somewhere at the edge of his blurring vision, Sam could just make out the tiny shaking figure of Rabbit, curled up in terror in a corner of the bus, still gasping into his crisp bag. Extra help from that quarter would not be arriving anytime soon, that was for damn sure.

Then the demon thrust another bulging arm through the bars. Hooked a second claw around the handle of the car-seat——

——and Sam felt the force they were pulling against double. Felt his feet begin to lose their grip. Centimetre by centimetre, Sam, Perdita, and L-Man started to slip forward, the car-seat edging ever closer to the snarling monster, Little Bruv still thrashing and howling inside.

Another heaving wrench——

—and the seat jerked closer again to the demon in the doorway—

Another wrench—

—and closer still.

Sam saw the monster hunch its shoulders for one final pull and knew that this time it was all over. That this time the creature would—

Then three things happened at once:

With a splintering crack, the car-seat's roll-bar handle gave way at the demon's end—

Sam, Perdita, and L-Man shot backwards, collapsing in a heap on the floor of the bus with car-seat and baby clutched between them—

And the creature tumbled back out through the vehicle's central exit, shrieking and flailing as it thudded onto the frosty ground of Cannon Street outside.

Sam leapt to his feet, whirling on the bus driver. "Go! You gotta get us— "

—but the driver was gone, his cab empty, door hanging open.

Sam swore. Grabbed a shell-suited shoulder. "L-Man, you gotta— "

But the bruv was way ahead of him. Leaping to his feet, L-Man charged headlong for the front of the bus, Sam and Perdita scrambling after him with the baby. The big lad threw himself into the driver's seat, grabbed the wheel, wrenched the ignition.

But even as the double-decker rumbled back into life and the central door hissed shut again, Sam could see the demon outside already clambering back onto its clawed feet.

"Go go go!" Sam screamed at L-Man, and with an ear-shredding screech of tyres, the bus took off, roaring away from the bus stop and accelerating hard.

But not hard enough.

Through the vehicle's back window, Sam watched the creature launch itself into a frenzied pursuit, and within seconds the thing had drawn level again with the central door. Then, howling in fury, the demon threw its arms forward and hurled itself at the speeding bus. With an ear-splitting crash, its massive, red-skinned bulk smashed straight through the glass of the door and slammed into the bus seat opposite, ripping the seat's entire metal framework right out of the floor.

Tangled in the seat frame, the demon hauled itself upright, roaring and writhing as it began to wrestle itself free of the thick steel tubing.

Sam whirled on Perdita. "Take cover!" he screamed. "Now! I got an idea!" And before the girl could object, Sam was gone, racing for the front of the bus, stuffing the car-seat down into the footwell of the driver's cab, telling L-Man the plan.

L-Man listened, nodded... and then floored the gas, tyres squealing yet again as the bus gave another brutal jolt of acceleration.

A split-second later, a deafening demonic howl pulled Sam's gaze back down the aisle, where he saw the raging creature finally tear apart the last of the steel tubing it was tangled in. Claws whipping and slashing, the demon in the Santa hat roared once more and began to stomp towards the front of the bus, black horns ripping ragged gashes in the metal ceiling, the very air itself shaking with the monster's rabid, howling fury...

And then, all at once, through the unholy noise, another sound rose up.

Another *roar*.

Not as loud as the demon's maybe. Not even close, if truth be told. But a roar anyway. And one that rang with a deep, primal rage.

A warrior's rage.

The revelation that Rabbit—*Rabbit!*—could even be *capable* of such a roar was astounding enough in itself, but the thing that *truly* took Sam's breath away was what the bro' with the 'fro did next. Because *that* was something *nobody* should be capable of. At least, nobody *sane*.

Still roaring with rage, Rabbit leapt up from his hiding place in the corner and darted straight into the path of the oncoming demon, bellowing right back at the monstrous, hulking thing, screaming up into its freakish, malformed face, two foot six of bad teeth versus eight foot twelve of certain death.

Sam gawped in total astonishment. More astonishing yet, so did the creature. Ear-shredding howl dying in its throat, the charging demon simply stumbled to a halt in the aisle of the hurtling bus and stood there, cocking its head at Rabbit in complete bewilderment.

In the end, that was all the bruv needed. Still roaring, Rabbit finally tossed aside the crumpled crisp bag in his trembling left hand, then grabbed the slider of the super-soaker water gun and hauled it back hard—once, twice, three times, four, and on and on and on. Pumping at the ridiculous plastic weapon in a frantic, relentless frenzy. Drenching the demon before him with jet after jet of salt water.

And, incredibly, it *worked*. Sam could barely believe it, but it did. The creature began to stagger backwards, howling in pain, red skin hissing where each burst struck. And with blast upon blast finding its mark, Rabbit's animal roar gradually became actual words:

"You like that, Hellboy? Do ya? Proper Saxa, man! None of your own brand crap! No expense spared, dude! Cos it ain't cool, get me? Picking on a little baby! It. Ain't. COOL!"

Crouched behind a seat less than a metre away,

Perdita watched with her jaw hanging.

In the driver's cab, L-Man shot a glance over his shoulder, and he too could only gape.

Gape as Roger "Rabbit" Crawford stood there in the aisle of the No. 15 to Trafalgar Square, a tiny Rambo with a toy water gun, soaking the writhing obscenity before him and screaming with an ever rising hysteria, "You is messing with the wrong crew, man! Get me? The wrong freakin crew! Walworth Warriors, man! Walworth Freakin Warriors!"

In the driver's seat, L-Man's head whipped front again, his shoulders tensing as he rammed the gas pedal even farther into the floor. In response, the bus juddered with yet more acceleration, streetlights flashing by ever faster outside, blurred streaks of yellow in the dark.

And still Rabbit stood there, bellowing his rage, super-soaker pouring salty vengeance upon the demon in the Santa hat. "Ain't no demon freak monster messes with the Warriors and gets away with it! Are we clear here, Hellboy? Are we freakin clear here? Ain't no— "

Then all at once, the super-soaker's pressure seemed to diminish, the jet of water thinning, dwindling, falling away to a trickle.

Two seconds later, it stopped completely.

Rabbit shot a startled glance at the water gun in his hands. Pumped again.

One further drop seeped from the barrel of the plastic rifle and plopped to the floor.

"Oh crap..." Rabbit whimpered, the water tank on his back now completely empty.

A blood-chilling moment of deathly quiet fell upon the speeding bus. Then the demon in the Santa hat reared up once more, threw its monstrous self forward—

—and Rabbit froze.

Just stood there in silent, wide-mouthed shock as half a ton of hell-spawned horror barrelled up the bus aisle towards him.

Sam launched himself at the fear-frozen Rabbit, knowing full well it was futile. No way could Sam cover the distance in time. He was already too late.

But Perdita wasn't.

Screaming her defiance, the girl hurled herself from the seat she was hiding behind and rammed into Rabbit shoulder first, dragging him clear of the charging monster. An instant later, girl and bruv thudded into the opposite wall of the bus and disappeared down behind another row of seats—

—leaving Sam, mid-dive and now fully airborne, hurtling headlong at the oncoming demon himself! With a shriek of terror, Sam threw out a desperate hand, somehow managed to snag a passing pole, his body slingshotting around it into the bus's wheelchair space.

"NOW!" Sam shouted—

—and saw L-Man's spine arch against the backrest of the driver's seat as the big lad stomped down hard with a hefty size ten… straight onto the bus's brake pedal.

Shredding tyres screamed against tarmac as the bus jolted to a sudden, brutal stop, and howling in shock, the charging monster cannoned the rest of the way down the aisle to smash horns first into the bus's front windscreen. Glass exploded outwards, the demon in the Santa hat now a howling, flailing red blur at the centre of a twinkling silver cascade…

… then the creature slammed into the road, and the howling stopped dead.

Silence.

Sam let go of the poles he'd braced himself against and took a step towards the front of the bus. Through the gaping hole in the smashed windscreen, he could see the demon in the road ahead, sprawled and unmoving, its flashing musical Santa hat now dangling limply from a shard of remaining window glass.

Sam's eyes whipped to L-Man in the driver's seat. "GO!"

L-Man's kind of language. The big guy cranked the shift then floored it, and as the bus took off again, swerving its way past the demon in the road, Sam stumbled back up to the driver's cab, reaching down into the footwell there. Heart hammering crazily, terrified now of what he might find, Sam hauled the car-seat back out and set it down to examine the baby inside.

But he needn't have worried. Little Bruv was okay. No longer crying, the kid just lay there staring back at Sam in a kind of fretful, confused silence. Frightened? Yes, no question. But apart from one tiny cut on his right cheek, the baby boy looked to be completely unharmed.

Sam heaved a sigh and was just reaching out to remove a lone piece of broken glass from the padding of the car-seat when, all of a sudden, yet another ear-shattering howl rang out from behind him.

No, not a howl. A *whoop*.

And even unseen, the identity of the whooper was no mystery.

Sam turned to find a wild-eyed Rabbit punching the air in triumph and shaking his empty super-soaker at the gods.

"Walworth Warriors!" Rabbit bellowed between whoops. "Walworth Freakin Warriors, man!"

So saying, the bro' with the 'fro thrust out a single fist, and before Sam even knew what he was doing he'd slammed his own down on top of it. L-Man followed instantly, reaching out from the driver's seat to complete their three fist "tower of power".

"Walworth Warriors!" the three boys chorused, and out of the corner of his eye, Sam could see Perdita looking on, watching all with a kind of bemused half-smile.

Autopilot pretty much took care of the rest of it, guiding them flawlessly through the insane choreography of the Warriors' Handshake, while L-Man steered a wobbly one-handed course down the broad empty lanes of Cannon Street.

And as the bus rumbled on into the darkening night of Christmas Eve, the Warriors' voices rang out, bright with triumph:

"All for one, one for all, two for a tenner and three for the show!"

14

Warriors Got a Plan

They ditched the bus pretty damn sharpish, of course. Priority Number One now was getting the hell out of sight as quickly as possible—something of a big ask in a bright red London double-decker, Sam had pointed out. No one had argued (though L-Man may have allowed himself a mournful sigh), and barely ten minutes after making their escape in it, they'd dumped their ride in a neglected side street south of the river. Less than five minutes after that, all four of them were hopping down onto the narrow gravel shore of the Thames's south bank, ducking into the shadows beneath the southernmost arch of Blackfriars Bridge. Sam had clocked the spot as they'd driven past. Quiet. Deserted. Hidden from view. And as close to St.

Paul's as they dared get for the moment. A good place to regroup, Sam had reckoned. To sit down together. Talk things through. Come up with a plan.

And had they come up with a plan? Yes, they had. Did Sam believe it was a plan that would actually work? Well... best wait till L-Man got back from his little side quest, see if he really had been able to get his hands on what he said he could...

In the meantime, as Sam waited, he found himself growing oddly talkative. The exact opposite of Perdita as it turned out, who sat beside him in complete silence, hugging her knees and listening. At least, Sam *thought* she was listening. Cloaked as they were in the deep shadows beneath the old Victorian bridge, it was kind of hard to tell.

"So yeah," Sam continued, "in our house we still do Santa. And presents and stuff. And too much TV and chocolate. Don't have to be Christian for that, right?" He glanced up at Perdita. Maybe she nodded. Maybe she smiled. Who the hell knew? In the end, Sam wasn't even sure why he was rabbiting on like this at all. Wasn't as if she'd asked.

A silence fell then. And not the first one since they'd pitched camp here.

Plucking a wet wipe from his pocket, Sam turned to Little Bruv—currently snoozing in the car-seat beside him—and began to dab gently at the tiny cut on the baby's face. Nearby, the Thames lapped listlessly at the muddy strip of south bank beach, a spectacular upside-down London glittering in its rippling waters, while a little further off, by a steeper section of the riverbank, Rabbit squatted with his super-soaker, refilling the thing's water tank from the shallows...

Balling up the used wet wipe, Sam glanced at his watch. Twenty-five past eleven. They had less than thirty-five minutes now. If L-Man didn't get back soon...

Sam shoved the thought aside and turned back to Perdita. "So what about you?" he said.

A pause. The girl sounded a little taken aback. "Sorry? Me?"

"Yeah. Christmas. Your house. You got aunties come round and stuff?"

Again, that hesitation. "Well... um... no, not really."

"Just you and Travis then, is it?"

"Well, um... I... I normally, you know... give Travis the day off."

Sam frowned.

"It's fine. He leaves food for me to microwave. Fortnum and Mason. It's not as if he wouldn't have better things to do."

"Ever asked him?"

Perdita didn't reply, and an odd tension hung in the air between them. Again.

The moment was broken by a sound. A sound as unmistakable as it felt out of place there in the shadows beneath the bridge. It was the merry TING-TING of a bicycle bell.

Leaping to their feet, Sam and Perdita whirled in the direction the sound came from.

"S'okay. Only me," a voice chirped...

... and there was L-Man, seated astride a bright red pedal rickshaw, grinning broadly as he rode the three-wheeled contraption down a ramp from street level onto the gravel beach.

Sam raised an eyebrow. Then another. Lacking further eyebrows, he strode over to examine the rickshaw more closely. Lightweight, twenty-four-speed gears, room for three in the back plus one driving. Exactly what they needed. How L-Man had even found one of these things at all, let alone nicked it without getting caught, Sam had no idea.

"Okay, cool," Sam said. "That oughtta do the job. And what about the— "

L-Man whipped out two white plastic tubular containers. Salt. "Burger van by the London Eye," he said, hopping off the rickshaw. And with a bottle of salt in each hand, the bruv began to amble his way down the shore to the waterline, where the small, dark figure of Rabbit continued to crouch, filling his super-soaker from the Thames.

As Sam watched L-Man go, he shook his head in amazement. Maybe, just *maybe*, this nutzoid plan of theirs was gonna work after all...

•••

Squatting by the muddy shoreline, Rabbit hauled the super-soaker's backpack water tank out of the river for what must have been the hundredth time, squinting yet again at the water level inside. And finally, Rabbit smiled, because now, at last, it was at maximum.

Perfect timing, too. Cos here came L-Man with the salt.

"Bruv, you is the man!" Rabbit said with a grin, in response to which L-Man offered a somewhat unreadable nod, before squatting down and plonking the two containers of salt onto the gravel by Rabbit's feet. Still grinning, Rabbit snatched up one of the containers, popped open its plastic spout, and began to pour salt directly into the super-soaker's now water-filled tank, jiggling the whole thing back and forth to help the stuff dissolve.

After a moment, Rabbit looked up again.

And frowned.

Because L-Man was still there.

No big deal really, but Rabbit had kind of expected the guy to just drop some sort of lame quip and amble off again. Maybe resume the "moves" on Perdita. Not that he had any kind of chance there, of course.

But L-Man hadn't budged. Bruv was still just crouching there. In total silence. Watching.

Which was weird.

"You okay?" Rabbit said.

L-Man mumbled something that might have been *yeah, fine*.

But still the big guy made no move to go.

Several more seconds of silence followed— again that *weird* silence—before eventually, L-Man's gaze shifted upwards, coming to rest on the object that now sat atop Rabbit's head.

Okay, Rabbit thought, *here it comes.*

Now, granted, Rabbit was not ordinarily your hat-wearing kind of dude, but somehow, when he'd seen the thing just dangling there from the bus's broken windscreen, bleeping out its neverending *Rudolph the Red-Nosed Reindeer* while the bobble on its end flashed a jolly Christmas red, Rabbit simply hadn't been able to resist. Some weird instinct had compelled him to pluck the demon's Santa hat free, and he'd been happily wearing the thing ever since, its cheap red fabric now locked in a titanic life-and-death struggle to contain the mighty afro beneath. Rabbit was pretty sure he knew which would win in the end. But hey, until then...

L-Man continued to ponder the flashing,

bleeping Santa hat on Rabbit's head.

"All right, *what?*" Rabbit said finally and waited for the smart arse response.

For reasons unknown though, said smartarsery didn't emerge, and after a few more seconds, L-Man just dropped his eyes.

Okay, seriously, there was only so much weird a bruv could take, right?

But then, at last, L-Man seemed to find his voice. "Unbelievable," he muttered.

Rabbit glowered, pulling the Santa hat down tighter over his afro. "Look, just leave it, okay? It's a trophy, innit? A warrior thing, get me?"

"Not the hat."

Rabbit paused. "What then?"

Shifting a little on his haunches, L-Man looked up again and this time met Rabbit's eyes. "'Proper Saxa, man. None of your own brand crap.'"

An angry pout puckered the remainder of Rabbit's already frowning face. "Hey, didn't hear you come up with nothing better," he said and was on the verge of appending some appropriate middle-finger signage when something made Rabbit stop...

And study his friend a little closer...

Because L-Man wasn't smirking. Wasn't taking the mick. He actually looked serious.

Deadly serious.

"Coolest thing I ever seen," L-Man murmured.

"Coolest. Ever."

Once again, Rabbit found himself waiting for a punchline that never arrived.

And once again, L-Man just lowered his eyes. "Bravest an' all," he mumbled. "I mean, like... like *superhero* brave..."

Okay, this really was starting to freak Rabbit out. "L-Man? *What?*"

Time-travelling babies. Magical swords. Demons in Santa hats. A lot of weird crap had happened to Roger "Rabbit" Crawford in the past twenty-four hours. But what happened next was so utterly off-the-wall it left all that crazy X-Files stuff on the starting blocks.

Crouched there on his haunches, L-Man shot a single nervous glance over his shoulder—as if checking to see that Sam and Perdita weren't looking—then drew in a faltering breath, leaned forward, and kissed Rabbit quickly on the lips.

Time slowed.

Then stopped completely.

Rabbit fully expected it to go into reverse and erase what had just happened. Turn it into a figment of his clearly short-circuiting imagination.

But then he saw that L-Man was trembling. Shaking with terror. The big lad actually looked more scared than Rabbit had ever seen him. More scared than he'd been facing those demons even.

Suddenly, Sam's voice rang out through the

darkness: "Bruvs!"

"I AIN'T GAY!" L-Man blurted.

A pause, then Sam's voice again: "What?"

"Um... nothing."

Sam stepped out from under the bridge. "Over here, guys. We gotta go over the plan."

And in a hurtling blur of polyester, L-Man leapt to his feet, charged over to the bridge, and disappeared into the shadows beneath it.

While Rabbit...

Rabbit just squatted there on the gravel shore of the Thames, slack-jawed and speechless.

"Oi! Rabbit!" Sam called.

Slack-jawed.

Speechless.

"Rabbit! Shift it! Now!"

It took another few seconds—more than a few actually—but in the end Rabbit shifted it.

● ● ●

Huddled there in the shadows beneath Blackfriars Bridge, the four of them went over the plan again. Not that there was much to go over, Rabbit thought. As plans went, it wasn't big and it certainly wasn't clever. Simple as they come, in fact. Everyone had agreed that their main problem was gonna be the crowds—St. Paul's would be crazy busy by now, both inside and out—so basically, the entire plan relied on just two things:

speed and timing.

"Long as we got a clear run at it, the rickshaw oughtta give us the speed we need," Sam said. "Reckon it should get us past most folks fast enough, before the change got a chance to kick in proper, yeah? And hey, if any of 'em *do* manage to go the full horns and homicidal... Rabbit, you'll be there riding shotgun, right?"

Rabbit gulped but gave his super-soaker a quick test blast and then nodded.

"Otherwise, it's pretty much gonna be a straight ride all the way," Sam said. "Over Millennium Bridge, up Peter's Hill. If there's a disabled ramp at the south entrance we roll right on up that, too, and straight into the cathedral itself before anyone got a chance to touch us. If there *ain't* a disabled ramp, we might have to leg it for the last bit."

Perdita nodded. "Either way, we then just carry on up the cathedral's south transept. Spiritual energies focus naturally beneath the dome, so that's where we need to end up. At midnight precisely. Not a second sooner. Not a second later."

"That's where the timing gets kinda crucial," Sam said. "Get there too early, someone gonna grab us, stop us, and then it's all over. Get there too *late,* we miss this surge thing, the ritual don't work, and... well, again, all over, yeah?"

"And we're gonna time all this *how* exactly?" Rabbit said.

"Reckon if we try and hit the entrance just when Big Ben's *starting* to chime, that *should* get us under the dome right when it's ringing the actual first stroke of midnight."

"*Should?*"

"You got any better ideas, I'm listening."

Rabbit didn't, and after another moment, Sam looked around again at them all. "Okay then. Ain't much more to say really. Everybody clear?"

Rabbit and Perdita nodded.

"L-Man?"

At first, L-Man didn't reply, just squatted there looking at no one, eyes fixed on the gravel at his feet. But then the big guy seemed to realise that some input was required and nodded, too.

"Good, so let's do it," Sam said, reaching down into the rucksack beside him to pull out the front-loading, papoose-style baby carrier that Little Bruv would be making this final little road trip in. Yet another genius piece of forward thinking by Travis, Rabbit mused. You really had to hand it to that guy. Butler dude knew how to shop.

Without another word, Sam got to his feet and began to thread his arms through the papoose's tangle of straps.

"Here, let me," Perdita said, moving in to help him.

And as Rabbit sat there watching Sam and Perdita sort out the papoose—the pair of them centimetres apart, almost nose to nose—he couldn't help but notice a few things. Three in particular. The first was that when Sam was looking at Perdita, she was pretty much doing everything she could *not* to look at him. The second was the same as the first but the other way round. And the third was all that stuff they *weren't* saying to each other.

Rabbit glanced over at the silent L-Man...

Yeah. Lot of that going about at the moment.

"Okay, that's you," Perdita said finally to Sam as she snapped the last of the papoose's clips into place. "Now we just need to— " But then she paused.

They all did actually. Paused where they stood as the sonorous wave of sound rolled up the Thames towards them from the south west—a deep, mournful clanging, dense with resonance, picking out maybe the most famous four-note melody in the world.

It was the sound of Big Ben chiming three-quarters of an hour.

Sam checked his watch. "Quarter to midnight," he said. "Five minutes and we do this, yeah?" and without waiting for a response, he turned on his heels and headed beneath the bridge, where the rickshaw stood cloaked in shadow, a sleeping

Little Bruv cocooned in the shelter of the vehicle's zipped-up passenger canopy.

After another moment, Perdita turned too, following Sam into the dark beneath the arch.

Only Rabbit and L-Man now.

Silence dropped in like a ton of awkward.

Rabbit fired a nervous glance L-Man's way, but the big lad seemed in no hurry to get moving. Just continued to squat there, saying nothing, eyes still focused on whatever lay between his trainers...

Rabbit got up. Began to head past L-Man for the rickshaw—

—and at last the guy spoke: "Listen, Rabbit, about— "

"We gotta go, man," Rabbit said, head down, hurrying on.

But two steps later, Rabbit found himself stopping...

... and frowning...

... and then turning back to look at L-Man.

To look at his friend.

His fellow Warrior.

His *bruv*.

As Rabbit stood there watching the big lad finally haul himself to his feet, a million questions swirled through his brain. But the only one he could pull from the turmoil was:

"Since when...?"

L-Man just shrugged.

"I ain't gay, man," Rabbit said.

"Okay, yeah, I get that, but…" L-Man shuffled where he stood, fiddling with his Ray-Bans. "But we're still cool, yeah?" and with a shaky sigh the guy proceeded to raise a single hand to head height, palm facing forwards.

A further fifty kilos of awkward thudded down silently between them.

L-Man was waiting for Rabbit to high-five him.

Rabbit frowned. It wasn't like he had any problem with bruvs being gay. It was just—

Then all at once a piercing yell obliterated the silence: "Oh God, no! NO!"

It was Sam's voice—a shrieking, throat-shredding rasp of pure horror—and for a moment Rabbit and L-Man just stood there, the pair of them frozen in dumb shock.

Then both boys whirled together, bolting into the darkness beneath the arch.

Rabbit got there first to find Sam hunched over the rickshaw's back seat, a frantic Perdita jostling at his shoulder, trying to see. "Samar! Samar, what is it?"

"Something's wrong! Something's *wrong* with him!" Sam gasped, hauling the baby's car-seat out of the shadows into a pool of streetlight.

And what Rabbit saw then all but stopped his heart.

Little Bruv's face was like something out of a

horror film—a bloated mass of angry red welts, the worst of them clustered around the tiny cut on his right cheek. Pain and confusion burned bright in the baby's eyes, his infant fingers clawing at weeping patches of ravaged, blistering skin, his swollen tongue poking out from between two hideously distended lips.

But if the *sight* of the little boy was a jolting nightmare, the *sound* he was making was worse still—a harsh, papery wheeze that Rabbit knew only too well.

The baby was struggling to breathe. His throat was closing up. And fast.

There was no doubt in Rabbit's mind. No doubt whatsoever.

Unless they did something right away, Little Bruv was gonna die.

15

Adrenalin

DI Devine stood at the foot of Samar Chowdhury's bed, watching in grim silence as the last of her forensics team finally left the room. A seething frustration roiled deep in Devine's gut now, curdling both her stomach and her mood. And why? Because, after almost ten hours of meticulous searching, what had forensics found here of value?

Nothing.

Absolutely nothing.

Never in her entire career had Devine felt so utterly lost. Lost in a world of... of *crazy*. Dragged there not even an hour ago by a mad old butler with a sword-shaped key. And the most frustrating part of it all? Even allowing that some kind of

222

bizarre paranoid conspiracy fantasy seemed to be at the root of everything here, there was still so much that defied easy explanation. Officers with amnesia. Acid that turned out to be salt. Babies from nowhere. Let's not even get started on the contents of that weird "safe" the butler's key opened. Or the recent sighting of the suspects in Cannon Street—a totally incomprehensible case of apparent vandalism involving some "famous" historical artefact that Devine had never even heard of.

Alone now in the Chowdhury boy's bedroom, Devine stifled a sigh and found her tired eyes drawn yet again to the walls around her. To the sheer *oddness* of them. Above the boy's bed, not a single poster. No football scarves or pennants. No band memorabilia. Nothing whatsoever to indicate who this boy actually *was*. What he aspired to *be*. While above the little blind girl's bed—both walls *and* ceiling—that garish gallery of superheroes. Batman, Spiderman, Wonder Woman. Plenty of others Devine didn't even recognise. All battling heroically for the attention of a child who would never be able to see them...

A soft voice spoke from behind: "They used to be Sam's..."

... and Devine turned to find Mrs. Chowdhury in the bedroom doorway, her husband by her side. Between the couple, little Asha Chowdhury huddled nervously, still clutching that badly wrapped Christmas present—the one she'd asked Devine to give to her big brother when they caught him.

"He was going to throw them out," Asha mumbled, and it took Devine a further moment to realise that the little girl was talking about the posters, though how Asha had even known that those were what her mother had been referring to Devine had no earthly idea.

Waving the family back into the room, Devine stepped aside and watched Mrs. Chowdhury lead a shuffling, bleary-eyed Asha to her bed, where she tucked the little girl in and kissed her goodnight. As Mrs. Chowdhury rose again, Devine caught her eye and nodded to the room's divider curtain, currently bunched up at the end of its rail by Devine's shoulder. "You want me to…" Devine began to pull the curtain closed but had drawn it only a few centimetres when Asha yelled, "NO!" leaping out of bed to haul it back open again.

Mrs. Chowdhury offered Devine a strained smile. "Sorry. She likes to keep it open. It drives Samar mad, but… well… I suppose he just makes her feel safe. He always has."

And once again, Devine felt that strange, disorientating detachment from reality. That *world of crazy*. Because absolutely none of what she was learning here, not one detail, in any way tallied with the picture Devine had constructed for herself in her mind—the picture of Samar Chowdhury, teenage thug, poster boy for "bloody kids" everywhere. Not even his—

Just then, a sound rang out—the unmistakable chime of an incoming Skype call—and Mrs. Chowdhury paused, shooting Devine an apologetic look before pulling out a phone. With a puzzled frown, the woman flipped open the phone's cover, tapped its screen once…

… and her mouth fell open. "Samar!"

Devine felt her heart stutter, her entire body snapping onto high alert as a young, male voice emerged from Mrs. Chowdhury's phone:

"Mum, please, you gotta help us!"

Ali Chowdhury gasped in shock then stumbled over to his slack-jawed wife, Little Asha right behind him, scrambling from her bed in a wild rush and flying to her parents' side.

"Oh, God, Samar, where are you?" Mrs. Chowdhury said. "What's going on?"

"Please, mum, you gotta listen," the voice on the phone said. "We need your help. And you can't tell the police. I mean it. No police. You just gotta trust me on this, Mum."

Devine saw Mrs. Chowdhury go completely rigid, her face a frozen mask of confusion.

"Mum?" the voice on the phone said. "Mum, what is it? Speak to me!"

As gently as she could, Devine extracted the phone from Mrs. Chowdhury's clutching fingers and looked down into the panic stricken eyes of the teenage boy onscreen. "Samar, my name is Detective Inspector— "

Raw horror overwhelmed the boy's face in an instant. "Oh God... no... NO!"

"Samar, listen to me," Devine said. "Whatever this is, it's over. Tell us where you are and we'll— "

"NO!" The boy almost screamed the word. "Look, there's no time. Put Mum back on. Put her back on NOW! Or he's gonna die!"

And all at once, the image on the phone's screen blurred and pixilated as the camera on the other end of the call swung around wildly, before coming to rest on a new subject. It took several seconds for the screen image to catch up with the camera move, but eventually the last of the pixels fell into place, and when they did, Devine felt her throat go dry.

She was looking at a baby. Logic told Devine that it had to be the same baby from the CCTV footage, but if it was, the child was now all but unrecognisable, its face grotesquely swollen, covered in some kind of angry red rash. Even worse, the tiny infant lay there so completely still that Devine honestly couldn't tell if it were alive or dead.

Then, as if in answer, the camera jerked a little closer, and as it did, Devine heard something—a kind of thin, laboured wheezing. Oh God... was that the baby's *breathing?*

At Devine's shoulder, Mrs. Chowdhury gasped, "Samar, you have to call 999!"

"Mum, we *can't*. Please just listen, okay..."

"Jackson!" Devine bellowed, her eyes still riveted to the phone's screen. Because there was something about what was *behind* the boy... the background... white and chrome and—

And then it hit her.

"An ambulance!" Devine barked. "Is that an ambulance? You're in an *ambulance?* There must be somebody there you can— "

"Just shut up and *listen!*" the boy on the phone shouted, camera swinging back again to his desperate, terrified face. "We *can't* call 999. We *can't* have any adult in here to help. It's just us. It can only *be* us. Put my mum back on."

Jackson tumbled in the bedroom door. "Ma'am?"

"Mrs. Chowdhury's phone," Devine snapped. "Skype call. I need it traced. Now!"

"Put my *mum* back *on!*" the boy shouted again as the wide-eyed Jackson reached for his radio and darted back out into the hall. "Now! Or do you want this baby to die?"

Devine thrust the phone back into Mrs.

Chowdhury's hand, and words began to spill from the boy on its screen in a frantic, fear-fuelled rush:

"Mum, you have to tell us what to do. His face, it got cut by... by something. We thought he was okay, but... I think it's that... you know, like that peanut allergy thing."

"Anaphylaxis. Samar, I'm just a nurse! You need to find someone who— "

"Just *tell* me! Or he *is* gonna die!"

"Okay, okay. Just let me..." Mrs. Chowdhury squeezed her eyes tight shut, pulling in a deep, slow breath. And when she spoke again, the woman could almost have been a different person—her voice now calm, steady, in control. Devine recognised the sound of it immediately— the measured, reassuring tones of an experienced medical professional.

"You need to find some adrenalin," Mrs. Chowdhury said. "Small glass bottle, about the length of your thumb. Shout when you find it."

Behind the boy on the phone's screen, two more figures suddenly darted into view and began to rake through the ambulance's drawers and shelves. Positive I.D.s on both, some distant part of Devine's detective mind noted—the Love boy and the girl called Perdita.

"Okay, we're on it," the boy on the phone said. "Oh God, Mum, his breathing..."

"Stay *calm*, Samar," Mrs. Chowdhury said. "Do

228

you have oxygen there?"

"There's cylinders, yes."

"All right, listen carefully… " and still in that measured, professional tone, Mrs. Chowdhury began to relay instructions to her son.

As she did, Jackson stumbled back into the room, panting and goggle-eyed, but Devine cut the young detective off before he could say a word. "Let's go. Now."

"Go? Where?"

"The Cannon Street sighting, that was what? Forty minutes ago?"

Jackson nodded.

"So we head that way and pray to God we get a trace on the Skype call before it's too late," and whirling on her heels, Devine began to make for the door.

"Wait!" It was Mrs. Chowdhury again, the woman's free hand now clutching urgently at Devine's arm. "I'm coming with you!"

Devine shook her head. "No. You're staying here."

"Inspector, there's a baby dying. I can do more if I'm there."

On the smartphone, the boy's voice surged in alarm: "Mum, no! Stay where you are! You can't come here!"

Mrs. Chowdhury ignored him. "Inspector, I'm not a doctor, but at the moment I'm all that baby's

229

got."

Devine thought hard. "You're right," she said finally. "Come on."

On the phone, the boy's voice rose to a full scream: "NO! MUM NO!"

"But I want a full medical team there the instant we trace that call," Devine said to Jackson, and was just turning again for the door when another hand grabbed at her elbow. It was *Mr.* Chowdhury this time, little Asha now sobbing in his arms.

"Tell me where you're going," the man said. "I can follow you in my— "

"Absolutely not," Devine snapped. "You'll have to stay here."

"Please, Inspector, this is *our* son. I can't just— "

"I do *not* have time to argue. Stay. *Mrs.* Chowdhury, with me. Now!" and shaking herself free of the man's grasping hand, Devine charged out into the hall with Jackson, Mrs. Chowdhury hurrying after them, talking into her smartphone as she ran:

"Okay, now I don't want you to put the oxygen mask directly on his face. Chances are he won't like it, and he might start to cry. That would be a bad thing. Crying is just gonna make it harder for him to breathe, understand? You have to keep him calm, yes? Calm is good."

• • •

Sam nodded, forcing himself to focus on his mum's face, bright and clear on L-Man's iPad. Forcing himself to *listen*. Because right now, a blind panic was raging in Sam's mind. Raging like some kind of ferocious caged monster. And at this precise moment, the only thing keeping that monster *in* its cage was his mum's voice:

"What you need to do is waft the oxygen at him from a short distance, yes?"

His mum's steady, reassuring voice:

"Just a few centimetres. You understand me, Samar?"

Sam nodded again, waving the plastic oxygen mask gently back and forth over Little Bruv's face. Oh God, his *face!* And once more Sam's heart clenched in horror at the sight of the baby lying there on the ambulance's stretcher. The little boy was barely recognisable now——a cruel, bloated parody of the beautiful thing he'd been not even twenty minutes ago. Worse still, he'd hardly moved since they'd got here. Hardly moved at all. Just lay there as if——

No! Sam gritted his teeth and caged the panic monster. They could *do* this. They had *everything* here they needed to *do* this. The ambulance had been Perdita's idea. Twenty seconds of iPad surfing had located Waterloo Ambulance Station, only ten minutes from Blackfriars Bridge. On the rickshaw they'd made it in seven, arriving to find the street outside the station lined with parked and unattended ambulances. All locked, of course, but not a problem when you had L-Man on the team.

"You're doing great, people," Sam's mum said, her cool brown eyes peering out calmly from the iPad's screen while a terrified Rabbit did his best to hold the tablet steady and point its camera at Sam and Little Bruv. "Really great. Just stay calm, yes? Calm is good…"

Opposite Sam, on the other side of the ambulance, L-Man and Perdita continued to rake through cupboard after cupboard, drawer after drawer, searching for the adrenalin…

"And *keep* wafting the oxygen," Sam's mum said. "Not too close though. Maybe just a little farther away, yes?" Her voice composed, measured, in control. "That's good," she said. "Very good Samar. And try not to— "

But her next words were lost, drowned out all at once by a series of loud thuds on the iPad's speaker—the unmistakable sound of car doors shutting. Three rapid slams were followed immediately by the growl of a starting engine, and a glance up at the iPad confirmed Sam's worst fears—his mum was now in the back of a car. A *police* car. Two seconds later, the vehicle's emergency siren began to wail, ringing out over the iPad's tinny sound system, and once again, panic slammed itself at the bars of Sam's mental cage. Because if the police did manage to trace this Skype call, that patrol car could be here in minutes. And then——

"Adrenalin! Got it!"

It was L-Man's voice—a piercing cry just one notch down from a full-on scream—and Sam whirled to see the big guy standing right behind him, a tiny glass drug bottle clutched in his trembling hand.

"Okay, good," Sam's mum said. "Now there should be a number on the label. Right after 'adrenalin'. A ratio."

L-Man squinted at the bottle. "Yes. One in... ten thousand."

"You're sure? Four zeros?"

L-Man rechecked the bottle. "Yes."

Sam's mum frowned, but her voice never wavered. "Wrong strength."

Sam could almost *see* the wave of despair surge through them all.

"You need one in *one* thousand," his mum said. "*Three* zeros. Keep looking."

L-Man and Perdita spun, lunging once more for the ambulance's cupboards——

——while at the exact same moment, Sam felt something soft flap against his right hand—the hand he was using to waft the oxygen. Starting in surprise, Sam whirled towards the baby on the stretcher beside him... and then gasped in shock.

Because Little Bruv was now wide awake. Wide awake and batting his tiny fists at the oxygen mask in Sam's hand. The oxygen mask that Sam had let drift *too close,* its soft plastic rim now all but touching the baby's face!

Heart jolting in horror, Sam yanked the mask back...

... but too late.

Little Bruv began to cry.

"Oh God... Oh God, Mum, what do I do? What do I— "

"Stay *calm*, Samar. Try to keep *him* calm. Calm is good. Hold his hand. Sing to him. And *keep* wafting the oxygen."

Calm is good.

Calm. Is. Good.

Sam took Little Bruv's flailing hand in his and began to croon quietly, singing along with Rabbit's flashing, bleeping Santa hat: "Rudolph the red-nosed reindeer, had a very shiny nose. And if you ever saw it, you would even say it glows..."

After a moment, Little Bruv turned to look up at Sam, cocked his head in something like puzzlement... and then all at once stopped crying.

Sam could barely believe it. Actually had to remind himself to keep on singing.

"Okay, good," his mum said. "That's good, Samar. Best keep him warm, too. As warm as possible. Cover his head if you can."

Rabbit yanked off his flashing Santa hat, threw it to Sam, and Sam pulled it down over Little Bruv's swollen head, singing along all the while with its looping electronic bleep:

"Then one foggy Christmas Eve, Santa came to say..."

Across from them, L-Man and Perdita raked through still more cupboards, still more shelves, hauling out drug bottle after drug bottle. Dozens now lay discarded on the floor of the ambulance. Hundreds even. What if there *was* no adrenalin here? What if—

"Got it!"

It was Perdita's cry this time, and an instant later, the girl was by Sam's side, a single glass drug bottle clutched between her fingers.

"Adrenalin!" she said. "One in one thousand!"

● ● ●

Outside the hurtling patrol car, the lights of Cannon Street flashed by ever faster, Devine's accelerator foot flat to the floor, the car's shrieking siren clearing the way ahead. In the passenger seat, a wide-eyed Jackson clung grimly to the police radio's handset, while in the back, Mrs. Chowdhury's eyes remained locked on her smartphone, her voice even now a model of professional calm:

"Okay, so one of you will have to draw up the

right dose, yes? You need to find a 1 mil syringe. It'll have a blue end."

Flinging the patrol car around a hairpin bend, Devine shot a glance in her rear view, catching a further glimpse of a now familiar Ford Fiesta speeding along in their wake.

The boy's father.

In her heart, Devine couldn't blame the man one bit. After all, the guy only wanted to—

Suddenly, a burst of static erupted from the police radio, and a crackly, distorted voice followed: "Sierra Six, this is Sierra Bravo. We have a trace on that Skype call."

Jackson crunched the handset: "We're listening."

"Waterloo Ambulance Station."

Of course. Where else.

Stamping on the brakes, Devine threw the patrol car into a lunatic left-hand turn, the vehicle fishtailing wildly before careering onwards, heading south now for Blackfriars Bridge.

In the passenger seat, Jackson squinted at the car's GPS.

"How long?" Devine asked him.

• • •

On L-Man's iPad, the other policeman's reply was faint but clear. Shockingly clear—

"We'll be there in four minutes, ma'am."

——and in the ambulance, a horrified silence fell.

"You guys heard that, right?" Rabbit whimpered.

"Yeah," Sam said. "Four minutes and we gotta be outta here."

L-Man looked like he was gonna throw up. "No way, man. No *way*."

"Shut up," Sam hissed. "We *focus*, and we *do* this!" He turned to Perdita. "You ready?"

Perdita plucked the protective cap from a tiny, blue-tipped syringe. "Ready," she said.

But Sam was far from sure that she was. The girl was shaking. And badly. Worse yet, Little Bruv had just drifted back into unconsciousness, his chest barely rising and falling at all now. Sam was wafting the oxygen as close as he dared, but it seemed to be making no difference. The baby's breathing had degenerated to little more than a thin, piping wheeze. Life leaking away through a straw.

From the iPad, Sam's mum spoke directly to Perdita: "Okay, now you need to push the syringe into the top of the adrenalin bottle. Take it easy. You don't want to bend the needle."

Perdita's hands trembled as she followed the instructions.

"What's your name, honey?"

"Perdita."

"Mine's Karuna."

Then all at once, the police siren howl on the iPad's speaker seemed to surge massively, and Sam's heart lurched. How far away were they now? Three minutes? Less? Sam wanted to scream at Perdita and his mum, tell them to get a freakin move on.

"You're doing great, Perdita," Sam's mum said. "Really great. Now I need you to— "

But before she could say more, Little Bruv suddenly jerked awake again, retching in distress, and with a startled gasp Perdita fumbled the syringe and the adrenalin. Both fell clattering to the floor.

Sam saw tears well in Perdita's eyes. "I can't do it," she whispered. "I'm so sorry..."

"It's okay, I got it," Sam said, passing her the oxygen mask. "Here, take over."

The girl nodded, drew herself together, and began to waft oxygen at the crying baby.

"Sing to him," Sam said.

Perdita began to sing: "...and if you ever saw it, you would even say it glows." Her voice was sweet, melodic, *angelic* even, and Little Bruv began to quieten again almost immediately.

Sam snatched up the adrenalin bottle from the ambulance floor, the tiny, blue-tipped syringe still stuck in its rubber top, needle unbent, thank God.

"Okay," his mum said, "so I want you to draw up one full mil of the adrenalin, yes? Fill the whole

238

syringe, understand?"

Sam nodded, pulling back the syringe's plunger and filling the barrel completely. "Is that it?"

"No. Now you have to lose most of that. Squeeze out enough to take it down to 0.15 mils. Use the markings on the side of the syringe. And *don't* rush."

Don't rush. Sam almost laughed in hysterical despair. Any second now, at least one patrol car's worth of London constabulary—not to mention his own *mum*—would be bursting in through the ambulance's back door, and the instant any of them got near Little Bruv—

"Samar! *Focus!*"

Sam caged the panic monster yet again and squeezed the syringe's plunger, easing up as it reached the 0.15 mil mark.

"Okay, now flick the syringe a couple of times with your fingers."

Sam did so, but just as his fingernail clicked against the syringe a second time, he saw Little Bruv's back arch again in a further fit of distress, yet another retching gasp fighting its way out of those tiny closing airways. A second later, the baby's eyelids fluttered closed...

... and then his entire body went limp.

"Oh God, Mum, we're losing him!" Sam yelled.

Still his mum's voice didn't waver: "Use your

other hand to pinch his upper arm, insert the needle half a centimetre, then pull it back, just a little."

Battling the urge to scream, Sam pinched Little Bruv's arm. Pinched it hard. The baby didn't respond. Just lay there, chest barely lifting, wheeze now all but inaudible.

L-Man and Perdita stood by, ashen and helpless.

In Rabbit's hands, the iPad shook.

Sam pushed the needle into Little Bruv's arm. Pulled it back a bit.

"Do you see any blood?" his mum said.

"No."

"Okay. Give him the shot."

Sam pressed the plunger. Watched the tiny dose of adrenalin sink into the baby's arm. Withdrew the syringe. "Is that it?"

"Yes. The adrenalin should start to work really quickly."

"His breathing... Oh God, Mum, it's almost— "

"Keep wafting the oxygen. We'll be there any minute."

And that was it. Blind, howling panic finally ripped apart the cage in Sam's mind. "NO!" he screamed back at the iPad. "You *can't* come in here, Mum! You *can't!* You have to— "

And that was when they heard it.

The staccato wail of the patrol car's siren.

Only this time it wasn't just coming from the speaker of the iPad.

It was coming from right outside the ambulance.

16

Full Dark

Devine hurled the patrol car around yet another perilous bend, siren howling, rear tyres throwing up twin fans of grit. She saw a sign flash by to her left—WATERLOO AMBULANCE STATION— then just beyond it, the sprawling concrete complex of the station itself. Five seconds later, Devine's right foot slammed into the brake pedal, and the car screeched to a brutal halt by the building's main entrance.

Killing the siren with a punch to the dashboard, Devine threw open her door and tumbled out with Jackson and Mrs. Chowdhury onto the ambulance station's floodlit forecourt—

—where her rising hopes took an immediate and gut-wrenching nosedive. The entire street outside the vast building was lined with parked ambulances. *Dozens* of the things.

"Dammit, which *one?*" Devine barked, then whirled in shock as a further screech of brakes tore through the night, and another car came skidding onto the station's forecourt, juddering to a stop just a few metres away.

Mr. Chowdhury.

And as the man himself leapt out and raced towards them, Devine noted with yet more dismay that he had *not* come alone. Turns out little Asha Chowdhury was *also* here to join this merry little party, strapped into the rear seat of her father's car.

Great, Devine thought. *This just gets better and—*

"What the hell is going on here?"

Whirling again, Devine saw a scowling paramedic standing in an open doorway farther down the street. "We just got a call from your lot," the man shouted over. "Telling us we've got some kind of paediatric emergency in our own building. There's no— "

"Not in the building, you idiot!" Devine yelled back. "In a— "

"There!" Jackson shouted, jabbing a finger at a parked ambulance less than ten metres beyond where the paramedic stood. Abandoned next to it, for no reason Devine could imagine, was a bright red tourist rickshaw, but that wasn't what had drawn Jackson's eye. The ambulance the young detective pointed to was different from the others in one crucial respect.

It had a light on inside.

•••

Sam's mind raged and raced, his entire body numb with terror. The police siren had stopped. The cops were here. Making a run for it now would be suicide. Sam spun on L-Man:

"Tell me you can drive this thing! Tell me you can— "

"No keys, man!" L-Man babbled. "No freakin keys!"

Raised voices outside. Pounding footsteps. Getting closer. Heading straight for them.

Sam shrieked into the iPad, "Mum, please, you have to stop them! They can't come in here! They can't! You have to— "

And then, with a jolting crash, the ambulance's rear doors flew open. Framed in the doorway was a lone figure in a green paramedic's uniform, and for a moment the man just stood there, gaping in disbelief. Then his eyes found Little Bruv on the stretcher, and he leapt up into the ambulance, bellowing at Sam and the others, "You lot. Out! Now!" Scrambling forward two more steps, the paramedic arrived at the foot of the stretcher, reached for his stethoscope… and froze where he stood.

Darkness began to swirl into the man's eyes.

"NO!" Sam screamed, hurling himself headlong at the green-suited figure, slamming into him shoulder first. If he could just get the guy back outside before he changed. Before he——

But even as the paramedic tumbled backwards, hook talons sprang from his flailing hands, sinking into the walls of the ambulance, and with a shriek of tearing metal, the man's thrashing, swelling bulk jerked to a dead stop in the vehicle's rear doorway.

Perdita and L-Man came barrelling in from behind Sam, screaming in terror and fury, ramming the spasming, partially-transformed creature in the midriff. But still the half-man-half-monster held on, writhing and convulsing. Howling now, too.

Then *another* sound—pounding footsteps again—and over the creature's heaving shoulder Sam saw four more people racing up the sodium-lit street, heading straight for the ambulance: his mum, his dad, the policewoman, a younger man Sam didn't recognise.

"No!" Sam roared at them. "Stay back! Don't come any closer!"

They didn't. Ten metres away, all four of them stumbled to halt, their eyes widening in utter horror at the incomprehensible scene before them.

From behind Sam, yet another scream of fury rang out—Rabbit—and shooting a glance over his shoulder, Sam saw the wild-eyed bruv raise his super-soaker to take aim...

... but this time the bro' with the 'fro was too late, and within seconds it was all over.

A claw—fully-transformed now—shot forward. Snagged Rabbit. Hurled him backwards out of the ambulance. Rabbit slammed into the road outside and lay still, super-soaker a twisted wreck of shattered plastic beneath him. The same claw flashed again. Flung L-Man at the ambulance's side window. The big guy smashed into the pane head first, tumbling through in an explosion of safety glass. And even as L-Man's feet were disappearing over the rim of the shattered window, the demon made a third lunge, this time for Perdita. Seizing her by the throat, the creature tossed the girl aside with brutal contempt, and Sam saw her head crunch hard into one of the oxygen cylinders. Perdita sagged unconscious to the floor.

Alone now and completely defenceless, Sam stumbled backwards, made a desperate grab for Little Bruv, swept the baby up into his arms. He staggered back farther. Farther still. Thudded hard into the rear of the ambulance's cramped interior.

Metal wall panels surrounded Sam on all sides

now.

There was nowhere else to go. No way out.

Snarling with glee, the demon took another lurching step forward...

In Sam's arms, Little Bruv lay exposed and helpless...

Then three metres of hate-fuelled abomination reared up and roared its triumph, an ear-splitting bellow that shattered the last of the glass in the ambulance's windows. Glittering shards of it fell tinkling to the floor as the demon drew back one nightmare claw.

Drew it back for the final time, Sam had absolutely no doubt.

Because it was over now.

All of it.

He had failed. Just like he always did.

Sam bowed his head, huddling in closer still to Little Bruv, hiding the baby from the demon with his own body. A last futile gesture of protection.

Closing his eyes, Sam waited for the final blow...

And waited...

And waited...

Sam looked up—

—and felt his pounding heart stutter.

Because the demon was still just standing there, frozen to the spot, rigid as a statue, one claw raised high over its head in preparation for the killing blow.

The killing blow that had never fallen.

Then all at once, the creature slumped to the ambulance floor and began to spasm, horns and talons receding into convulsing flesh, bloated red torso rippling as it shrank.

Sam just sat there, slack-jawed, utterly dumbstruck.

The demon was reverting. *Un*-transforming.

Why, Sam had no idea. No idea whatsoever.

And didn't care.

Elation exploded through him, relief and joy and triumph bursting like fireworks in Sam's mind. Dazzling and overwhelming and—

—and then the truth hit him.

Hit him like a black tsunami. A rushing, icy darkness that sucked all the air from Sam's lungs, all the warmth from his body.

Already knowing what he would see, Sam looked down at the tiny bundle cradled in his shaking arms.

The baby wasn't moving. Wasn't breathing.

The little boy just lay there, limp and lifeless against Sam's chest.

That was why the demon was changing back.

Because there *was* no baby anymore.

Little Bruv was dead.

17

Black Christmas

Devine just stood there frozen with shock, her disbelieving eyes locked on the scene ahead, her reeling mind entirely unable to process what she was seeing:

The *creature* in the back of the ambulance... towering over the boy and the baby... raising its claw to strike... then falling to the floor...

The boy... turning to the baby his arms... his look of horror... his howl of anguish...

And then...

Then the darkness.

The lights in the ambulance winking out all at once, its interior plunged into deepest shadow. The streetlights *around* the ambulance wavering, dimming, fading to black.

And then the darkness—somehow that *same* darkness—spreading outwards, racing down the road in both directions, snuffing out still more streetlamps, snatching light after light from the windows of nearby buildings. On and on until the entire street outside the ambulance station was cloaked in a black so deep Devine could see nothing in front of her at all.

But of course, the advance of the Darkness didn't stop there.

If only it had.

Though she did not—*could* not—see the rest of what happened in the moments that followed the baby's death, Devine would come to know everything all too soon, and her blood would chill as she pictured each terrible scene:

Cars, buses, vehicles of every kind, all across London, rolling to a stop, their engines stalling, their headlights failing, *all* of their internal workings ceasing to function.

Piccadilly Circus, with its towers of dazzling dancing neon, falling victim in near identical fashion—every light there first flickering, then dimming, then dying completely.

A sickening surge of inky black racing across the Westminster skyline.

The glowing face of Big Ben vanishing into the dark at one minute to midnight.

The heaving crush of Trafalgar Square on

Christmas Eve plunged into utter blackness, mystified revellers pulling dead and dying mobile phones from pockets while all around them the Darkness rolled onwards, a relentless, spreading wave of primordial night claiming the entire City of London.

And not just London.

Claiming it all. Across the globe—in every country, every city, every town and village—the Darkness hurling humanity back into a literal and terrifying Dark Age. And all of it in the moments that followed the baby's death.

In the moments themselves though, Devine could know none of this. Could *see* only what she saw. But with her mind still reeling from the horror of the creature in the ambulance, what Devine *saw* was enough. Enough to prompt in her a swift and radical reassessment of all that an old-school butler had told her, along with a fervent, if unexpected, prayer of thanks. Thanks that, until very recently, Marjory Devine had been a smoker.

•••

"A lighter!" Sam shouted. "A torch, matches, anything! Somebody get me a *light* in here!"

Silence. And a darkness so complete—so *dense*—Sam could feel it press in on him, stifling as a straightjacket.

"Somebody *speak* to me!" Sam screamed.

"Anybody! One of you's gotta have a— "

"Yes... I... I've got a..."

Sam heard several faint clicks, each accompanied by a spark of light, and finally, just past the open rear door of the ambulance, a cigarette lighter flicked into life, its pale yellow flame pushing back feebly at the darkness around it. The hand holding the lighter belonged to the policewoman. Devine.

Completely unable to stop himself, Sam turned to look at the tiny, sagging bundle in his arms, and once again he felt despair crush the shattered remains of his heart. "Oh God... Mum! What do I do? There's gotta be something we can— "

"Bag valve mask!" It was his mum's voice, punching in from the darkness beyond the lighter flame. But her words meant nothing to Sam. They were random syllables. Gibberish.

"What? I... Mum, I don't know what that— "

Sam's mum barged past the policewoman and leapt up into the back of the ambulance. "Bag valve mask," she repeated and began to rake through the vehicle's wrecked interior. "There should be one in here. It looks like a— " Her voice rose, "*This!*" and she snatched up something from a corner—a transparent face mask attached to a large rubber bulb. "Okay, we don't have much time," she said and started to stoop towards the baby. "I need all you to— "

"No!" Sam shouted, grabbing the bag valve mask from her. "Everybody move *back!* You too, Mum. Get too near this baby and you seen what happens. Everybody *back!* Now!"

Sam's mum didn't move. Just stood there blinking in bewildered silence.

A second later, Devine's shaking voice cut in. "I think you should do as he says," the policewoman said, seizing Sam's mum by the arm and pulling her backwards out of the ambulance.

Sam shot a glance at the paramedic on the floor. "Him as well!"

"Jackson!" the policewoman shouted, and a man appeared at Devine's shoulder—the younger guy that Sam hadn't recognised. Jumping into the back of the ambulance, the two police officers grabbed the groaning paramedic and quickly dragged him out into the pitch black of the street. A moment later, Devine thrust her lighter back through the rear door, illuminating the ambulance's interior again. "Is... is this... far enough away?"

Sam nodded, and once again some sadistic, irresistible force dragged his eyes back to the tiny, motionless form in his lap. "Oh God, Mum, what do I do? I just put it over his mouth and squeeze, yeah?" Sam began to jam the bag valve mask onto Little Bruv's face—

"Wait!" his mum said, her head darting back

into the glow of the lighter. "Samar, you *have* to stay calm here. You have to be *careful*. *Gentle*. Press the mask down over his mouth and nose. Make sure there are no leaks around the edges. You need a *good* seal."

With wave upon wave of heartbreak crashing over him, Sam fumbled the bag valve mask onto Little Bruv's lifeless face. "O-o-okay," he stammered finally. "I think that's it."

"Now squeeze the bulb *gently*. Just once."

Hands trembling, Sam squeezed the rubber bulb on the bag valve mask. But his fingers met instant resistance. It felt wrong. Very wrong. The air in the bulb was going nowhere. Panic rising, Sam clenched his fist hard around the bulb, *forcing* the air into Little Bruv's lungs.

His mum's voice rose in alarm: "No! *Gently*. *Don't* force it. The adrenalin should be kicking in any second. You'll *feel* his lungs start to release. Okay, squeeze. But *gently*."

Battling an almost overwhelming urge to just pump wildly at the rubber bulb, Sam pressed the mask into Little Bruv's face... and squeezed.

"Good. You should be able to feel it getting easier each time. Once more now..."

Sam squeezed the bulb a third time. But still there was that resistance, and yet again Sam's heart clenched in despair. *Nothing* was happening. It *wasn't* getting easier. Not even a little. The baby just lay there in Sam's lap, limp and unmoving and... "Mum, it ain't working. He ain't even— "

"Stay *calm*. And squeeze."

Sam shut his eyes. Fought back the terror. Began to squeeze the bulb for a fourth time. But again, that same resistance. No difference. No difference *at all*. If it was meant to be getting easier, why wasn't—

And then something changed. Something *released*. Just like his mum had said. Beneath Sam's fingers, the bulb depressed with sudden ease, and Sam actually *heard* the air sigh its way into Little Bruv's lungs. *Saw* the baby's chest rise.

"Okay, good," Sam's mum said. "And again."

Heart pounding, Sam squeezed. And this time there was almost *no* resistance. The air whooshed instantly into the baby's lungs, and once again his chest rose—higher this time.

"Good, Samar. That's good. Maybe just— "

But before his mum could finish, Sam saw one of Little Bruv's legs give a tiny kick. An instant later, his two chubby arms began to twitch, baby fingers groping for the mask pressed against his face. With a gasp of surprise, Sam yanked the mask away—

—and heard a loud, rattling wheeze as Little Bruv pulled in a huge lungful of air. Barely a second later, that same air found its way out again in a long and lusty wail of infant distress.

It was the most beautiful sound Sam had ever heard, and a blaze of near overwhelming euphoria lit up Sam's entire body. A whiteout of pure and perfect joy.

Sam scooped the howling baby up into his arms and hugged him. Hugged him as close and as hard as he dared. "It's cool," Sam whispered into the baby's ear. "It's all cool, Little Bruv. We got ya, yeah? Warriors got ya. It's all cool..."

Sam had an idea he might actually be crying himself now. Was pretty sure of it, in fact.

He didn't give a damn.

Tears coursing down his battered, bloodstained face, Sam rocked the wailing Little Bruv in his arms and sang to him:

"Rudolph the red-nosed reindeer, had a very shiny nose. And if you ever saw it, you would even say it glows..."

18

A Paradox and a Present

Detective Inspector Marjory Devine sat alone on a bench outside the ambulance station, brooding in the darkness of the silent street. A single candle burned beside her, fixed by its wax to a makeshift candle-holder—a lid from an old coffee jar—and huddled there in the feeble, flickering glow of that one tiny flame, Devine found her exhausted mind replaying the same terrible scene, over and over, like some kind of mental CCTV loop from Hell:

The paramedic... leaping up into the ambulance... rushing to the baby on the stretcher... and then changing. Changing into...

Beside Devine, the candle guttered, casting monstrous capering shadows on a nearby wall, and glancing down at the gnarly stump of wax, Devine frowned, startled to see how little of it there was left. How long had she been sitting here? Half an hour? Longer?

A thought occurred to her then. And not a happy one.

It would be past midnight now. Well past.

It was Christmas Day.

Christmas Day, for Christ's sake!

As if in sympathy, the sibilant sound of muffled cursing suddenly whispered its way past Devine's ears, pulling her out of herself and drawing her attention down the street.

Jackson.

The young detective sat in the front of the dead patrol car, wrenching at its ignition and swearing in muted fury. After a moment, Devine picked up her candle and strode over.

For several more seconds, Jackson continued to twist at the car's ignition—back and forth, back and forth—while in response, the vehicle made not a single sound. No electrical click. No grumbling, winter-weary engine trying to kick in. Absolutely nothing.

Eventually, the scowling Jackson gave up on the ignition, yanked open the glove compartment, and pulled out a torch. He flicked its switch. Click click click. Dead too. He tossed the torch aside. Snatched up the police radio's handset. Thumbed it repeatedly. Not even a whisper of static. Finally, he slammed both fists into the centre of the steering-wheel and slumped back in the driver's seat, his eyes dull with defeat.

"At first I thought it was just the lights," he said. "It's not. It's... it's *everything*."

"It's not even just electrical," Devine muttered, pressing her wristwatch to her ear and then shaking her head. "My grandad's old wind-up. Barely missed a tick in eighty years..."

Jackson said nothing. Just sat there staring back at Devine with those dull, defeated eyes.

"Keep trying," Devine said to him. "You never know."

With a weary sigh, the detective constable hauled himself upright once more. "Yes, ma'am," he mumbled and began again to wrench at the patrol car's ignition.

For a moment or two longer, Devine continued just to stand there, chewing her lip and frowning. Then she turned to look across the street, where one of the parked ambulances now sat with its rear doors open, its hospital white interior lit by dozens of candles. Inside the vehicle, a lone paramedic— the only one of the ambulance station's crew who'd stayed behind—crouched before three bruised and battered children, tending to their various injuries. Their various "demon"-inflicted injuries, Devine reminded herself. Injuries sustained while attempting to protect a mysterious baby. A baby that these kids insisted was *actually*...

But no. Just...

Just *no*.

Shaking her head in exasperation, Devine crossed the road and stopped by the ambulance's open back door, studying the trio of teenagers inside—the girl, the big lad, and the little kid with the huge afro. For almost a full minute more, Devine stood there in complete silence, frowning at the three children in the back of the ambulance. Finally, she shook her head. "It makes no sense," she said. "Nothing you've said here makes *any* sense. If that baby really is who you say he is... if he really *has* been removed from our past, then why is he still a part of our history? Why are we still celebrating Christmas here? That *must* mean you find a way to fix this, right? That you're *destined* to fix this. That you've *already* fixed this."

It was the girl who answered. The brains of the outfit, Devine had by now concluded.

"Or it's all just some kind of cataclysmic temporal paradox," she said. "Something the Darkness can use to undermine the foundations of our reality. To destroy us completely."

Devine opened her mouth to speak... but nothing came out. How the hell was any sane person supposed to respond to something like that?

The girl continued, her voice weary but

adamant, as if daring Devine to object: "Inspector, I can't pretend to know exactly how this works, but if you think we are somehow on the winning side here, I would suggest that you are not paying attention. The Darkness has one aim—the complete and utter destruction of, well, everything. A descent into primordial chaos. Look around you, Inspector. However this works, that descent has already begun."

And as if on cue, a low rumble suddenly welled up from somewhere deep below them, rolling out across the darkened street. Moments later, the very ground itself began to shake.

"Mother of God…" Devine whispered.

For another ten or so seconds the earth tremor rumbled on. Slates slid clattering from a nearby roof, crashing to the ground just metres away. In the building opposite, an entire row of windows shattered all at once, glass falling like deadly rain. And from all around, distant screams rang out, dozens of them, male and female, young and old, echoing through the dark.

At last, the tremor began to abate, sinking slowly back into the depths it had come from, leaving only silence behind.

Dead silence.

Devine just stood there, shell-shocked and shaking.

● ● ●

Exactly one hundred and three candles lit the cavernous interior of the ambulance station. From his vantage point on a chair at the centre of the room, Sam had already counted them twice. They cast a rippling golden glow over everything. Over the baby boy in Sam's arms, fast asleep and snoring contentedly, the swellings on his face now almost completely gone. Over the circle of chairs that had been arranged around Sam and Little Bruv as a kind of makeshift cordon. Over Sam's dad, pacing the perimeter of that cordon in grim contemplation. And over his mum and a tearful Asha, huddled together in the nearby tea and coffee area, Asha still in her dressing-gown and slippers.

No one spoke. No one had spoken for at least ten minutes now. Which was fine by Sam. He didn't much feel like talking anymore. Didn't much *feel* anything. Just numb. Empty. The last genuine emotion Sam could remember experiencing—that wild rush of euphoria he'd felt when they'd saved Little Bruv—seemed like ancient history now. A horn-blasting, flag-waving juggernaut of joy that had rolled on past almost as quickly as it had rolled up, vanishing over some bleak horizon when everyone had finally begun to accept that the lights weren't coming back on again after all. That despite everything—despite them succeeding against all the odds in snatching

Little Bruv back from death—the Darkness had still somehow managed to snag itself a hooked toehold on reality.

Because in the end, such a hold could really only mean one thing, couldn't it?

The birth of the apocalypse. The anti-nativity.

Black Christmas.

Where the treetops glisten, and children listen to hear...

Sam squeezed his eyes shut, but there was no derailing that unholy train of thought now. To hear what exactly? The shriek of monsters? The diminishing screams of the tortured and the dying? And then, finally... nothing at all?

Was that really how this was gonna go? How it was all gonna—

"You have to tell us what to do."

Sam looked up.

The police detective, Devine, stood in an open doorway, deathly pale and shaking.

"You *have* to tell us what to *do*," she repeated, louder this time.

Sam looked the woman up and down... and felt nothing. "What you asking me for?"

"There must be *something* you can— "

"Don't you get it?" Sam said. "He *died*."

"For a minute. Not even that! Seconds!"

"Long enough."

"You can still try! If we can somehow get you

to St Paul's, maybe you can— "

"Did you even listen to *anything* I told you? We *had* to be there at midnight. *Midnight*. That was half an hour ago. It's over."

Devine opened her mouth to object again, but before she could speak, another earth tremor welled its way up from the concrete floor, rumbling through the vast ambulance station like the passing of some gargantuan invisible army. All around, windows rattled and doors shook. Over in the tea and coffee area, a lone mug shimmied off a high shelf to smash at Asha's feet, and whimpering in fright, the little girl clung tighter still to Sam's mum.

Eventually, the shaking subsided, though somehow the silence it left in its wake seemed even worse to Sam. A cruel lie. A blatant threat of more to come.

"So… *what* then?" Devine said at last, her anger seething now like a mini tremor all its own. "We just sit here? Sit here and wait for… for…"

Sam said nothing.

Did nothing.

Felt nothing.

Devine turned on her heels and walked out.

After another moment, as the last of the policewoman's footfalls finally echoed into silence, Sam breathed out and let his gaze fall to the floor once more.

Then a soft voice spoke:

"Samar?"

Sam looked up to find his mum standing there just beyond the cordon of chairs. Sam's dad was by her side, while in front of them both stood a silent Asha, her solemn face streaked with tear tracks, though the actual flow itself did seem to have stopped for now.

Sam stared back at his family, unsure what they wanted.

Eventually, Sam's mum pulled away one of the perimeter chairs, guided Asha through the resulting gap, and with the gentlest of motherly nudges ushered the little blind girl forward.

Slowly, step by careful step, Asha began to shuffle her way towards the centre of the circle of chairs, finally stopping directly in front of Sam and the baby.

And still Sam just stared. At Asha. At his family. Back to Asha again.

What his little sister could possibly want, Sam had no idea. None whatsoever.

But what Asha did next might well have been the last thing Sam was expecting.

Sagging visibly, a picture of utter exhaustion in Spider-Man jammies and Wonder Woman bathrobe, Sam's little sister took one final shuffling step forward... then raised her hands.

Clutched in them was a spectacular mess of

crumpled giftwrap and twisted Sellotape, all scrunched together around some unidentifiable object about the size of Sam's fist.

"I wrapped it myself," Asha said, a residue of pride surfacing on her tear-streaked face.

For several more seconds, Sam just continued to stare, gawping down at the Christmas present his wilting and traumatised little sister was apparently offering him. Sam honestly couldn't tell if the moment felt tragic. Or funny. Or sweet. Or embarrassing. Or what…

He felt nothing.

But clearly he had to say *something*. "Look, Asha, can we maybe not— "

"*Take* the present, Samar," his mum said, the steely tone of her voice adding an unmistakable *or you will be sorry, my lad*.

With a sigh of resignation, Sam took the present from Asha and began to unwrap it.

A bad move apparently, because Asha immediately let out a shriek. "No! Not yet! It's not Christmas yet!"

Okay, enough, Sam thought. If no one else was willing to face the truth here… if he *really* had to be the one to spell it out for them all, then so be it. "Asha, look, I'm really sorry, okay, but it's never gonna *be*— "

"STOP IT!" and this time Sam's mum's voice rang with a barely contained fury. "You hear me,

Samar Chowdhury? Just... *stop!*"

For Asha that was the last straw, and croaking out a dismal whimper she turned and ran back out the circle of chairs, throwing herself headlong into her father's legs.

Silence fell yet again, and in it, some form of wordless communication seemed to flow between Sam's parents. Eventually, Sam's dad nodded, scooped the sobbing Asha up into his arms, and began to carry her back to the tea and coffee area.

Sam watched the pair of them go.

And felt nothing.

"Okay," his mum whispered, "now you listen to me, Samar Chowdhury. I may not fully understand what's going on here or what's going to happen next, but I will *not* let your little sister see you like this. Do you understand me?"

"Mum— "

"It's *Asha*! She *needs* you to be strong. She *needs* you to make her feel *safe*."

"Safe? Mum, wise up! It's the end of the— "

"You don't *know* that!"

Sam looked up and forced himself to meet his mother's brimming eyes. Why wouldn't she just *accept* this? Why wouldn't *any* of them accept it? How could he make them *see*?

Eventually, Sam just sighed. "I'm sorry, Mum," he said, "I really am, but I *do* know that. It *is* the end of the world. I know it because *I'm* one of the

267

people that was asked to save it. And I screwed up. I *screwed up,* Mum. Just like I always do."

A long silence followed, and in it Sam could see his mum struggling to find words. He could have told her not to bother. There *were* no words. Of that Sam was absolutely certain. At least, none that could change anything. None that could—

"You were ten years old, Samar," his mum said.

And all at once Sam felt his shoulders tense—

"You were ten years old, and it was an accident."

Felt his lungs pull in a startled gasp of air—

"Did you hear me, Samar?"

Felt a flutter of panic in his belly. "No. I don't know what you're— "

"Yes, you do."

Midday sun filtering through leafy branches above...

And as Sam's mum continued, her voice began to grow steadier and her back began to straighten: "We should have talked about this a long time ago."

"Mum, please..." But it was too late. Images and sounds had already begun to trickle their way into Sam's mind. Into the emptiness...

Splotches of golden sunlight crawling over ten-year-old Sam as he...

"We *wanted* to talk about it," his mum said. "We thought about it often, but— "

Sam's dad stepped up then. "But that was my

fault. I... In the end I thought it would be best to... well... just to try and forget about it. Let the past be the past."

Not a trickle now. A *flow*. Filling the void. *Pouring* its way into Sam...

... as he climbed the tree, hand over hand, branch by branch.

The feel of the bark, rough beneath his palms.

The sound of Asha's merry, tinkling laughter, drifting up from below.

Higher and higher Sam climbed. Then higher still.

And now he wasn't ten-year-old Samar Chowdhury anymore.

Now he was Super Commando Dhruva, rescuing the president's daughter, hearing the captured girl's screams ringing out across the Peruvian jungle...

Screams of comic book terror that...

... that suddenly didn't sound like screams of any kind at all.

That sounded more like...

Like laughter...

Laughter that should have been a distant, merry tinkle...

... but wasn't.

"Samar, you're not to blame," his mum said, her hushed voice growing steadier still, absolute certainty shining bright in her eyes. "You were *never* to blame."

Sam glanced over at Asha sitting alone in the tea

and coffee area... and the rest of it came now. The last of it. Flooding into Sam's exhausted mind. Every terrible moment:

His head whirling towards the sound of that laughter. That too loud laughter.

His heart lurching as his eyes found what he already knew they would:

Asha, grinning up at him from a branch below. Four-year-old Asha, who could barely walk two steps without falling over. Now ten metres up a tree, following the big brother she still believed might grow up to be an actual superhero one day.

Then, of course, his biggest mistake of all.

Yelling down at her, "Asha, no!"

And watching his little sister jerk with fright.

Watching her miss her footing.

Watching her...

Sam looked over again at Asha, sitting there by herself in the tea and coffee area, her eyes clouded, unfocused...

Cortical blindness was what the doctors had called it. Physically, Asha's actual eyes were fine, but the head trauma from the fall had been severe. There had been significant damage to Asha's brain, to its visual cortex, and in the end, that damage had never fully healed.

"It shouldn't have happened," Sam said. "It *wouldn't* have happened. Not if I'd been looking out for her. Not if— "

"You were *children*," his mum said, and still that iron certainty rang in her every word. "You're both *still* children."

"I wasn't paying attention. If I *had* been she'd never have— "

"Samar, it was an *accident*. That's all. A terrible, tragic *accident*."

There was no stopping them now. Freakin tears. Freakin useless, stupid waterworks. "I'm sorry," Sam finally choked out. "I'm just so sorry."

But his mum simply shook her head. "Samar," she said, "don't you see? It's not *us* that need to forgive you. And it's not Asha either."

Sam looked up.

"Open your present," his mum said.

"What?"

"*Open* your present."

Sam had actually forgotten that Asha's present was still in his hands, and glancing down at it again—at that colourful catastrophe of scrunched up giftwrap and Sellotape—Sam still had absolutely no idea what he should feel about the thing. In the end, he simply hauled in another deep breath and, in one rapid motion, ripped off the entire wrapping.

Inside was a mug. A novelty mug. On the front of it was a cartoonish drawing of Super Commando Dhruva, but where Dhruva's face ought to have been, a photo of *Sam's* face had been printed. And beneath this, in bright gold lettering, were two words: MY HERO!

"Know what?" Sam's mum said. "There's some things Asha sees just fine."

Sam had no idea how long he must have stared at that mug. At that stupid, beautiful, tacky, priceless piece of pound-shop pottery. Long enough for his throat to turn sandpaper dry. Long enough for the waterworks to finally give it a damn rest.

Maybe long enough for other stuff, too.

Eventually, Sam dragged his eyes away from the mug and looked up...

... and there was Asha, standing right in front of him once more.

"Hey," Sam said, "it's..." He glanced down again at the mug. "It's really cool, Asha."

Asha pouted. "But I *told* you not to *open* it. It's not Christmas yet."

"Yeah yeah, all right. God, sometimes you really are a pain in the arse, you know that?"

A deadly scowl darkened Asha's face. "Hey! That's swearing! Dhruva would *never*— "

And suddenly Sam was pulling his little sister into him. Pulling her in and hugging her tight. Hugging her in a way he hadn't done for... since...

But it didn't matter. For some reason, none of that stuff seemed to matter anymore.

And then he was hugging Asha tighter still, crushing her to his heaving chest and holding her there, his face buried in her hair...

... while between them both, in Sam's lap, a little boy in a Teletubbies onesie slept on, jostled and squished but entirely oblivious.

After another one of those no-idea-how-long-it-was moments, Sam finally let Asha go.

"You still shouldn't have opened it," she grumbled. "It's not Christmas yet."

"I know, I know," Sam said. "I just thought— "

And that was when it hit him.

Except *hit him* didn't really do the sheer intensity of the thing justice, did it?

Nope, not even close. Then again, what *would* exactly?

A "eureka" moment, maybe? A thunderbolt? An epiphany? (Ooh, *fancy!*)

Even those fell short.

The Almighty Sledgehammer of Truth was what it *actually* felt like, smashing its way into Sam's world and battering down the wall of assumptions they'd bricked themselves up behind.

"Oh..." Sam mumbled finally. "Oh... my God..."

Asha's lips pursed with instant disapproval, while over by the perimeter of chairs, Sam's mum cocked her head in puzzlement. "Samar?" she said. "Samar, what is it?"

Sam's jaw hung open, speech having all but vacated the premises now.

He turned to his mum, eventually managing to choke out four words:

"It's not Christmas yet…"

"What? But it's… Samar, what are you…?"

Sam said no more. Just scooped the sleeping Little Bruv back into his arms, leapt up from his seat, and bolted for the door.

19

The Lights of Ludgate Hill

Barging his way out of the ambulance station's main exit, Sam plunged headlong into the near total darkness of the street beyond. Across the road, a candlelit ambulance sat with its back doors open, and Sam sprinted straight for it, the sleeping Little Bruv cradled tight to his bouncing shoulder. In the back of the vehicle, Sam could make out Devine and the paramedic alongside Perdita and the boys. "Hey!" Sam shouted to them as he ran, slowing a little in his final approach to let the two adults leap clear and get themselves a safe distance from the baby.

"Your watch," Sam gasped at Perdita. "What does it say?"

Perdita stared back at him in confusion. "What?

What are you——?"

"Your watch! What does it say on it? The time!"

"I-i-it's the same as everyone else's," Perdita stammered. "Clocks and watches stopped when everything else did. At midnight. Samar, what's—— "

Sam grabbed Perdita's wrist. Looked at her watch. Compared it to his own. "No," he said. "Not quite. Not *quite* midnight."

L-Man moved in behind Perdita. "Sam, bruv, what you on about?"

"Big Ben," Sam said. "Anyone hear Big Ben chime the hour? Cos I didn't."

Perdita shook her head. "Samar, I don't understand. I don't see how that makes any difference. The ritual—— "

"——is powered by a surge," Sam said. "A surge of spiritual energy at midnight. I get that. But think about it. It ain't the *time* that's important, is it? It's the *surge*!"

Perdita frowned, looked for a moment as if she was about to voice another objection... but then paused. Half a second later, the girl's eyes flashed wide, and her mouth fell open to form the shape of the lone syllable that came out of it: "Oh..."

Sam grinned. "Centre of London, Christmas Eve, thousands of people—*tens* of thousands even—all of them poised, on the verge. They're seconds away from midnight, ready for the big

276

moment, and then... no Big Ben. No TV, no radio, no internet, no clocks that work, no watches, no phones. Just darkness and silence."

Perdita's voice fell to a murmur. "The surge," she said. "It never happened. It was interrupted before it really started. The spiritual energy, it's..."

"It's still there. It ain't been released yet."

Sam could feel all eyes on him now. The boys. Devine. The paramedic. It was Rabbit who eventually said the actual words: "So how do we release it then? What do we gotta do?"

Unfortunately, that was a question Sam had no answer to.

But Perdita did. Her voice dropping further still—almost to a whisper now—the girl suddenly shifted her gaze to stare over Sam's shoulder. "I don't think we have to *do* anything," she said. "Look!" and eyes widening, she raised a hand to point down the street into the darkness.

As one, they all turned, squinting into the pitch black where Perdita indicated.

Except that it *wasn't* actually pitch black. Not anymore. Not completely.

At first, Sam had no idea what it was he was actually seeing—all he could really make out was a series of faint, flickering pinpoints of light, right at the very end of the street, bobbing along past the junction with the main road in a long ragged line…

Then all at once Sam's eyes seemed to adapt, sucking just that little bit more information from the darkness ahead. Enough for him to finally make sense of what he was looking at.

It was people. *Dozens* of people. Hundreds even. There were family groups with young children, elderly couples, gangs of teenage friends. They shuffled along on the main road, hand in hand or arm in arm, four or five abreast, an apparently endless stream of them. All were wrapped up tight against the cold. All were heading in the same direction.

And all were carrying candles.

Once again, it fell to Rabbit to nail the unspoken: "What the freakin hell?"

An instant later, Perdita let out a gasp, leaping from the ambulance and racing up to the startled paramedic. The girl's eyes were ablaze with excitement now. "Is there any way we can we get up onto the roof here?"

"What? Um… well, yes," the paramedic said. "Why?"

"Just show me."

Mystified but nodding, the paramedic grabbed a nearby candle, pulled out a ring full of keys, then began to head back towards the ambulance station's main entrance.

"Come on," Perdita said to Sam and hurried

away after the departing paramedic.

Clutching the sleeping Little Bruv tighter to his shoulder, Sam exchanged baffled looks with L-Man and Rabbit, then quickly fell into step behind Perdita. Without another word, the two bruvs followed, Devine bringing up the rear.

Candle held high, the paramedic led the group back into the eerie world of the darkened ambulance station. Through a maze of winding corridors they hurried in silence for several minutes before finally they arrived at a stairwell and began to head upwards. Sam lost count of how many flights they ascended, but eventually, at the summit of a particularly narrow staircase, the paramedic unlocked a final door and stepped through. Perdita was right behind the man, and had only just put a foot over the threshold when Sam heard her inhale sharply.

Clearing the last step himself, Sam jumped out onto the roof of the ambulance station... and straightaway found that he too could only gasp.

Inevitably, three further gasps followed—from Rabbit, L-Man, and Devine. Then, last of all, and surprising everyone present, the smallest member of the group proceeded to add his own unexpected response. Because it was at that moment that Little Bruv, still nuzzled tight against Sam's neck, let out a kind of keening sigh and finally began to stir. As if curiosity were getting the better of even *his* ability to sleep though anything. As if he too wanted to see.

Approaching the safety barrier that edged the building's flat roof, Sam stared out at the spectacle before them.

By rights, they really shouldn't have been able to see anything. Not with a citywide blackout. Not on this darkest of all dark and moonless nights. London should barely have been visible at all. But it was. Not so much its bricks and mortar, though Sam could certainly make out such detail in a few of the nearer streets. No. What was *truly* visible—and in breathtaking, almost starlike clarity—was something else entirely.

The city's lifeblood, Sam thought.

Because that was exactly what it looked like.

From the roof of the ambulance station, the veins and arteries of London lay revealed for miles around, picked out in shimmering threads of golden light, all the way to the horizon.

People. People by their thousands. By their *tens* of thousands. All carrying candles.

On the closer streets, Sam could make out individuals. There were young and old. Able-bodied and wheelchair bound. Skin tones of every variety. Some were carrying lighters rather than candles. Sam saw one man with an actual flaming torch. And once again, all of them seemed to be streaming in the same direction. Converging upon a point somewhere to the north-east of the ambulance station.

On Sam's chest, Little Bruv gave another restless wriggle, another fitful moan, then finally he raised his weary head, turning to look at the streets below. And as he did, he laughed. A gurgling baby laugh that sounded like *Ga-ha!* Infant eyes widening in wonder, the little boy in Sam's arms reached out with two chubby hands, as if trying to grab at the distant threads of light. *Ga-ha!* he blurted again.

Devine shook her head in bewilderment. "Where are they all going?"

Perdita smiled. "Isn't it obvious, Inspector?" she said... and told her:

"They're going to a place where they can *fight...*"

Two streets away, Sam saw the door of a terraced house open and an elderly Sikh man step out. He was wrapped in an ancient trench coat, collar raised to the base of his turban.

"A place where they can make a stand against the Darkness. *Together...*"

A young white girl in ripped denims approached the old Sikh, offering him a candle, and smiling, the old man took it then joined the stream of candle-bearers shuffling down his street.

"The same place that has drawn them for thousands of years..."

One road over, a party of black girls—all high heels and wonky party hats—staggered from a restaurant and fell into step with a group of Asian lads, dinner table candles held aloft.

"Since long before Christianity. Long before Islam. Long before *any* modern religion…"

Sam hugged Little Bruv to him. Felt the baby's warmth against his skin.

"Where are they all going? They're going where they've *always* gone, Inspector."

Sam looked to the north-east. He could see it now. Even from here. The edges of its famous architecture highlighted in the glow of the countless candles now descending upon it.

"They're going to Ludgate Hill."

And they were. To the astonishing monument that now stood atop it. Just one of who-knew-how-many that had occupied that same spot since people first came to this place.

They were going to St. Paul's.

20

Chariot of Fire

In the cavernous main hall of the ambulance station, the light was growing dimmer by the second, fewer than half the one hundred and three candles there still burning. Huddled close over Little Bruv and squinting in the gathering darkness, Sam blew again on his icy fingers then finally pressed the last of the poppers on the infant snowsuit that now cocooned the baby from head to toe. Their paramedic friend had dug out the all-in-one thermal suit when he'd seen the kid start to shiver in the plummeting cold, and Sam was relieved to see that the thing already appeared to be doing its job. Shivering no longer, Little Bruv was fast asleep once more, muffled infant snores drifting out from somewhere deep within the suit's quilted hood.

With a weary sigh, Sam slipped his arms beneath the dozing baby, then lifted him up, and gently laid him back in the battered car-seat, draping an old blanket over him for good measure. Shaun the Sheep grinned out from the blanket's fleecy surface, offering an enthusiastic thumbs up—*Baaaaaa–rilliant!*

"Samar..."

Sam stiffened. It was his mum's voice, and he'd been waiting for this moment for the last half hour, ever since they'd all finally agreed on the plan. Sam was acutely aware that what they were about to attempt here was not going to be easy on his mother. Okay, fair enough, it wasn't exactly gonna be a trip to Disneyland for any of them, but for his mum...

Sam took a deep breath, got to his feet... and turned to face her.

She stood there alone, rigid as a statue, anguish chiselled into her every feature.

"Samar, I can't," she said. "I can't just... *leave* you. I'll stay. Stay with you here until... until..." Her voice trailed away into silence.

Glancing over his mum's shoulder, Sam saw the rest of them waiting by the ambulance station's main exit—Sam's dad, Asha, Perdita, Devine, Jackson, the paramedic...

"Mum, you can't," Sam whispered, taking a

step forward and putting his arms around her. "You have to go. You *know* you do. Right at this moment, St. Paul's is probably the safest place in London. Maybe the safest place anywhere."

Trembling in Sam's embrace, she opened her mouth to object, and as gently as he could, Sam cut her off: "Mum, no. You *have* to go. For Asha. There's nothing more you can do here. *Please, Mum.*"

Her eyes dropped, but still she made no move. And as she stood there shaking in Sam's arms, yet another earth tremor rolled through the room, rattling doors in their frames, sending chairs skittering across the floor. By the exit, Asha whimpered and hugged into her dad's leg.

"Mum... *please...*" Sam urged over the rumbling clatter. "You *have* to."

Finally, the tremor began to subside, and just as the last growling shudder of it sank back into the floor, Sam felt his mum shift a little in his embrace then pull back. Looking up once more at Sam, she dried her eyes, kissed him... and nodded. Then without another word, she eased her way out of Sam's arms and went to join the group waiting by the exit.

Just as she got there, the door itself banged open, and L-Man and Rabbit stumbled in, the two boys carrying armfuls of what looked like rubbish. What in fact *was* rubbish—twenty or so empty plastic juice bottles, the large two litre kind, all of them scrounged from nearby bins.

Staggering the rest of the way through the door, the lads let their mucky payloads clatter to the floor and then moved in to take up positions on either side of Sam. Sam acknowledged each bruv separately with a sombre nod, before turning once more to the group by the door and catching Perdita's eye. After a moment, the girl took the hint, broke away from the group, and stepped up to Sam and the boys.

Sam kept his voice low: "What if you're wrong about this?"

"I'm not," Perdita said. "It's building. Building by the minute. Can't you feel it?"

Sam glanced about him and nodded. Of course he could feel it. They all could. It was everywhere. All around them. A kind of otherworldly *potential*. To Sam, it felt a little like that breathless thrill you'd always get first thing on Christmas morning when you were little. But cranked up somehow. *Dangerous* almost.

Perdita shivered. "Energy like this?" she said. "It *will* find its own release."

"Critical mass…" Sam murmured.

"Exactly. We just have to make sure you're *there* when it happens. You and Little Bruv."

Sam smiled. "First time you've called him that. Sounds funny when you say it."

A smile stole onto Perdita's lips then too, and her eyes darted to the sleeping baby in the car-seat, lingering there for several long seconds before finally looking up again at Sam.

"He did, you know," Perdita said. "He chose right."

The girl was close now. Very close. Her face just a hand's width away. Sam could smell her hair—strawberries. See the smudged remains of her eye makeup. Her lips only inches from his...

Sam gulped, his eyes flicking to his parents watching silently from the doorway.

Then Perdita's gaze dropped, one of her slim pale hands darting in to hook a stray lock of hair over an ear.

"All right," Devine called, "let's go."

And just like that, the moment—had there even *been* a moment?—was gone.

Perdita turned, re-joined the company by the door, and headed off with them into the darkened street outside the ambulance station.

Sam and the boys followed the group as far as the main exit, watching from the doorway as Perdita and the five adults each extracted one of several short lengths of timber standing in a petrol-filled bucket by the door—wooden chair legs, their submerged ends wrapped in thick layers of cotton bandages. Moments later, six flaming torches were burning bright in the darkness, and moments after that, following a final exchange of murmured goodbyes and anxious handshakes, Devine led the company away down the street.

Sam stood watching them go, Rabbit and L-Man by his side.

Within seconds, the hurrying group had reached the junction with the main road, where they merged quickly with the ever-thickening throng of candle-bearers streaming past. Sam saw the group's six flaming torches become one with the shimmering river of light…

… and then they were gone.

Silence.

Sam glanced round at his mates.

No one spoke. They didn't need to. As one, the three boys turned to look at what stood there waiting for them in the street.

The rickshaw.

"Okay," L-Man said finally, "so let's pimp this ride."

The Walworth Warriors set to work.

● ● ●

In the end, it really didn't take that long. The paramedic had already gathered most of the stuff the boys needed—salt from the ambulance station's kitchen, surgical rubber gloves, rolls of duct tape, a compressed air powered emergency siren. Someone—Sam's dad maybe?—had even found time to make up four extra chair leg torches for them. In fact, the empty juice bottles that L-Man and Rabbit had collected had actually been the very last item on the boys' list, so with everything already to hand, the work itself turned out to be a dawdle. In under half an hour, the job was done, and the three of them stood back to admire the results.

To admire the rickshaw transformed.

The juice bottles—sixteen of them in total, all filled with salt-water—were now arrayed cannon-like down each side of the rickshaw's frame, secured there by copious quantities of duct tape. Above the vehicle's front wheel hung a large basket, overflowing with bulging surgical gloves, each one filled with yet more salt water and tied off at its end (anti-demon water bombs, or so the theory went). Duct-taped to the handlebars, where a bell would normally go, was the compressed air powered siren, ready to blast forth and clear the way ahead, should the need arise. And finally, thrusting skyward from the rickshaw's passenger canopy were the chair leg torches, one fixed to each corner, all four of them blazing away even now, sending defiant embers up into the black sky above the deserted street.

Well all right then, Sam thought.

Their carriage awaited.

Their "Chariot of Fire" (name non-negotiable,

copyright Roger "Rabbit" Crawford).

Of course, if the rest of the plan came together—if Devine and the others did manage to clear the route to St. Paul's for them—none of what the boys had just done to the rickshaw would even be necessary. These were all "just in case" deals. Precautionary measures. In the wise words of R. Crawford, better safe than get your balls ripped off by the spawn of Satan.

Chewing his lip, Sam began slowly to circle the rickshaw...

He pressed a fist into one of the plastic juice bottles and watched a jet of salt water squirt horizontally from the tiny hole punched in the bottle's cap...

He snatched up one of the surgical glove water bombs and lobbed it at the wall opposite. It burst on impact, salt water splashing the brickwork in a wide circle...

He climbed aboard the rickshaw's driver's seat, grabbed the handlebars, gave the brakes a squeeze, the pedals a kick...

All good.

Nodding his satisfaction, Sam looked down at the tiny, snowsuited figure of Little Bruv, now strapped securely into the papoose-style baby-carrier on Sam's chest.

Kid was fast asleep again. Of course.

But maybe not for much longer...

Bringing one hand up over the handlebars, Sam spread his fingers wide and let his open palm hover above the activator button of the compressed air siren...

He glanced round at his friends.

After a moment, L-Man nodded.

Rabbit did, too.

The Walworth Warriors were ready.

Then with one final nod—there might even have been a hint of a grim smile there—Sam brought his hand slamming down onto the siren—

—and a blunt, ear-bludgeoning honk punched its way out into the darkness...

21

Ready or Not

Devine heard it straight away—a distant, echoing bleat coming in from the south, cutting through the noise of the swarming crowds of candle-bearers in St. Paul's Churchyard.

"That's them," she said to Perdita. "They're ready."

Listening for just a moment, Perdita nodded her agreement then handed Devine a fresh roll of perimeter tape. Behind the pair, two parallel lines of the striped plastic tape, ten or so metres apart, stretched back through the churchyard to the steps of the cathedral, looped around trees, lampposts, traffic lights, anything they could find. Opposite Devine and Perdita, Jackson and Mr. Chowdhury were hard at work taping the second line, while

292

the paramedic was doing everything he could to clear the area in between of people.

"We need to work faster!" Devine bellowed across to the others.

One *serious* understatement, and they all knew it. Currently, their supposed people-free "safe corridor" covered a paltry twenty-five metres, from the cathedral's south entrance barely to the middle of the churchyard. The bulk of the route the rickshaw would be forced to negotiate—the entire stretch of the Millennium Footbridge and all the way up Peter's Hill—still remained totally impassable, packed with ever more incoming candle-bearers.

Fighting back her rising despair, Devine wound tape around yet another lamppost and yelled at the approaching crowds, "Everybody stay back! Back *behind* the tape, people! The south entrance is closed! Stay *behind* the tape and make your way to the— "

A hand came to rest on Devine's arm— "Inspector, you *have* to tell me what's going on."—and with a grunt of frustration, Devine turned to face the elderly figure loitering at her elbow. It was the Dean of St. Paul's, the cathedral's most senior cleric, but senior or not, it was by now abundantly clear to Devine that the man was not coping. Not coping at all.

"Nothing you've told me here makes any sense

here," the Dean said. "If this is some kind of terrorist attack— "

"Oh for pity's sake, terrorists do *not* cause earthquakes," Devine shot back, anger and fear hardening her words. "Now please, I need you to— "

"Inspector..." It was Perdita's voice this time, breathy and uncertain and edged with some *new* fear, if such a thing could even be possible tonight. "Inspector, are you seeing this?"

Devine turned, opened her mouth to ask Perdita what she was talking about...

... and then closed it again. Because yes, Devine certainly *was* seeing this. Though exactly what it was she was seeing Devine had not the least idea.

Drifting in the air between her and Perdita, caught in the flickering light of the girl's flaming torch, were countless tiny... *flakes* was the only word Devine's mind saw fit to supply. The only word for them really. They fell in swirling flurries, fluttering down from the starless darkness above. Tiny, drifting *flakes*. Like snow.

But black.

Devine looked up... and felt herself stagger.

Because the air above her—the entire *sky* in fact—seemed now to be filling with the stuff. It was everywhere. All around them. For as far as Devine could see.

A blizzard.

A blizzard of black snow.

Reaching out with a trembling hand, the ashen-faced Dean of St. Paul's let one of the drifting flakes settle on his palm, and for a long moment, the old man just stood there staring down at the thing in dumb disbelief. They all did.

Then, for no reason Devine was able to comprehend, the Dean brought the black snowflake up to his nose... and sniffed it. Instantly, his face twisted in revulsion.

"It smells like... death," the old clergyman said, and when he looked back up again at Devine, his eyes were wet, quivering with horror. "Tell me what I can do."

Devine looked around at the crowds of candle-bearers still swarming in from all directions. "Your security team," she said to the Dean. "I need you to round them up for me."

●●●

Rocketing from the momentary shelter of a pedestrian underpass, the rickshaw hurtled once more into the full force of the black blizzard, Rabbit's despairing monotone ringing out from the back seat. As ever, the bruv managed to nail the mood of the moment: "Seriously? Black snow? Man that is just unnecessary."

Bearing down still harder on the pedals, Sam

drove the rickshaw onwards, the four flaming torches above its passenger canopy lighting the way through the storm of darkness.

"Gonna be fine, Little Bruv," Sam whispered to the tiny sleeping figure in the papoose on his chest. "All gonna be okay. Gonna see your mum and dad soon, yeah?"

The rickshaw flew around a tight corner. And another. Then another still. One last hard left and Sam hit the brakes, the vehicle skidding to a stop by a small copse of trees set back from the broad pathway that hugged the south bank of the Thames.

Huffing and panting, his thigh muscles burning brightly, Sam peered out into the darkness ahead. Clearly visible now, less than forty metres away, was the unmistakable sci-fi swoop of the Millennium Footbridge, the graceful, arcing span of it picked out in flickering candlelight as streams of pilgrims shuffled north along its narrow walkway, heading for St. Paul's on the other side. Squinting harder still through the black blizzard, Sam could make out something else too—several ribbons of broken perimeter tape, fluttering from either side of the bridge's entrance ramp. Devine's group had obviously tried to seal the bridge off as they passed, but with no one to police such a flimsy barrier, the cordon simply hadn't held. In truth, Sam wasn't surprised. The move had been a long shot at best.

With his gasping lungs finally starting to ease up, Sam shot a further glance behind him to check on L-Man and Rabbit in the rickshaw's back seat... and saw immediately that they too must have clocked the broken perimeter tape. Both boys sat there rigid with terror.

"Keep it together," Sam told them. "They'll get back to clear the bridge eventually. Priority was always to clear the other end first, yeah? *Inside* the cathedral, too. Cos hey, let's face it, they ain't cleared the decks in *there*, we're dead anyway."

● ● ●

The cathedral was beyond crowded now. Wherever Devine looked, frightened candle-bearers were crammed into every seat and pew. Packed cheek by jowl into every aisle and side chapel, every recess and bay. How the cathedral's security team were ever going to clear the heaving area beneath the dome, let alone the entire south transept, Devine really had no idea. But they had their orders now, and Devine had no option but to trust them to their task.

As the guards set to work, Devine turned to head for the south exit...

... and yet again she found herself reeling. Reeling at the incredible spectacle of it all—the shimmering, yellow glow from what must now be ten thousand flickering candles rippling over the cathedral's epic vaults and arches, glinting off its extravagant baroque adornments. Gold leaf and gilt trim shone like slivers of sun. Frescoes and mosaics glowed bright as a child's colouring book. The effect was beyond dazzling—nothing less than a full-scale assault on darkness itself—and at the sight of it Devine couldn't help but feel a spark of hope.

But then, as if in response—as if sent wilfully forth to snuff out that spark—another earth tremor shuddered its way up from the depths. All around, ancient joinery creaked and groaned. Statues toppled and plaster dust rained down. And with a shriek like tearing metal, a lightning-bolt shaped crack split the towering stained-glass window behind the high altar, sending hundreds of multi-coloured panes crashing to the tiled floor.

● ● ●

Wrapping one arm tight around Little Bruv in the papoose, Sam braced himself against the rickshaw, holding onto it for dear life as the ground heaved and rocked beneath his feet. All around him, paving stones shifted and cracked, lampposts rattled, trees came crashing to the ground. Sam shot yet another desperate glance towards the bridge ahead, hoping—*praying*—for some kind of sign. Anything at all to indicate that Devine and the others were at least *starting* to clear the walkway there.

But no. *Still* those endless streams of candle-bearers shuffling across. What the hell was going *on?* Where *were* they?

Eventually, as the gut-churning tremor finally began to abate, Sam forced himself to let go the rickshaw, drew in a deep breath, then took a further moment to look around, peering hard through the dark blizzard in all directions.

Because something else was beginning to worry Sam now.

The black snow.

It was starting to lie. Building up layer by layer in ever-widening patches of pure, impenetrable darkness. For some reason, those patches made Sam very nervous indeed...

And mere seconds later, that reason became horrifyingly clear when a cry rang out ahead:

"Look out!"

Sam whirled... and saw two young men halfway up the bridge's entrance ramp, yelling and gesturing as they raced towards someone ahead of them—an elderly woman, trudging along by herself and clearly oblivious to the men's cries. As Sam watched, the old woman took two more shuffling steps forward, at which point her front foot strayed into one of the larger drifts of black snow. Almost instantly, the woman's foot and lower leg vanished, sinking into the patch of gathering darkness as if it were a hole. Screaming in terror, the old woman toppled to the walkway, the rest of her starting to slip forward, over the edge of the patch of black, into whatever void lay beneath. Both her legs disappeared. Then her lower torso. Her flailing upper body had just begun to follow when the two men finally reached her, grabbing the old woman by her underarms and hauling her shrieking and sobbing back out of the darkness.

Beside the rickshaw, Sam stood reeling in mute horror. From behind him, in the vehicle's back seat, he could hear L-Man and Rabbit's trembling gasps of shock.

Sam shut his eyes. Took a second to let his hammering heart recover. *Keep it together, bruv. Just keep it together.* Then he opened his eyes again and scanned the length of the bridge, finally seeing what he hadn't seen before—that the candle-bearers were all avoiding the places where the black snow had begun to lie, stepping carefully around each dark drift.

But for how much longer were they gonna be able to do that? The areas of black... there were just so *many*—gathering, building, broadening, one beginning to join with another...

Finally, Sam nodded... and glanced around at his friends.

Once again, words were unnecessary.

Rabbit looked like he was gonna puke all over his hand-knit hoodie. "No! NO! We have to *wait*! We have to *wait* till they clear the bridge!"

"Wait any longer, we ain't never getting across," Sam said. "Wait any longer, maybe there ain't no St. Paul's left to get across *to*. We do this, bruvs. We do this *now*!" and heart revving once more, Sam leapt up onto the rickshaw's driver's seat, grabbed the handlebars, then turned again to his mates in the rear. Both of them looked utterly petrified now—as heroic as two puppies in a basket. Sam was pretty sure he looked no better.

"Ready?" Sam said.

L-Man gulped but reached down and snatched up a salt-water filled juice bottle from the floor of the rickshaw. Grasping it with both hands, the big guy raised the bottle to his shoulder and then pointed its cap end forward, wielding the thing like it was some kind of badass machine-gun—a Coca-Cola Kalashnikov.

For a moment, Sam thought Rabbit was gonna dig his heels in, but in the end he didn't. The bro' with the 'fro simply sagged a little, grabbed himself a juice bottle too, and lifted the improvised weapon to his own shoulder. Finally, both boys nodded.

Yeah. Ready.

Sam glanced down at Little Bruv, still asleep in

the papoose on his chest. Gently, he brushed a few flakes of black from the baby's cheek, stroked his infant face. Then, with a final grim nod of his own, Sam turned once more to his mates... and did what absolutely could not be avoided here.

He stuck out a fist. "Walworth Warriors, bruvs."

They went through it all with impeccable, machine-like precision. Every dip, swish, clench and bump. The Warriors' Handshake.

And it was good. Stupidly good. *Insanely* good.

Did it suddenly feel like they *weren't* all gonna die a horrific, agonizing death by demon claw? No. But it was good anyway.

The three of them just being there.

His bruvs.

The Warriors.

The stuff they'd done together.

The stuff they were about to do.

And their voices. Kicking it out into the dark:

"All for one, one for all, two for a tenner, and three for the show!"

Sam slammed a foot down onto the rickshaw's raised pedal, and with a clatter of gears the vehicle took off. Less than five seconds later, the Walworth Warriors' Chariot of Fire hit the slope of the entrance ramp and hurtled onto the Millennium Footbridge.

302

22

Bridge of Darkness

Sam had tried to steel himself against what was coming. He really had. But when the rickshaw rocketed from the end of the entrance ramp, and the actual walkway of the bridge finally rose into full view, all Sam felt was terror, crushing his guts like a demonic fist.

So many people, stretching all the way to the other end of the bridge. So much darkness, gathering in ever more of those unholy patches, while the black blizzard raged all around.

Behind him, L-Man gasped and Rabbit whimpered. They knew it as well as Sam did. This was impossible. Insane. Sam almost hit the brakes right there and then. But instead, he just dragged in a lungful of ice-cold air, choked back his fear, and bore down on the pedals.

The rickshaw shot forward, hit the flat of the bridge's main walkway, and ploughed on, hurtling straight for a straggle of candle-bearers ahead. Sam yanked the handlebars, left, right, left again, the rickshaw slaloming wildly between clumps of walkers, swerving around a blanket-sized drift of black snow. In the papoose on Sam's chest, Little Bruv jiggled and bounced crazily, his infant eyes starting open with fright. Oh yes. Kid was awake now. No question.

Heart hammering, Sam pumped the pedals harder still, and the rickshaw rocketed onwards through the black blizzard. Ahead of them now, a huddle of teenagers. The group whirled. Saw the vehicle careering towards them. Leapt aside. For a moment it actually looked like they were all gonna make it, until a jolt rattled through the rickshaw and a cry of pain rang out from behind as the vehicle's rear wheel clipped a single trailing ankle, toppling one of the terrified kids like a bowling pin.

Sam risked a glance over his shoulder and caught a glimpse of the unfortunate teen now sprawled on the ground behind. Was he convulsing? Transforming? Sam couldn't tell. Either way, that had been too damn close. And Sam clearly wasn't the only one who thought so. In the back seat of the rickshaw, Rabbit and L-Man sat wide-eyed with sheer terror, hugging their juice bottle weapons to their chests and gripping the vehicle's frame like they were riding the world's scariest roller-coaster. Which pretty much summed it up, right? Cos let's face it, *nobody* was tall enough for this freakin ride.

Gathering still more speed, the rickshaw powered on through the black blizzard, Sam's legs pounding at the pedals. On either side of him, group after group of walkers flashed by in a candlelit blur, while ever more storms of black snow tunnelled straight at Sam's exposed face. The blizzard was getting worse. Sam was sure of it. Even with the rickshaw's four flaming torches, he was struggling to see more than a few metres ahead now.

Then an extra dense flurry of black snow hit Sam full in the face, and all of a sudden he could see nothing at all. Panic exploding through him, Sam clawed clumps of the black flakes from his eyes, shook his head to clear the last of it, then turned forward again—

—and felt his heart jolt with a million volts of horror. All Sam could make out ahead of him now was an impenetrable mass of dark uniforms and shiny musical instruments! A brass band! Salvation Army! Blocking the way and utterly oblivious to the rickshaw barrelling straight at them!

Screaming his shock, Sam slammed a fist onto

the compressed air siren fixed to the rickshaw's handlebars, and as the blaring honk blasted out, the entire band whirled as one... then parted, the rickshaw rocketing safely through their stunned and stumbling ranks.

A tidal wave of relief surged through Sam—

—before blind terror came crashing back in again.

Because that was when he saw it. The biggest black snowdrift yet—straight ahead of them, spanning almost the entire width of the bridge, and less than five metres away!

Heart leaping, Sam crunched the brakes, and the rickshaw rocked with a bone-shaking jolt of deceleration. L-Man and Rabbit yelled in shock, slamming forward into the back of the driver's seat, and then the world began to spin as the vehicle pitched into a sickening, slo-mo skid, frame rattling, rear wheels throwing up ragged arcs of black snow. Completely out of control, the rickshaw slid onward for a full five seconds more, before finally juddering to a halt right at the very edge of the huge patch of darkness.

Sam breathed out. Okay, now that really *had* been too damn—

And then the rickshaw's front wheel slipped forward into the black.

With a stomach-turning lurch, the entire front of the vehicle dropped like a plummeting elevator, and before he knew what was happening, Sam was tumbling over the handlebars, plunging straight for the lightless void below. Screaming in terror, he threw out a desperate hand, somehow managed to snag the inner rim of the front wheel. An instant later, he screamed again—in pain this time—as his falling body jerked to a brutal, shoulder-wrenching stop, the weight of himself and Little Bruv threatening to rip Sam's arm clean out of its socket.

Twisting his fingers into the spokes, Sam bit back the pain and clung on one-handed to the rickshaw's front wheel, the lower half of his dangling body lost in darkness, the rickshaw half-in-half-out of the huge drift of black snow. In the papoose, Little Bruv's eyes were wide open now, shining with terror as Sam's legs kicked and flailed, searching for some kind of purchase beneath him. But there wasn't any. Of course there wasn't. There was nothing beneath Sam at all.

Literally nothing.

A yell rang out from above: "Hang on, Sam!"

L-Man. Student of the bleedin obvious.

Together, the big guy and Rabbit leapt out of their seats, stumbled to the back of the rickshaw, and began to haul on its rear frame. Sam felt the vehicle jolt backwards, and hope flared in his chest. The boys could *do* this! Roaring with the effort, L-Man and Rabbit dug in their heels, took the strain, heaved again. And slowly, centimetre by centimetre, the front of the rickshaw began to jerk upwards, edging its way out of the darkness...

Then came the very last words any of them wanted to hear:

"Hey there! You guys need some help?"

Sam whirled towards the sound of the voice... and felt his heart wrench with horror. Because over the rim of the patch of darkness, he could now see a gang of maybe a dozen candle-bearers heading straight for them.

"Just hang on!" a tattooed guy at the front of the group yelled.

Popular subject, the bleedin obvious.

L-Man bellowed back at the man, "No! Stay there! Don't come any closer!"

But Tattoo Guy didn't listen. Of course he didn't. None of them did. They just kept on coming, hurrying towards the rickshaw, their faces furrowed with concern, all of them eager to help.

L-Man yelled again, "No! Please! You gotta stay back! We got this!"

Four more steps was all it took. One by one, Tattoo Guy and his group of good citizens froze mid-stride, fell into spasming, convulsive fits, then began to transform.

L-Man screamed and Rabbit shrieked, the pair

agape now with raw terror. But maybe some kind of adrenalin-fuelled power-up kicked in then too, because all at once, with one last heave, the two boys finished the job, dragging the rickshaw the rest of the way out of the void, taking Sam and Little Bruv along with it.

Sam swung his legs up, slammed his feet down onto solid ground, leapt back aboard the rickshaw. Behind him, L-Man and Rabbit hurled themselves into the vehicle's rear.

And behind *them*, Tattoo Guy and the Happy Helpers of Old London Town completed their shuddering transformations.

Gasping in horror, Sam kicked down hard on a raised pedal, and the rickshaw took off. But even as the vehicle sped away into the black blizzard, a blood chilling riot of screams and roars from behind told Sam that they had company now. And a single glance over his shoulder was all he needed to confirm it:

The demons were following, a dozen or more of them, barrelling along behind the rickshaw with that grotesque, simian gallop. Candle-bearers everywhere screamed in shock, scattering like sheep as the howling creatures hurled themselves forward—monster after monster, meathook claws raised high, ready to strike the instant their tiny target got within range.

Which, at the rate these things were gaining,

could only be *seconds* away.

Heart slamming in his chest, Sam hammered still harder at the pedals, zig-zagging the rickshaw between patches of black, left hand battering at the siren to clear the way ahead.

He threw another terrified glance over his shoulder... and instantly wished he hadn't.

The nearest demon was now barely three metres behind.

Head lowered, shoulders hunched, Sam urged yet more power from his pounding legs, but it was useless. His muscles were at their limit, the pain in them already close to unbearable. Sam could do no more. Rabbit and L-Man were just gonna have to deal with the problem themselves.

Rabbit and L-Man did.

As the demon pack galloped closer still, Rabbit raised his juice bottle, gave himself a moment to take aim, and then squeezed the bottle hard. A thick jet of salt water hit the nearest demon square in its leering face, and with a howl of shock, the creature fell tumbling to the ground, vanishing into the darkness behind.

Eyes narrowing, L-Man took aim with his own juice bottle. Fired. Missed. Fired again.

Shot number two hit home, and with an ear-splitting roar a second demon dropped away, battering off the bridge's safety barrier to disappear into the night.

"Good job, bruvs!" Sam yelled.

"Yeah!" Rabbit bellowed back, all but grinning. "These things ain't so— "

Then the demon at the front of the pack launched itself from the pursuing horde and slammed down onto the rear frame of the hurtling rickshaw. Shrieking in terror, L-Man and Rabbit raised their juice bottles, but before either of them could get off a shot, the creature batted the makeshift weapons right out of the boys' hands. And even as the two bottles went flying into the black, the monster on the back of the rickshaw roared again then lunged for the now defenceless Rabbit. Screaming in shock, the bruv threw himself to one side, but too late, and with a sickening smack, a massive red-skinned claw closed around Rabbit's throat, hauling the guy bodily out of the back seat.

"No!" Sam screamed, snatching a fistful of surgical glove water bombs from the basket in front of him and hurling them over his shoulder at the demon on the rear of the rickshaw.

Two of the bombs burst on impact, and with an ear-shredding bellow, the shocked creature thrashed and writhed in a sizzling, blistering frenzy, before finally tumbling backwards and disappearing into the dark...

... with the screaming Rabbit still clutched in its monstrous claw!

For an instant, time itself seemed to stop, snapshotting the utter horror of the moment...

... and then, with a howl like some kind of tortured animal, L-Man threw himself at the opening above the passenger seat's backrest, screaming out into the night behind them:

"Rabbit!"

Black despair crushed Sam's soul. Rabbit was lost! Rabbit was gone! Rabbit was—

L-Man's mouth fell open. "Rabbit!"

Rabbit was clinging to the back of the rickshaw.

Sam could barely believe it, but there the guy was, hanging onto the rear frame of the hurtling three-wheeler, the toes of his trainers kicking up a spray of black snow as they trailed behind him on the bridge.

How long Rabbit would be *able* to hang on though was another matter entirely. Because right behind him, less than a metre away, at least ten galloping demons were again closing in, their swinging claws slashing ever closer to Rabbit's trailing feet.

The demon leading the pack surged forward. Gained a few more centimetres. Took yet another vicious swipe. With a yell of terror, Rabbit hauled his legs in, but not fast enough, and a hooked talon snagged the bruv's left trainer, ripping it right off his foot. Shaking the gutted Nike from its claw, the lead monster snarled with glee, summoned yet another burst of speed, edged closer still...

... and once again, a wave of black despair swept through Sam. Because this time there was no way the demon could miss. Sam saw it. L-Man saw it.

And Rabbit saw it, too. The guy's eyes seemed to dim, some last flicker of hope leaving them as he looked up one final time into the faces of his fellow Warriors.

Then the galloping creature behind Rabbit raised its murderous claw—

—Rabbit closed his eyes—

—and L-Man lunged over the rickshaw's back seat, straight into the path of the plunging claw. With both hands, the bruv grabbed Rabbit by the collar and heaved, Rabbit's featherweight body jerking up and over the seat's backrest just as the demon's flashing talons sliced through the empty air where Rabbit no longer was. Screaming their combined terror, the two boys tumbled backwards, collapsing into a heap on the floor of the hurtling rickshaw, while at the same time, in the road behind them, the galloping demon howled its fury and flailed at the surrounding night.

Rabbit dragged himself upright, gaping at L-Man in utter disbelief.

But if the bro' with the 'fro said anything then, Sam didn't hear it, because right at that moment another monstrous shriek pulled Sam's attention left—

—and there was yet another demon, coming up the side this time, drawing level with the front of the rickshaw, its black eyes lasering in on Little Bruv in the papoose on Sam's chest.

Sam grabbed another fistful of water bombs. Lobbed them hard at the monster. Watched them explode in a huge arcing splash. But even as the demon fell away shrieking into the dark, Sam saw still more of the creatures—ten of them at least—now galloping up on *both* sides of the rickshaw, as if trying to get directly to Little Bruv at the front.

Sam turned to yell at L-Man and Rabbit—

—but the guys were already on it. Back on their feet again, the two boys slammed fists and forearms, chests and knees, down onto the juice bottle cannons fixed to either side of the rickshaw. Multiple sprays shot left and right, cutting a brutal swathe through the nightmare horde, and an ear-shattering clamour of demonic shrieks and howls ripped through the night as the creatures jerked in agony and fell away in a thrashing, tumbling blur of claws and fangs and monstrous red flesh.

Not even five seconds later, the last of the demon pack finally disappeared into the darkness behind the speeding rickshaw, and a split-second after that, the vehicle hurtled off the end of the bridge's exit ramp, out onto the pedestrian precinct beyond.

Sam could barely believe it. They were through! They'd made it over the bridge! The hardest part of this was surely over! Bellowing in triumph, Sam rammed a fist down onto the compressed air siren in front of him, partly to keep clearing the way ahead, but mostly just to hear its raucous blare—a joyous, trumpeting blast of pure victory.

He really should have known better.

With a jolting crash, the rickshaw came to a sudden and complete stop, and all at once, Sam's world was a tilting, spinning blur as momentum catapulted him from the driver's seat. Sailing through the darkness, his mind stuttering in shock, Sam somehow managed to curl himself up into a ball and wrap his arms tight around Little Bruv in the papoose, protecting the baby's head as best he could. Then WHAM! Hunched shoulders hit planet earth and Sam began to roll, over and over, bones crunching on concrete—knees, elbows, skull, knees, elbows, skull—tumbling onwards. Finally, when there seemed to be nothing left to crack or bruise or strip the skin from, an upright world lurched back into place, and Sam lay there sprawled on the paving slabs, dazed and battered and bleeding.

Head still reeling, Sam struggled to his feet.

Somewhere, a baby was crying...

Little Bruv!

Panic stabbing at his heart, Sam looked down at the papoose... and almost sank to the ground again in relief. Little Bruv was okay. Distressed, yes—bawling his lungs out, in fact—but as far as Sam could see, the little guy was unharmed.

So what the hell had just happened?

Sam glanced behind him... and saw exactly what.

Set across the path that exited the bridge was a line of bollards, presumably there to stop vehicle access to the pedestrian precinct. And the freakin things were painted black. Black! Sam had had no chance of seeing them in time. None whatsoever. Entirely oblivious, he'd simply gone hurtling onwards at full-speed and slammed headlong into the bollard in the centre of the line, the rickshaw now all but completely wrapped around the heavy cast iron post.

"Sam! Sam, are you okay?"

It was L-Man, staggering up through the black blizzard, Rabbit by his side. Both boys looked shaky as hell, but at least they were still walking. At least they—

And then, once again, the inevitable happened.

Candle-bearers began to approach.

At first, just one wide-eyed old lady: "Oh my! I saw what happened! Is your baby all right?"

But then more of them, the sound of Little

Bruv's distress pulling them in from every direction, all of them frowning with honest, human concern, all of them just wanting to help:

"Poor little thing…"

"Is he gonna be okay?"

"Here, I'm a nurse, let me look at him…"

Bruised and bloody and still reeling on his feet, gasping with terror and utter exhaustion, Sam didn't even *try* to argue with them. Instead, he just turned to look up the street.

Because there it was.

St. Paul's.

It was *there*. *Right there*. Its southside entrance only two hundred metres away up the gentle incline of Peter's Hill. Sam could sprint that distance in under a minute, no problem.

But not tonight.

Because tonight, impeding any and all further progress, was a jostling, surging mob of yet more candle-bearers—thousands upon thousands of them, crammed together in a totally impassable bottleneck at the entrance to St. Pauls churchyard.

Only two hundred metres or not, the way ahead was nothing less than a road into Hell…

… while closing in from every *other* direction… that gathering army of the caring and the kind-hearted, all of them pouting their sympathy, crooning their concern:

"Poor little guy…"

"Is his mum around?"

"Here, I'm good with babies…"

No way forward.

No way back.

And a nightmare of razor-taloned horror only moments off.

What Sam chose to do next went way beyond desperate. In fact, knowing what he already knew, Sam had no doubt whatsoever that it was sheer insanity.

But maybe, in a world of darkness, insanity was the only sane choice.

Wrapping both arms tight around the screaming Little Bruv in the papoose, Sam turned towards the impenetrable mass of humankind blocking the way to St. Paul's…

… and ran headlong at the heaving crowd.

23

Demons Demons Demons

Lowering his head and dipping one shoulder, Sam hurled himself full-tilt at the seething mob crowding the slopes of Peter's Hill. At the same time, he began to roar—a guttural, throat-shredding, get-the-hell-outta-my-way bellow, as loud as his pain-wracked lungs would allow.

Up ahead, the nearest clump of candle-bearers whirled at the sound, but too late, and Sam slammed into the group shoulder first, sending bodies flying in all directions.

Farther up the street, others began to turn, their mouths falling open as they caught sight of this shocking new spectacle—of this crazed and bloodstained teenage boy barrelling towards them, roaring like a rampaging gorilla while a tiny shrieking baby kicked and thrashed against his chest.

Some of that crowd did manage to get out of the way in time. Others didn't.

And a few of those that didn't... began to change.

Sam caught glimpses of them out of the corner of his eye as he battered his way on through the crowd. A spasm here, a tremor there, a chilling flash of demonic black eyes. Were the transformations taking hold? Sam didn't dare look behind to see.

What he *did* see was L-Man and Rabbit moving in on either side of him, their own heads lowered, their own shoulders dipped, ramming their way forward with Sam and the baby.

"Just keep moving!" Sam yelled at them. "Whatever happens, don't slow down!"

Rabbit and L-Man began to roar now too, all three of them ploughing onward through the stunned crowds, hands and elbows and shoulders clearing the way ahead with brutal, battering-ram efficiency, slamming terrified walkers to the ground, throwing others aside.

Don't slow down don't slow down don't slow down...

Ten seconds later, Sam knew exactly how impossible that was gonna be. Because with every few metres of ground the boys covered, the crowds ahead grew denser...

... and denser...

... and then denser again.

Still the Warriors hurled themselves forward, barging their way on up the people-choked slope of Peter's Hill, parting the crowds like a three-man human snow-plough.

Don't slow down don't slow down don't slow...

But they *were* slowing down. They *had* slowed down. Sam knew it. They *all* knew it. The people the boys were trying to shove aside simply had nowhere to go now, ever more closely packed clusters of them pressing in from all directions. *Way* too many people, *way* too close and for *way* too long. Raging panic hammered at Sam's heart. How long till the first full-scale demon transformation? How long before one of these people finally—

Rabbit screamed, and Sam whirled to see a man with dreadlocks lying spasming at the bruv's feet. A split-second later, an Asian woman beside the man froze where she stood, darkness swirling into her eyes. Then the old guy that Sam was shoving against fell thrashing to the ground, a horrified little girl clinging to his hand and shrieking, "Grandad! Grandad!"

Still the Warriors rammed their way onward, screaming their terror, roaring their fury. But ahead of them now was just a single solid wall of unyielding humanity, the boys' momentum down to little more than a grinding, shoulders-to-the-wheel crawl.

And all around, ever more candle-bearers fell shuddering to the ground.

Parkas and anoraks split and tore, burst apart by bloating demon torsos—

Distending limbs punched at the sky, reddening with each new spasm—

Horns erupted, talons sprouted—

Those not transforming began to shriek. To run. But in the heaving mass there was nowhere to run *to*, and utter chaos came crashing down in a screaming, stampeding frenzy.

Finally, from somewhere behind the Warriors—how *far* behind, Sam had no idea—a sound rose up. The nightmarish animal howl of the crowd's first fully-transformed demon. As loud as a chainsaw. As raw as torn flesh. And heading straight for them...

•••

"Everybody get *back!*" Devine roared, forcing her way on through the heaving masses in St. Paul's Churchyard, a fresh roll of perimeter tape unspooling behind her. "The cathedral is now *full*, people! I repeat, the cathedral is *full!* Keep *behind* the tape and make your way to..."

Devine stopped. Shook her head. This was utterly futile. The crowds were just too much.

322

Even with the cathedral's security team on the case, progress was agonisingly slow—they must have been at it now for close to half an hour, and still their supposed people-free "safe corridor" barely reached the end of the churchyard. Yet somehow they were supposed to extend the thing all the way down to the Millennium Footbridge? And then *clear* the bridge itself? No way, Devine thought. Absolutely no way. Not in the time they had left. Because at the rate the black snow was now falling...

Unable to stop herself, Devine turned once more to look behind her—

—and yet again she felt her heart clench at the sight of it.

At the sight of St. Paul's.

Or what *remained* of St. Paul's.

For centuries a symbol of London pride— survivor of the blitz, a monument to hope and humanity—the cathedral was finally succumbing to enemy attack, its dome now almost completely gone, erased by the black snow. *How much longer?* Devine wondered. *How much longer before the Darkness takes the rest of it? Before the last of St. Paul's finally—*

And that was when she heard it.

The screaming.

It seemed to be coming from the south, from the direction of the Millennium Footbridge, near where a dense mass of candle-bearers was bottlenecked at the entrance to the churchyard. In the middle of the heaving throng there, something seemed to be happening. And whatever it was, it was nothing good.

Peering harder into the candlelit gloom, Devine concentrated, trying to make sense of what was going on down there, and after a moment, her eyes finally seemed to adjust. She thought she could make out movement now, right at the centre of the crush of candle-bearers. Yes, definitely. Jerky, erratic movement. Screaming people throwing themselves wildly against each other, as if trying to get away from something. As if—

And then another sound entirely cut through the commotion, rising above the screams. A sound Devine had heard only once before and had prayed she might never hear again.

It was the blood-chilling howl of a demon.

Almost instantly, a second howl joined it. Then a third. A fourth. A fifth. And on and on, a nightmare crescendo of demonic fury.

Then all at once, just fifty metres downhill from where Devine stood, the front of the bottlenecked mob scattered in a shrieking frenzy, and a figure burst out into the open.

Samar Chowdhury.

The teenager exploded from the screaming

crowd like a rocket from a silo, wailing baby strapped to his chest, his two friends hurtling along at his side.

And Devine? Devine just froze where she stood, the sheer shock of the moment taking every last drop of air from her lungs in a single, gut-crushing gasp of horror.

What happened next though... *that* very nearly took Devine's sanity.

The three boys had made it barely five metres from the jostling chaos behind them when, almost literally, all Hell broke loose. Devine couldn't even begin to count how many creatures there were. They poured from the terrified crowd in a neverending stream, a howling demonic army, claws reaching for the sprinting boys only four steps ahead of them.

It was a vision from the End of Days itself.

And yet, even as terror slammed a booted foot into Devine's chest, she felt something else, too. The tiniest flicker of *hope*. Because right now, the boys could be only eighty metres from the cathedral's south entrance, and with the partially-completed cordon in place they had a clear run the rest of the way! Yes, the demons were gaining, but not fast enough! As long as no one took a tumble, Sam and his friends were gonna make it! They were gonna—

And with a sickening jolt of horror, Devine

remembered.

The south entrance door! The door the boys were racing towards! It was closed! Locked and bolted in order to dissuade arriving candle-bearers from trying to use it!

Adrenalin lighting up her entire body, Devine whirled, charging across the churchyard for St. Paul's. With her heart slamming, she flew down the perimeter tape corridor. Rocketed through the gateway in the cathedral's surrounding wall. A dozen desperate, stumbling strides took her up the building's main steps. Five more carried her over the broad stone landing. And then she was hurling herself headlong at the massive wooden door, ramming into it shoulder first, pounding furiously at its heavy oak panels:

"Open up! Open up now! OPEN UP IN THERE!"

No answer. Fists hammering in blind terror, she shot a glance over her shoulder—

—and saw Sam and his friends hurtling through the churchyard below, the demon horde now all but upon them. With a roar of rage, the creature leading the pack lashed out, raking its talons across Sam's left shoulder, and Devine heard the boy scream. Saw his face twist in agony. But still he ran. Plunging headlong for the south entrance door. The door to safety.

The door that was *locked*.

Again Devine threw herself at the massive slab of oak, battering on it with both fists, both feet, screaming and yelling for someone inside—

—while in the churchyard below, the lead demon edged closer still to the sprinting boys. Devine saw its monstrous claw slash out once more, and this time, the blow must have sliced right through the papoose's shoulder straps, because the entire baby carrier, wailing baby still inside it, fell from Sam's chest, plummeting towards the ground.

Barely breaking stride, the boy flung out a single desperate hand and somehow managed to snatch papoose and baby back up again, mere milliseconds before they fell into the path of the stampeding demon army now less than two metres behind. Pulling the screaming infant tight to his chest, Sam hurtled onwards, launching himself through the gateway in the cathedral's outer wall, his two friends still flying along at his heels. And as the other boys cleared the gateway themselves, the pair made a grab for the edge of the open gate, hurling it back into the pursuing horde. With a startled howl, the lead demon crashed head first into the gate's wrought iron bulk and went sprawling. A second creature followed suit, tripping over the first, and for a moment, the two monsters lay there, jamming the narrow gateway in a writhing red tangle. Then both creatures leapt once more to their clawed feet and went powering up the steps after the boys, the rest of the demon horde following in a howling fury of flailing talons and thrusting horns.

But the monsters' momentary stumble had done it. Had secured Sam and his friends a few precious seconds. The boys now bounded up the steps with a clear ten metre lead, hope blazing bright in their eyes.

Hope that was about to be dashed against half a ton of solid oak!

Still Devine hammered at the closed cathedral door. Still she shouted. Still she screamed.

And still there was no answer.

Clearing the final step, the boys leapt up onto the stone landing... and Devine saw Sam's eyes widen in shock as he finally took in the horror of the closed door ahead.

Heart pounding, Devine threw her entire body at the huge oak slab, over and over, battering and kicking at it, bellowing at the top of her lungs. But still nothing. Absolutely nothing. Not even a—

And then the clunk of a lock from inside!

Gasping in terror, Devine hurled herself at the door yet again. And this time the towering wooden panel flew inwards, slamming back into the alcove beyond. With a cry of shock, Devine tumbled through the open doorway, her legs a treacherous tangle beneath her. And even as she collapsed at the feet of the terrified Dean of St. Paul's, Sam and his friends came rocketing through after her. Arms pinwheeling, totally unable to stop themselves, the three boys skidded wildly across the smooth tiled floor and smashed headlong into the closed door at the opposite end of the alcove, slumping in a heap against its dark oak panels.

But the demons! The demons were still coming! Still barrelling up the cathedral steps!

"Shut the door!" Devine yelled at the Dean. "Shut the door!"

Nothing. No response. The old clergyman just stood there, paralysed with fear.

Scrambling to her feet, Devine lunged for the door, grabbed its edge—

But she was too late. The army of demons cleared the top of the cathedral steps, thundered across the stone landing, and surged forward into the open doorway.

24

Warriors Five

Sam shrank back into the floor, Little Bruv clutched to his chest, the pair of them screaming in terror as the creature leading the pack hurled itself at the open doorway, hit the threshold—

—and then smashed to a complete and sudden stop, its entire monstrous body flattening against apparently empty air in a fleshy triple-smack of face-torso-limbs.

An instant later, the rest of the howling horde thundered up after their leader—

—and in rapid-fire succession, met exactly the same fate.

Sprawled there on the tiled floor of the south entrance alcove, Little Bruv still howling in his arms, Sam watched in open-mouthed astonishment, struggling to process exactly what it was he was seeing here—creature upon creature *slamming* into some kind of invisible barrier across the cathedral doorway and then *thudding* unconscious onto the stone landing outside. On and on it went, demon after demon after demon—SLAM-THUD SLAM-THUD SLAM-THUD—the landing gradually filling up with their slumped red bodies. The whole thing was bizarre and shocking and...

... and altogether freakin *hilarious*. *So* hilarious in fact that, for one insane moment, Sam actually found himself wishing he could be outside again, watching the rest of it unfold from there. Cos seriously, this had to look *damn* funny from sideways on, yes? Full-on, Loony Tunes funny. All those who-knew-how-many demons, piling up like cartoon cats hitting a brick wall.

And that was when Sam began to laugh. Not just a single ha-ha either. All of a sudden, this was the funniest thing Sam had ever seen, and once the first snort of amusement had escaped him, he somehow found that he couldn't stop, the laughter rolling out of him in long, loud, lung-busting barks.

Heads began to turn Sam's way, everyone in the alcove gawping at him now as if he'd gone completely crazy. And hey, right at this moment, Sam was *not* inclined to argue. "They can't get in!"

331

he finally managed to gasp between guffaws. "They can't get in here!"

For just a moment longer, Rabbit and L-Man continued to stare back at Sam in complete bewilderment. Then, as one, both boys turned again to watch the demon army still face-planting into the invisible barrier... and suddenly the bruvs were laughing, too. No timid giggles from them either. Genuine, gut-busting howls of hysteria.

And it didn't end there. All at once, in Sam's arms, Little Bruv stopped crying, looked around at the three laughing boys... and then let them have it with his own excellent effort—a raucous and gurgling infant chortle, full-throated and merry and...

... and exactly what Devine needed to start *her* off. The policewoman's chest began to heave with breathless, almost silent hee-haws. Two seconds later, she stuck out a hand to steady herself against a pillar, stared down at the shredded knees of her tights, and proceeded to hee-haw her police heart out.

In the end, the old vicar guy—the one who'd finally opened the door for them—was the only person there who failed to catch the giggles. Poor old dude just stood in a corner, staring at them all in total confusion as the crazed laughter rolled on and on.

Eventually, almost a full minute later, long

after the last of the demon horde had slumped unconscious onto the landing outside, the spontaneous hysteria finally began to abate, sheer physical exhaustion getting an upper hand once again.

Wiping tears from her eyes, Devine stepped up to Sam and pulled him to his feet. Next to them, Rabbit and L-Man climbed unsteadily to theirs, a last burble of giggles escaping the two boys before fading away on their weary sighs.

By now, a kind of blissful quiet had eased its way into the space left by the laughter, and almost as if by some mutual telepathic agreement, everyone there, the old vicar guy included, began to gather around Sam, peering down at the tiny bundle in his arms.

In his turn, Little Bruv beamed back at them all, hitting them with one final yelp of baby laughter— like a comedy full-stop—before following through with a yawn of truly epic proportions. Two seconds later, his infant head sagged once more onto Sam's chest.

"Yeah. I know how he feels," L-Man said. "Is he okay?"

Sam looked Little Bruv over. "Think he's fine. Totally fine. Kid's a fighter."

Rabbit grinned. "Super flyweight, yeah!" he said, clenching one hand and bringing it down gently to fist-bump the baby. And maybe it was just his imagination, but Sam could almost have sworn he saw Little Bruv make a tiny, sleepy fist to accept the gesture. Either way, it looked pretty damn cute. The world's smallest boxer's handshake.

With a smile tugging once more at his lips, Sam turned again to the cathedral doorway and the piles of unconscious demons now littering the broad stone landing beyond it. Some of the creatures there—*most* of them in fact—had actually begun to shudder where they lay, already starting to morph back into the poor sods the Darkness had possessed. Hopefully, in another minute or two, they'd all be completely human once more.

"They won't remember, will they?" Devine said. "None of it."

Sam shook his head. "No. I don't think they will. They'll just— "

And at that exact same moment it hit them both.

Devine was standing *right next* to Little Bruv, her arm all but touching the baby's head!

With a gasp of shock, Sam leapt backwards to get to a safe distance. Devine did exactly the same, thudding heavily into a pillar behind her. But they both knew it was already too late.

Or at least, it *should* have been too late...

Sam frowned at Devine. "You... you ain't...

changing…"

A soft voice sounded from behind them:

"No. She won't. Not in here."

Perdita.

Sam turned to find the girl poised in the archway of the alcove's inner door, the door itself open now, golden candlelight spilling through from the packed pews beyond.

"I suppose I should have known, really," Perdita said, her rich girl self-assurance doing little to hide the choked tremble of relief in her voice, or indeed the tell-tale sheen of moisture in her make-up smudged eyes. "We're *all* safe in here. You said it yourself, Samar. They can't get in. The *Darkness* can't get in."

Sam nodded and was just opening his mouth to ask if Perdita was okay when, all at once and completely unexpectedly, he found the words catching in his throat, his gaze—his every waking sense, it seemed to Sam—transfixed somehow by the girl standing before him. Framed there in the elegant stone arch of the cathedral doorway, backlit by ten thousand flickering candles, Perdita looked… well, long blonde hair, shining blue eyes, graceful as a ballet dancer…

She looked like an angel.

Perdita's brow wrinkled. "What?" she said.

Sam lowered his eyes. Felt blood rush to his cheeks. "Nothing."

Clearing her throat, Devine stepped up to them both. "Is there anything else I can do here?"

"Yes," Perdita said. "You can open all the doors, Inspector. Let everyone in now. As many as possible anyway."

Firing back a curt nod, Devine turned, stepped over the threshold of the outer door—no invisible barrier for cops, apparently—and began to thread her way carefully through the dazed ex-demons now staggering to their feet on the landing outside. A few seconds later, the policewoman disappeared from view down the cathedral steps.

In the silence that followed, Sam turned back to the sleeping baby on his chest and began to extract him from the remains of the papoose, wincing a little as he did so—Sam's demon-slashed shoulder was beginning to throb quite a bit now, but hey, there didn't seem to be *too* much blood, so Sam reckoned he would live.

"Here, let me," Perdita said, moving in to help with the baby.

"Thanks," Sam replied, holding Little Bruv out at arm's length for her. And as Perdita set about untangling the baby from the shredded papoose, Sam took a moment to draw himself together then shot a glance over his shoulder, intending to speak to Rabbit and L-Man behind him. When his eyes actually located the two boys though, he found himself pausing.

And frowning.

In truth, Sam wasn't sure quite what to make of the scene before him—basically, a silent and brooding Rabbit staring with an odd intensity at a slouched and oblivious L-Man, studying the big guy with... well, again, Sam wasn't exactly sure with what. Something on Rabbit's mind though, that was for certain.

Eventually, Rabbit tapped L-Man on the shoulder, and the big lad turned.

"Thought I was a goner, man," Rabbit mumbled, shuffling a bit and staring hard at the tiled floor beneath his one surviving trainer. "Thought I was Monster Munch."

In response, L-Man offered Rabbit a brow-puckering frown before coming back with some world-class shuffling/floor-staring of his own.

Thereafter, the cryptic proceedings seemed to grind to a halt.

In the end though, as if finally realising that shuffling/floor-staring alone might not cut it here, Rabbit jerked out a single, decisive nod, then lifted one hand to the high-five position.

And there he stood, eyes lowered, palm raised, solemn as a monk whose dog just died.

"I was a numpty," Rabbit said. "Total numpty. I shoulda been more— "

But the rest was lost as a beaming L-Man slammed Rabbit with an arm-jolting handful of white-boy skin.

Sam got the distinct feeling he was missing something here...

"There you go," Perdita said at last to Sam, untangling a final twisted papoose strap from the baby's left leg. "All done." And with a grimace of distaste she tossed the ruined baby-carrier aside before moving back to the alcove's open inner door and picking up something from the floor there. Her rucksack. The one with the pieces of broken sword inside.

Hooking the bag over her shoulder, Perdita drew in a deep breath then turned once more to Sam and the boys. "Come on," she said to them. "Everyone's waiting."

With a weary nod, Sam tucked the sleeping Little Bruv back into the crook of his arm before looking up again at Perdita...

... and only then became aware of something that must surely have been there for some time—a sound, soft and low, drifting through the inner door from the cathedral beyond.

It was the sound of singing—*carol* singing—and as Sam listened, its gentle lilt seemed somehow to soothe his battered and aching body. To seep into his bones, warming them with melody.

Silent night, holy night, all is calm, all is bright...
In Sam's arms, Little Bruv slept on...

Smiling again, Sam strode forward and joined

338

Perdita beneath the cathedral's inner door.

A moment later, L-Man and Rabbit moved in beside them.

A moment after that, all four of them joined hands.

And together, the Walworth Warriors—new blood and all—stepped through the doorway into the vast candlelit interior of St. Paul's Cathedral.

25

Two Become One

Sam and the Warriors emerged from the doorway to find themselves looking out over a shimmering sea of candlelight that filled the entire cathedral right to its farthest corners. All around them, the melodic murmur of the carol singing echoed softly through the building's towering arches, dipping softer still as the Warriors took their first steps along the south transept. It was almost as if the entire ten-thousand strong congregation had somehow seen what lay sleeping in Sam's arms. As if they were afraid of waking him.

Up ahead, the circular floor area beneath the cathedral's dome lay only fifty or so paces away. Maybe not even that. But Sam had taken barely three of those paces when all at once he stopped—

stumbled almost—filled with the sudden crazy certainty that he wouldn't be able to make it. That his aching, trembling legs would give out on him before he actually got there.

Then... Sam felt Perdita's hand in his, firm and supportive... saw his bruvs by his side, terrified too but standing tall... and the feeling passed.

Drawing in a deep breath, Sam nodded to his friends then turned front once more.

And hand in hand, the Warriors began to make their way up the aisle, four abreast, slow but steady, while ten thousand pairs of bewildered, fearful eyes watched from all around.

Fifty paces, Sam told himself, *only fifty paces*, and began to count them as he walked...

He'd got as far as nineteen when another earth tremor rumbled through the building, candle-bearers everywhere shrinking into their seats and clutching each other in terror. But still they kept singing, every single one of them, soft and low, a lullaby of defiance.

Twelve more paces, and a series of echoing clunks drew Sam's eyes to the far corners of the cathedral as several doors there were hauled open, yet more candle-bearers beginning to file in. Where they were all gonna go, Sam had no idea, but in they came anyway, ushered into unseen alcoves, mysterious doorways, the narrowest of passageways and corners...

Turning forward once more, Sam willed another ten reluctant steps from his aching legs, shuffling past the epic girth of one of the dome's massive support columns...

... and suddenly there they were—Sam's family, huddled together in a front row just behind the cordon tape. Sam watched tears of relief spill from his mum's eyes as she spotted him. Saw his dad stoop to whisper something to Asha. Didn't take an Einstein to work out what: *It's Sam. He's okay.* Asha beamed in response—a grin of supreme smugness that somehow said, *Of course he is, silly*— then waved wildly in Sam's direction. Smiling through his exhaustion, Sam briefly released Perdita's hand to wave back, and then watched his dad stoop for a second time to whisper again into Asha's ear.

Finally, another nine paces later—to Sam it felt like nine *thousand*—the Warriors arrived at the spot directly beneath the centre of the cathedral's majestic dome...

... and there, just as *Silent Night* drew to its lilting conclusion, they stopped.

A grave, weighted hush fell upon the vast space, and once again Sam felt the near crippling pressure of expectation. He shot an anxious glance at Perdita, who returned him a brief but reassuring smile before pulling her rucksack from her shoulder and dropping gracefully to her knees.

Setting the bag down onto the tiled floor, Perdita removed from it the two parts of the broken sword and placed each piece carefully before her in the centre of the sunburst design that dominated the tiling pattern beneath the dome. This done, she rose and stepped back to take Sam and L-Man's hands again, restoring the Warriors' four-in-a-line formation by the edge of the sunburst.

All around, ten thousand people waited—row upon row of confused and fretful eyes, lasering into Sam and his friends, frowning at the mysterious baby asleep in Sam's arms.

Eventually, L-Man risked a whisper: "What now?"

Sam peered into the farthest corners of the cathedral, where ever more candle-bearers continued to be ushered in, cramming steps and side chapels, arches and window ledges...

"We wait," Sam said. "Critical mass, remember? As soon as we— "

"Get out of my way! Let me *through!*"

The voice—totally unexpected and shockingly loud in the hushed cathedral—had a grating, strident edge to it, and whirling towards the centre aisle where it had come from, Sam saw a group of candle-bearers there step hurriedly aside to reveal a lone figure standing just behind the perimeter tape barrier. It was a man. Middle-aged, average height, few distinguishing features of note, but glowering furiously at everyone around him, as if daring anyone there to get in his way.

No one did, and silence fell once again. *Complete* silence this time. Even the candle-bearers just entering seemed to pause where they were and hold their breath.

After a long moment, the man nodded, as if satisfied with the crowd's compliance. Then, still glowering in a fury, he turned front to face the Warriors, and as he did, that glower found itself a new target:

Sam.

With a single angry snatch of his hand, the man snapped the line of perimeter tape before him and began to approach. He moved slowly but with confidence—with *purpose*, Sam thought—the click of his footsteps echoing beneath the dome. Clearly this guy had something he wanted to say, but what that might actually be, Sam had no idea. Absolutely none.

A dozen stalking paces later, the man came to a stop directly in front of Sam and Little Bruv, the last clack of his footsteps echoing into silence.

Throughout the vast, overcrowded cathedral, no one spoke, and no one moved.

For another long moment, the man looked Sam over. First up and down... and then straight in the eye. Finally, he spoke:

"Get out," the man growled.

Sam frowned.

"Get out of our church," the man said. "This is your fault. All of it. Your fault! You and your terrorist friends!"

Silence pressed in. Stony with shock.

Thousands of pairs of eyes bored into Sam and the furious figure standing before him.

Sam kept his voice low: "Mate, this... this ain't no terrorist thing. This is— "

Then another earth tremor shook the building, and another window exploded into glittering shards.

"Get out!" the man yelled, and he slapped Sam hard across the face.

Gasps of horror swept through the congregation, and several security guards darted forward to intervene.

Sam stopped the guards with a look.

In his seat behind the perimeter tape, Sam's dad rose in a grimacing fury.

Sam caught his father's eye and stopped him, too.

Dead silence fell once more.

And still the man just stood there—proud, defiant, shaking with anger.

Sam moved in close, stooping a little to whisper into the guy's ear, "Look, you're scared, I know. But don't be," and with a subtle jerk of his head,

Sam indicated first his fellow Warriors, then the tiny snowsuited bundle tucked into the crook of his elbow. "Us and Little Bruv here, we got this."

Snorting in derision, the man finally turned his angry glare on the sleeping baby in Sam's arms and opened his mouth to reply—

—but before he could, Sam reached out quickly and clasped the guy's hand:

"Merry Christmas, yeah?"

Instantly, the man stiffened, the scowl on his furious face deepening further still. Seething with rage, he looked back up at Sam, drew in a rasping breath to speak again...

... and that was when it happened. That was when the deathly silence all around finally came to an end. Broken—*shattered* even—by a sound so faint it was scarcely audible at all.

At first, Sam had no idea what it was he was actually hearing, the sound itself muffled and indistinct. It seemed to be some kind of electronic beep, high-pitched and rhythmic and...

... and coming from *Little Bruv!*

Frowning in confusion, Sam stared down at the sleeping baby nestled in his arms.

Then, at last, something in Sam's numb and exhausted brain clicked, and his heart all but turned a summersault as he finally recognised it.

Recognised the *tune.*

Rudolph the Red-Nosed Reindeer!

In one frantic, disbelieving rush, Sam yanked down the front zip of Little Bruv's snowsuit, pulled back the suit's quilted hood—

—and there! There it was! Still perched askew atop Little Bruv's head!

Rabbit's musical Santa hat, bleeping out its merry little Christmas song once more.

In the end though, it wasn't the *bleeping* that truly sent Sam's pounding heart into full-on overdrive. At least, not *just* the bleeping. It was what *accompanied* it. Because while the Santa hat continued to chirp out its tacky little Christmas tune, the bobble on the *end* of it, currently draped over Little Bruv's chest, did its very *own* tacky little thing. Something it hadn't done since the Darkness had rolled out across London.

It *flashed*.

Flashed a gaudy Christmas red.

Together, Sam and the angry man stood entranced, the little LED bobble blinking between them, turning their faces red-white-red-white-red-white.

And all around, ten thousand people made not a single sound. An entire football stadium's worth of breathless silence, broken only by that cheesy little melody, tinkling out across the ocean of candlelight, faint as finger cymbals, loud as a symphony...

And if you ever saw it, you would even say it glows...

Eventually, Sam shook his head and turned to Perdita: "I don't understand. What— "

But he got no further. Because just then a *second* sound cut in. Again, another tinny electronic melody, but this time more a kind of brief synthesised fanfare.

Like the sound of a mobile device powering up.

And even as the dumbstruck L-Man began to extract his rebooting iPad from a shell-suit pocket, the rest of it kicked off.

In the hanging candelabra directly above the Warriors' heads, a lone electric light bulb started to flicker... before surging abruptly to full power. A second later, the rest of the bulbs in the candelabra followed. A second after *that*, another nearby candelabra began to shimmer into life. Then another. And another. Then the reading lamps in the choir stalls. Then spotlights in both transepts. Then the rest—bulb after bulb, in wall fittings and alcoves, atop pillars and beneath arches, all bursting into existence again in a dazzling pulse of light that surged outwards in a circle from Sam.

No, not from Sam.

From *Little Bruv*.

Beyond speechless now, Sam and the Warriors just stood there agape as the wave of artificial light rolled onwards through the vastness of St Paul's, neon and halogen and LED adding level after level of man-made sparkle to the already blazing glow of the candles. And it wasn't *just* a light show they were getting here, Sam now realised. There was a soundtrack, too—a crescendoing cacophony of bleeps and ringtones as, throughout the congregation, in ten thousand bags and coat pockets, ten thousand mobile phones powered up simultaneously.

Within seconds, the entire cathedral was ablaze. Incandescent. Every last electric light in the place burning at full power. But even then—even as he was shielding his eyes from the blinding spectacle of it all—Sam somehow knew that the show wasn't over. That there was more to come. *Much* more. And glancing round at the Warriors, it was clear to Sam that *they* knew it, too. "Come on," he said to his friends. No further elaboration was required. As one, the four of them turned, raced back down the transept, and stumbled on into the south entrance alcove to peer out at St. Paul's churchyard below—

—where they saw exactly what Sam knew they would: the wave of artificial light rolling on, spreading outwards from the cathedral, surging down every road that Sam could see. Streetlamps flickered then flared to full power. Christmas illuminations exploded into riotous colour. Headlamps of abandoned vehicles punched out bright cones of light into the dark blizzard. And all around, in the cathedral's grounds and surrounding streets, even while the black snow continued to fall, the crowds of candle-bearers began to cheer.

Clutching Little Bruv tight to his chest, Sam turned then darted back again into the heaving cathedral... and here too, people were finally letting the hope in. Cheering and applauding. Shaking hands and kissing. Holding each other in a cathedral ablaze with light.

And then...

Then Sam heard it.

How he was *able* to hear it, he had no idea. Through the reverberating roar of cheering and clapping in the crowded cathedral it really shouldn't have been possible. But hear it Sam did. And once again, he was not alone. From the looks on their faces, it was obvious that the rest of the Warriors heard it too—the sound they had all been waiting for, faint with distance but utterly unmistakable.

The chiming of Big Ben.

Within seconds—five at most—the rest of the cathedral seemed to catch on to the sound as well, the riotous clamour of cheers and applause fading with startling speed as ten thousand people paused to listen to those distant, throaty peals rolling in from the south.

Through shattered windows, the sound drifted

in—Big Ben clanging its ponderous way through all four bars of that famous melody. And when at last the lowest-toned bell rang the first peal of "midnight", a further titanic wave of cheering rose up all around, thundering through the vaults and arches of St. Paul's. The volume—the sheer *immensity* of sound in the vast cathedral space— was utterly heart-stopping, and Sam instinctively pulled the sleeping Little Bruv closer to him, cupping his hands over the baby's ears, waiting for that colossal, world-shaking roar to subside.

But it didn't subside. At least not right away. It just continued to grow. Louder... and louder... then louder still, till the very air trembled against Sam's skin.

And then, over the deafening noise, Sam heard Perdita yelling at him, "Look!"

Sam turned, looked... and felt his heart leap.

In the centre of the sunburst-tiled floor, the two pieces of broken sword were glowing.

"The surge!" Perdita bellowed above the din. "It's happening!"

Grabbing him by the arm, the girl began to drag Sam back towards the tiled circle beneath the dome, Rabbit and L-Man stumbling after them.

In the end though, they never quite got there. Because just as Sam and Perdita reached the outer edge of the sunburst, the two glowing sword pieces rose into the air and came together, their broken ends fusing in a single blinding flash. A split-second later, ten-thousand people gasped in unison as a two-metre wide column of swirling, multicoloured light exploded from the sunburst beneath the floating sword, shooting upwards into the dome above.

26

A Beacon Through Infinity

In the square outside St. Paul's, Devine clung to Jackson, reeling on her heels at the eye-popping spectacle of it all—at the dazzling world of electric light flickering back into existence all around. Between the pair of them, the two police officers managed not a single spoken word—just stood there, entirely transfixed, entirely astonished...

... and entirely unprepared for what happened next.

By now, the cathedral's dome was actually gone completely, erased by black snow. But from where Devine knew that dome to be—from the very crown of it in fact—a blazing, column of swirling, multicoloured radiance suddenly burst forth and shot skyward, lancing straight up through the black blizzard, disappearing into the infinity of darkness beyond.

Devine gasped. Jackson did too. From all around them, wild cries of astonishment rang out as people everywhere clutched each other and staggered in shock.

And even before the last of those cries had died away, it began.

Hardly daring to breathe, Devine watched in mute wonder as the tiny, impossibly delicate object fluttered down from the darkness above and landed on Jackson's shoulder.

A single flake of snow.

But not black.

Oh no.

This snowflake was *white*.

Wide-eyed and trembling, Devine let go of Jackson, reached up, and with the tip of one finger gently lifted the single white snowflake from her partner's shoulder. For another long moment, she and the young detective just stood there, gaping down at the tiny crystalline perfection of the thing before them. Then, finally, Devine glanced up again at Jackson, brought the snowflake up to her mouth... and licked it.

Water. Fresh, clean water. Icy, pure, and perfect.

Still trembling, Devine turned her eyes skyward once more... and yet again she had to steady herself against Jackson. Because all around them now, for as far as Devine could see, a swirling, sparkling whiteness was spreading through the black blizzard. Spreading *fast* too, billowing flurries of it surging into the plunging torrents of dark. Within seconds, the last of the falling black snow had actually disappeared completely, replaced entirely by twinkling flakes of perfect white, fluttering steadily to the street below...

... where, almost immediately, they began to lie, building up layer by layer on top of the scattered patches of accumulated darkness.

Devine fell to her knees, staring at the ground before her. Jackson did the same, the pair of them gawping in silent fascination as a dense patch of darkness was first mottled, then covered by virgin white flakes. When she could see no more of the black, Devine reached out, brushed aside the fresh white snowfall... and there beneath it, in all their glorious grey solidity, were the sturdy bricks of St Paul's Churchyard. No trace of the darkness whatsoever.

Climbing again to their feet, the two police officers stood looking at each other for a moment longer... and then Devine just threw her arms around her partner. For a second, the shocked lad remained rigid as a post. But then he was hugging Devine back and laughing, and the pair of them danced—actually *danced*—two or three jumbled hops and some kind of twirl, galumphing their way through the crowded churchyard in the falling white snow. Eventually, Devine had to force herself to stop before she took a tumble—the ground was already starting to get slippy, and Jackson had all the grace of a drunken gorilla. Laughing now too, Devine turned to look back at St. Paul's...

... and the sight that met her eyes then was the one image of this night which Devine knew would never ever leave her. The image of the cathedral's beautiful dome slowly re-emerging from the darkness, etched into silvery existence again, flake by twinkling flake, while above it, a swirling column of light beamed out into the snow-filled heavens.

Stunned and speechless, it was actually yet *more* light that brought Devine back into the now—a single, heart-stopping burst of it from *inside* St. Paul's itself. It blazed out through the cathedral's broken windows in a series of blinding, multicoloured shafts. And with it, there came a sound.

A cacophonous, ear-shattering blast of sound.

Part fanfare, part thunderbolt...

● ● ●

Heart leaping in his chest, Sam staggered

backwards, jerking his gaze away from the searing explosion of light. He saw L-Man reel. Rabbit and Perdita freeze in shock. Ten thousand candle-bearers cling to each other in terror.

And even as the retina-scorching flash was receding to a dancing afterimage negative, even as that stupefying roar of not-quite-music reverberated into silence, Sam knew what he was about to see. Knew *who* he was about see.

With Little Bruv still clutched to his shoulder, Sam blinked his vision back into some kind of working state, then turned once more to the circle beneath the dome.

The swirling column of multicoloured light was still there, beaming upwards from the tiled sunburst on the floor, but before it there now stood an angel. Not the angel they'd met before. He, of course, was long gone. This was someone new. And from the look of him, the dude was a whole other level of heavenly ass-kicker. If the angel they'd met in the alley had been a heroic, battle-scarred infantryman in some epic heavenly army, the one who stood before them now was a four-star general. He was just *more* in every way. Bigger. Grimmer. Shinier. Nearly ten feet tall, the warrior angel towered over Sam and his friends, light glinting off the vast gleaming chest plate of his armour, his deep green eyes shining with unknowable knowledge, unquestionable authority, unimaginable—

"'Ssup?" Rabbit said, raising an amiable hand.

L-Man whacked Rabbit upside the head. A little unfairly, Sam thought. Not like anyone else had stepped up, right?

Still the angel just stood there, looming over the Warriors, his watchful eyes taking in each of them one by one. *Inspecting* them almost.

At last, the warrior angel's roving gaze came to rest on the tiny bundle in Sam's arms, somehow still asleep despite the overwhelming sensory assault of the last few minutes.

Then the gleaming armoured giant spoke:

"You know why I am here," he said, and his voice echoed through the vaults and arches, low both in tone and volume yet somehow dense with power. Like distant thunder.

Sam gulped, nodded... and then for some inexplicable reason began to tremble.

With a ponderous, monumental authority, the heavenly warrior reached for the baby...

... and all at once Sam found himself stepping back, hugging Little Bruv tighter to him. "Wait..." Sam said. "Just... w-w-wait. Okay, first off, I need to know— " But somehow the rest of the words seemed to get lost, caught somewhere in Sam's thickening throat. Forcing himself to breathe deeply, Sam took a moment, coughed a little, and tried again:

"I need to know that you're taking him back, yeah? Back to his mum and dad?"

"Yes," the angel said.

"Like, straight there, right? Cos Little Bruv, he really needs his— "

"You have the word of Gabriel."

If ever a moment called for a stunned gasp followed by a respectful period of awestruck silence, it was this moment, and ten thousand people duly obliged.

Well, ten thousand minus one.

"Got any identification?" Rabbit said, scowling suspiciously.

L-Man whacked Rabbit upside the head again.

For several seconds more, Sam continued to study the astonishing figure standing there before them. Continued to absorb everything he could about this impossible being. The sheer, unearthly *enormity* of him. The staggering sense of power he seemed to radiate. All of that.

But something else, as well...

Something set deep in the angel's grim, almost sorrowful eyes.

Truth. Plain truth. Unmistakable and undeniable.

Finally, Sam nodded...

... and then glanced down once more.

Glanced down at the tiny, snowsuited figure asleep in his arms.

Little Bruv. *Their* little bruv. Just one baby boy. Beautiful and perfect and…

… and before Sam could even *think* about putting up any kind of fight, something vast and hot rose in his chest, welling up through his throat to settle just behind his eyes.

Trembling all over now, Sam drew in another wavering breath and tried to make sense of it. Of whatever the hell this was he was feeling. It wasn't as if he'd thought this moment would be *easy*. Truth be told, he hadn't actually *thought* about it at all. Not really. Cos, well… demons, magic swords, impending Armageddon… kind of slammed, you know? And now…

Now here it was.

And it was… *not* easy.

Sam swallowed. Watched three fat tears splash down onto Little Bruv's sleeping face. Wiped them away with the grimy sleeve of his hoodie.

"You be good for your mum," Sam whispered to the baby. "You be a good boy, yeah?"

And he kissed Little Bruv.

Kissed him gently. On the cheek.

Could it really be the first time he'd done that? *Really?*

Sam knew that it was, of course, and for a long moment, as if to make up for it, he let his lips linger there, pressed against the soft skin of Little Bruv's sleeping face, feeling that warm baby glow, smelling that sweet baby smell...

Eventually, Sam looked back up at the Warriors, and for a second or two, all three of them just stood there, staring back.

Then L-Man nodded, took a hesitant step forward... and kissed Little Bruv, too.

Rabbit followed, taking the baby's tiny hand in his and pressing it to his lips, before planting a second kiss—the gentlest of smackers—right on Little Bruv's forehead.

Perdita was next, touching her lips to the baby's cheek with a graceful bow of her head. Something in the way she did it told Sam that Perdita wasn't at all used to kissing. *Any* kind of kissing. But it was a real kiss anyway. A *true* kiss. That was also clear.

Then, turning once more to face the majestic figure standing there before them, Sam gulped back the last of his fears, drew in a slow, steadying breath...

... and finally offered up the baby.

With a single, grave nod, the angel reached out in solemn silence, and slipping his hands beneath the sleeping bundle, took Little Bruv gently up into his gigantic arms.

"Oh... and I think you may need this as well," Perdita said suddenly, stooping to pull something from the rucksack at her feet and then offering it to the warrior angel.

The angel stared down in confusion at the object Perdita held out.

It was this morning's *Metro* newspaper.

Sam finally managed a smile. "Trust her," he said, and with a further solemn nod, the angel reached out, took the newspaper, and tucked it carefully under one massive arm.

Then, with no warning whatsoever, and to Sam's utter astonishment, ten towering feet of gleaming, heavenly ass-kicker suddenly dropped to one knee, bowing his head before them.

Before the Warriors.

"Heaven and earth are in your debt," the angel said to them.

Silence. Even Roger "Rabbit" Crawford had no response to that.

At last, the angel rose again, Little Bruv now nestled in the crook of his mighty left arm.

And that was when Sam *really* began to shake. His entire body this time. Every cell in it screaming at him to reach out and grab Little Bruv. To snatch him back. Hold him close. Keep him *safe*.

But then Sam felt Perdita take his hand once more. Take it and squeeze it tight. It didn't stop the shaking. Not completely. Not even close, actually. But it helped a little.

And standing there beneath the astonishing dome of St. Paul's Cathedral, that dazzling column of multicoloured light still churning and swirling just one step behind him, the shining soldier of God turned his gaze on the Walworth Warriors for the very last time. Even then his solemn expression didn't really alter—at least, not that Sam could see anyway—though something in his eyes did seem to... to lighten perhaps. Just a little. To soften even.

And curled up tight in the corner of the warrior angel's colossal arm, a picture of perfect peace once more, Walworth's tiniest warrior slept on, snug in his bright red snowsuit, thumb jammed in his gob, snoring his cute little baby snores...

Then the angel took a single step backwards into the swirling column of light, and a vast storm of colour flared around him. Once more the sound rang out. That unmistakable sound. Part fanfare, part thunderbolt. A sound Sam knew he would never hear again...

Crushing Perdita's hand in his, Rabbit and L-Man gripping his shoulders in support, Sam battled the all but overwhelming impulse to shield his eyes. Fought with everything in him *not* to turn his gaze away from that final dazzling flash of fire...

... and maybe he saw Little Bruv's eyelids flutter open one last time. Flutter open to let two sleepy brown eyes peek out through the vanishing column of light.

Maybe Sam saw that.

Maybe he didn't…

Then the light, the angel, and Little Bruv were gone.

27

White Christmas

All things considered, Roger "Rabbit" Crawford was beginning to think that this might turn out to be a pretty decent Christmas after all. Okay, sure, homicidal demons, dying babies, narrowly averted Armageddons. All seriously bah humbug stuff, no doubt about it.

But there was the *other* stuff, too.

The *good* stuff.

Like now, for instance. Right at this very moment, the crush around Rabbit was insane—thousands of people streaming for the cathedral's exits, all at the same time, with Rabbit and the rest of the Warriors crammed together in the middle of the heaving pack. Yesterday, a situation like this would have had Rabbit wheezing into something small and crinkly, inhaling the refreshing tang of cheese and onion. Now though? Rabbit's lungs were free and clear and pumping their awesome asses off. Okay, so maybe not the best choice of phrases there, but Rabbit knew what he meant.

The *good* stuff, in other words.

And hey, the good stuff didn't end at the Miracle of the Kick-Ass Lungs either.

There was more. *Much* more.

Sam and Perdita were another fine example. Currently, the pair were just a couple of steps ahead of Rabbit and L-Man, shuffling their way towards the exit with Sam's family, and *still* holding hands. No surprise there, of course, but *good* all the same, yes? *Right,* somehow. Though at this precise moment, Sam did seem weirdly intent on giving the girl a hard time:

"Just tell me you ain't spending another Christmas Day on your own," he was saying.

As it happened, Perdita didn't even get a chance to reply to that one. Sam's mum just jumped straight in there, hooking her arm into Perdita's and announcing to all, "She most certainly is *not*. You will be coming to us for Christmas dinner, young lady. And *no* excuses."

Ha! See? There it was again! The *good* stuff! Right there! Doing its thing!

Then, of course, there was Walworth's Shiniest. Talk about an attitude transplant. Rabbit had genuinely never seen L-Man smile like he was smiling right now. Who knew the big guy had so many freakin teeth, right? *Looked* kinda different, too... though different *how*, Rabbit still couldn't exactly say. Maybe...

... and that was when it hit him. The Ray-Bans were gone. Rabbit had no idea when exactly L-Man had ditched the idiot-shades but ditch them he had. And one seriously smart move, in the opinion of Roger "Rabbit" Crawford.

So, yet again, the *good* stuff, yes? Though in this case something of a trade-off, seeing as how the world now had to deal with a whole lot more of the big-ass white boy's grinning mug.

And then finally... *finally,* there was that *other* thing. The thing Rabbit was still kind of struggling to get his head round. The thing he still couldn't *quite* bring himself to believe...

For the umpteenth time, Rabbit ran through his mental inventory:

Acne-ravaged skin? Check.

Embarrassing Christmas hoodie knitted by his gran? Check.

Poorly constructed Lego teeth? Check.

Mighty Afro? You betcha!

All still present and correct. Nothing different. Nothing new.

And yet...

It was the way people were *looking* at him.

Gawping almost. Crazy as it sounded, Rabbit couldn't quite ditch the outrageous notion that, at some point in the last twenty-four hours, he'd somehow managed to turn a mysterious corner and step into that mythical land where Usain Bolt was king and Idris Elba Prime Minister.

The land of the *not* not cool.

But how to test the theory? Rabbit glanced about him... and saw *exactly* how.

Up ahead, a girl of about Rabbit's own age was standing on a pew with a couple of friends, gaping down at the Warriors as they passed by. Pretty damn cute this girl was, too. Short and curvy. Dark curly hair. Big brown eyes...

... which suddenly shifted and met Rabbit's head on!

For an instant, Rabbit went totally rigid. Froze like an Xbox with a dodgy disc.

But then he shook off the fear, hauled in one mighty kick-ass lungful of air... and just hit those big brown eyes with the widest grin he could muster. Legoland was open for business!

And business, as it turned out, was booming! Because all at once, the girl's mouth fell open in complete astonishment, and Rabbit saw her turn away to whisper with her friends...

... before turning *back* again to fire at Rabbit the brightest, broadest, flat out *sexiest* smile he had ever been on the receiving end of.

The freakin *good* stuff indeed!

Yup, all things considered, this was turning out to be one *damn* fine Christmas morning.

An elbow in the ribs jerked the grinning Rabbit out of his thoughts.

It was L-Man, and as Rabbit turned to him, still on full-beam, the big guy recoiled a little in shock, before nodding towards Sam and Perdita in the crowd ahead. Still hand in hand, the pair had edged farther away, a couple of metres in front now, almost at the exit.

"Oi! Chowdhury!" L-Man shouted over to Sam.

Pausing in the archway of the cathedral door, Sam and Perdita turned.

"Ditching your bruvs already, are ya?" L-Man sneered.

Sam and Perdita eye-rolled in perfect unison, before Perdita smiled, shoved Sam back towards Rabbit and L-Man, and then headed out the exit with the rest of Sam's family...

•••

Halfway down the steps of St. Paul's, Devine stood shivering with Jackson, watching as the endless crowds continued to pour from the cathedral.

"That looks like them now, ma'am," Jackson said, pointing out a group just emerging onto the top landing. "Some of them, anyway."

369

The lad was right. It was the Chowdhury family. The girl Perdita too. And Devine couldn't help but smile as she saw their eyes widen in astonishment at the scene before them. You could hardly blame them, of course. When they'd entered the cathedral not even an hour ago, they'd left behind them a bleak, desolate London, half-consumed by the Darkness.

But now...

The transformation was almost impossible to comprehend. The snow—the *real* snow—had only just stopped falling, the cathedral's grounds and surrounding streets now completely blanketed in pure, perfect white. Several snowmen had already joined the crowds in the churchyard, while all around, excited children skipped and darted, hurling snowballs and making snow angels, laughing and playing in the glow of the candles and Christmas lights.

Raising a hand to the emerging group atop the cathedral steps, Devine eventually managed to catch Mrs. Chowdhury's eye, and only a few seconds later the entire party had joined Devine and Jackson on the middle landing.

For several *more* seconds everyone just stood there, no one knowing quite what to say, until finally, Mrs. Chowdhury simply smiled, threw her arms around Devine, and hugged her.

Somewhat wrong-footed, it took Devine a

moment to return the hug, but in the end, return it she did, and thereafter, all parties seemed happy to get in on the action.

Eventually, as the stumbling dance of hugs and handshakes began to wind down, Perdita's voice cut across the last of the heartfelt thank-yous, and some kind of emotional undertone in it made Devine take note:

"Um, excuse me, Mrs. Chowdhury..." Perdita said.

"Karuna, please. What is it, dear?"

"I was just wondering..." the girl paused for a second, took a breath, then continued: "Wondering if you might be able to squeeze in one more for Christmas dinner? Besides me, I mean," she added, whereupon her glistening eyes left Mrs. Chowdhury's to glance down the cathedral steps...

... at the foot of which, parked by the south entrance gate, there now stood a Rolls Royce stretch limousine. And standing to attention beside it, one impeccably besuited figure.

"I could bring some extra food to microwave," Perdita said. "Fortnum and Mason."

Mrs. Chowdhury smiled—laughed almost, though not unkindly—and even as she began to assure Perdita that one more for dinner would be no problem at all, the girl took off, rushing down the rest of the steps and fighting her way through the heaving crowds. Moments later, she was face to face with the elderly man poised by the limo.

For a long time, girl and butler just stood there staring at each other, the pair of them trapped in some kind of wordless limbo…

Then, at last, Travis threw his arms around Perdita and hugged her.

Devine smiled. *Lot of that going about tonight,* she thought. As there bloody well should be.

Eventually, Perdita extricated herself from Travis's arms and said something to him. Ever attentive, the old butler listened gravely for a moment, then nodded his agreement, and stepped smartly to the back of the limo to haul open its rear door. Turning once again to the cathedral, Perdita began to wave, beckoning for them all to come on down—Mr. and Mrs. Chowdhury, Asha, Devine, Jackson. Apparently they had a ride home if they wanted it.

Devine glanced about her, taking a professional moment to assess the good-natured but increasingly rowdy crowds cramming the streets and grounds around St. Paul's. "You go," she said eventually to the waiting Chowdhurys. "We better hang about for a bit yet."

Mr. and Mrs. Chowdhury nodded, exchanged one final round of hugs and handshakes with Devine and Jackson, then began to make their way down the rest of the steps with Asha.

For another long and distinctly meditative moment, Devine stood there on the cathedral steps, watching the Chowdhury family go. Then, at last, with her smile returning once more, she turned again to Jackson, opened her mouth to say something—

—and a flying snowball smacked her right in the side of the head, exploding in a shower of white, all over Devine and the young detective.

Jackson scowled. "Bloody kids," he muttered, glancing around to see which of the hundreds of running, playing children had thrown the offending projectile.

But that, as things turned out, was as far as Detective Constable Jackson's investigations got, because just then, a huge cheer rose up from the crowds in the street below, and the two police officers whirled to see the vast ocean of heads down there turn en masse to look back at the cathedral.

It really wasn't hard to guess why.

Shaking the remains of the snowball from her hair, Devine turned too…

… and there they were—Sam, Rabbit, and L-Man, framed in the cathedral doorway, blinking in astonishment at the cheering, applauding crowds in the street below.

Devine allowed herself one further thoughtful moment to study the three dumbfounded teenage

boys standing there atop the steps of St. Paul's...
and then she smiled again.

"Yeah..." Devine said to herself, "bloody
kids..." and began to applaud.

• • •

Sam knew he'd been lost for words several times
in the last twenty-four hours. But this? This was a
whole new world of dumbstruck. Stepping out of
St. Paul's into that picture postcard London-in-
the-snow had been jaw-dropping enough. But
now...

The cheering, the applause, everyone looking
at him and the Warriors....

And then, just when Sam thought it couldn't
possibly get any more nuts, a *band* starts to play.
Seriously. An actual brass band! Salvation Army.
Playing some carol or other. One of the jolly ones.
Lots of oompah-merrily-on-high. And the sound
of it just seemed to whip up the crowd still
further, ever more cheers and applause thundering
up into the star-filled sky.

Sam felt a hand clutch at his arm—L-Man, the
big guy's beaming smile frozen on his face. "What
do we do?" the bruv muttered through gritted
teeth. "What do we *do*, Sam?"

Good question, and not one Sam currently had
any kind of answer to.

Bizarrely though, the one who *did* seem to have

an answer was Rabbit. In fact, from what Sam could make out, the bro' with the 'fro appeared to be having much less of a problem with this whole "cheering masses" situation than either Sam or L-Man. Seemed, in fact, to be weirdly chilled about the whole deal. *Cool,* you might even have said.

"Just smile and wave," Rabbit drawled, and *then* Sam saw the guy actually flash a great big cheesy grin at a bunch of girls nearby. "Think the end of *Star Wars*, yeah? But without the robots and the big hairy dude." Rabbit began to raise a hand—

"Wait," Sam said. "Not yet." Because Sam's eyes had only now come to rest on the Rolls-Royce stretch limo parked in the street below, and the small group of people standing by its open back door. Asha, Sam's mum and dad, Travis the butler...

And Perdita.

Across the heads of the cheering mob, Sam managed to catch Perdita's eye and began to wave at her, beckoning for her to come up and join them.

For a moment, the girl seemed unsure, but then Sam saw Travis give her a gentle shove, and all at once she shot off like an Olympic sprinter, taking the cathedral steps three at a time, the crowd parting for her as she came through and cheering her all the way.

With a last effortlessly graceful leap, Perdita

joined Sam and his mates atop the steps of St. Paul's, and together the four of them finally turned to face the roaring, clapping crowds.

So what now?

Rabbit was right, Sam reckoned. Smile and wave. End of *Star Wars* minus robots and...

... and that was when the last of the magic happened.

Just as Sam was raising a hand to acknowledge the cheering throng in the street below, he saw the world before him drawn aside like a curtain...

... and suddenly Sam wasn't looking down at a crowded St Paul's Churchyard anymore. In fact, he wasn't even looking through his own *eyes* anymore.

Through the eyes of someone else entirely, Sam saw before him a swirling blaze of multicoloured light. Moments later, that light began to recede, to fade, revealing something else beyond it. Some kind of landscape. Bleak. Barren. Starry sky above. Desert sand below. Crouched in the sand were two people, a man and a woman, both dressed in robes of some sort. The mother (of course she was a mother) appeared to have been weeping, her husband's consoling arm still around her shoulders even while the startled couple shrank back from the blinding swirl of colour. But as the last of the light finally faded, the pair glanced up again. Glanced up at the owner of the eyes Sam was now looking through. And then... *then* the couple's faces lit up with their very own light, shining with astonishment and wonder and a relief so intense it almost hurt Sam's heart to look at it. The mother rose. Stumbled forward. Reached out with eager hands. She was weeping still, but tears of joy now. And through someone else's flesh, Sam felt warm arms enfold him. On someone else's cheek, he felt hot storms of kisses. With someone else's family, he felt safe and loved and...

... and suddenly Sam was back on the steps of St. Paul's, his own family waiting for him in the street below, his *other* family right by his side.

"Samar? Are you okay?" Perdita said. "What is it?"

Sam smiled. "Tell you later. Let's get this over with."

"Dibs on Han Solo," Rabbit said.

L-Man snorted. "Seriously? Bruv, you *ain't* Han Solo."

But Rabbit's eyes were already aglow. "Han Solo with a Mighty Afro!"

"Bruv, you is delusional. *I'm* Han Solo."

"Sorry, bruv. Han don't wear no shell suit. You're the hairy dude."

"I *ain't* the hairy dude!"

Rolling his eyes, Sam took Perdita's hand in his, squeezed it firmly, then stepped forward.

And together, with Sam leading the way, the

Walworth Warriors began their final descent—down the snowy steps of St. Paul's Cathedral, smiling and waving, as the crowds cheered in the streets below, and the band played oompah-merrily-on-high.

Dear Reader

Thank you for taking a chance on SAVIOURS DAY. I hope you enjoyed it. It's my first book, and I must admit that finally sending it out into the world feels just a little bit, well... *terrifying.*

If you did enjoy the story and felt at all inclined to leave a reader review on Amazon, that would be absolutely smashing (hey, I'm British, I'm allowed to say smashing). More than that, it would also be incredibly helpful. Books by famous authors have millions in marketing to support them, whereas independent authors like me have, for the most part, only their readers to spread the word.

Because of this, Amazon reader reviews really can make a HUGE difference to the success of a book like SAVIOURS DAY, so if you did indeed feel the urge to pen a line or two—heck, even just a *word* or two—go to it, I say!

And hey, if you would like to find out a little bit more about me and what I'm up to next, why not pop on over to my website at:
www.lewiskinmond.com
Or even go all in and join my mailing list at:
www.lewiskinmond.com/subscribe
That way you can keep up to date with all my latest

news (and I promise I won't bother you *too* much, or distribute your email to anyone else, or any of that other dodgy stuff).

Well toodle-pip then, Dear Reader, and I hope we shall meet again erelong (okay, sorry, maybe a bit *too* British there...).

Happy Reading
Lewis
December 5th, 2017